College Bound

Lilia Ford

In memory of my mom

Chapter 1

Here is an example of biography as Public Service Announcement:

"The Demon Booze: Johnny's Story"

Once Upon a Time there were two brothers, Johnny and Jackie, both former Eagle Scouts. One night, Johnny is out with some new friends and they talk him into trying Booze. When he wakes up the next morning, he discovers he's knocked up his girl. He ends up a drunk with eight screaming brats at a trailer park, until he's shot to death holding up a liquor store. All because of Booze! Meanwhile, Jackie, who didn't try Booze, went to college and medical school, and guess what: he just won the Nobel Prize for curing cancer!

So my version goes like this:

"One Dumb Decision: Natalie's Story"

Once Upon a Time there was a (bodaciously hot) orphan named Natalie who lived with her Evil Stepbrother in a McMansion in Saratoga County, New York. She fell in love with the class prince charming, a football player (also supremely hot) named Tim. They had sex! Then one night, she had a few shots of tequila and did something incredibly stupid, and thanks to that she got kicked out of the house and ended up living at the mini-mart where she worked with no money to pay for college, so she became a sex slave.

All thanks to that one dumb decision!

1

Okay, so to fill in the blanks on that little tale, we'll start with the orphan part: Mom died of cancer when I was seven, Dad remarried total bitch stepmother Angela approximately one day later, lived unhappily-ever-after until both were killed in February of my junior year driving our Mercedes off a cliff.

A bunch of estate lawyers and probate hearings later, and it turned out my dad had put most of his assets into Angela's name in case he got sued, and she had left everything to my stepbrother, Stephen.

In other words, me = royally shafted.

Stephen, an accountant who defines the phrase "uptight asshat," got named my guardian and generously allowed me to keep living in my own house while I finished high school.

So, the dumb decision: I started dating Tim a few weeks before the start of senior year. As I mentioned, he was seriously easy on the eyes, and we'd been going at it like rabbits all through those last days of the summer vacation. Since we'd not been all that discreet, Stephen found out and went into some accountant version of conniptions about how my total-slut behavior was humiliating him and costing him clients, and that if I didn't clean up my act he was putting me in a boarding school.

Needless to say, I told him where he could shove it and redoubled my efforts to have sex with Tim as often as possible. I think I even told myself that Tim and I had some sort of Harlequin Romance "deep meaningful connection," which when I look back on it has to be the most craptastically stupid thing I have ever thought in my entire life. I knew the guy wasn't getting his Mensa card anytime soon, and other than being super hot and a champion running back, Tim's resume wasn't

2

o'erbrimming with accomplishments, but I figured it was enough that he was a good guy who was really into me.

So Tim and I were at this party celebrating their big win at the first game of the season. I admit I was reeling after my nineteenth major fight with my stepbrother over the Tim business. I'd accused Stephen of jealousy since I was getting laid and he wasn't, which at the time had sounded like the best comeback in history but in retrospect represented "questionable judgment."

Continuing that theme, I let Tim talk me into doing some tequila shots, even though usually neither of us drank. He had his training rules, and I'd been a really hard-core ballet dancer up until my dad died and I couldn't pay for the lessons anymore, and any time I even thought about tasting alcohol, I would hear my ballet teacher, Rodrigo, yelling about decreased coordination (not to mention fat on my thighs). But the fights with Stephen were taking a toll, so I decided *what the fuck* and did a few shots.

Fast Forward: Tim and I started fooling around on a beanbag chair in the corner of the basement rec room where the party was being held, and somehow the suggestion was made that we let his best friend, Will, in on the action.

Look, I know it was incredibly stupid, but I did not sleep with both of them. It was just some kisses and gropes, and No One Even Got Off! But it was also not exactly private.

Bottom line: Stuff was posted. Gossip ensued. My name was bandied.

You'd think in this day and age, in a state like New York, it wouldn't be so bad. Well, think again. By the time Tim and his friends got through with me, pretty much every person I had ever met in my life was under the impression I'd starred in an Xtube video entitled *Football Team Gang Bang: Upstate New York Edition.*

The following Monday, I was pulled out of Calculus to attend an emergency meeting with the principal, vice principal, and "Call-Me-Heather" Saunders, the guidance counselor. Apparently, me kissing two guys was the most outrageously depraved act to happen in the history of Brandon High School.

Now I'll be the first to admit that I have anger issues. I did not handle the meeting well. I employed profanities. Trash-talking occurred. It is possible that the expression "fascist hippie cunt" was used.

You don't have to tell me! I know I acted like an idiot and that the situation represented a complete failure on my part to "consider the long term consequences of my actions." The tragedy of it was that up until then I'd been a top student at Brandon—I always made super high grades and did better than my whole class except for two chess club losers on the SAT. Now, Call-Me-Heather started throwing around terms like "conduct disorder" and "emotionally disturbed" and the end result was that I was suspended for a week and on some sort of permanent "conduct probation."

I wish that was the extent of it, but when my stepbrother got home that night, more words were exchanged—including repeatedly the words "slut" and "whore." Stephen gave me an ultimatum: if I wanted him to keep supporting me, I had to pull out of Brandon High School and attend a "special" boarding school for emotionally disturbed teens.

I responded basically how you'd think I would: by yelling out some really sweet profanities, which led to Stephen threatening to call the police on me. That finally got me to cool off enough to get the hell out of there. I called a friend, threw a bunch of clothes in a bag, and stormed out.

I had no idea I would never step foot in the house again.

I mean, I was mad enough at the time that I thought I'd never speak to the bastard again, but I also never imagined I'd end up homeless either. I was in my default mode—not thinking.

Two days later, my cell phone service got disconnected. I tried to sneak back into the house, but Stephen had changed the locks, though he'd been kind enough to leave a suitcase with the rest of my clothes on the porch along with a note that reiterated his threat about the boarding school, and added that since I was eighteen, he was under no obligation to support me. I had no idea whether that was true or not, but I also had no idea who I could ask or who might help me.

I don't know how much you need to know about the next part, which makes for pretty depressing writing, to be honest. I can't say I handled any of it well, and I got angry and shot my mouth off way too often, alienating even those people disposed to take pity on me. My only excuse is that everything just seemed to fall apart at once.

I had no idea how to fix it and with three notable exceptions, no one wanted to help me. Turning eighteen might have made me legally an adult, but I was utterly clueless about how an adult actually *lives*. And I don't think even a boatload of money would have rendered me unclueless. You need actual adults to show you how it's done.

As far as the school and most of my parents' old friends were concerned, I was practically a meth-dealing homicidal prostitute. The kids at Brandon who'd formerly been my friends were all obsessed with getting into college and seemed to think they might catch failure from me as easily as they caught chlamydia from each other. The futon offers dried up precipitously, and by October I was reduced to camping out at the Athletic Center at school and then in the town library, which really needs better security. That lasted until Thanksgiving break of my senior year.

I said there were three people who did a lot to help me, and I hope this next part means they go down in history as the stand-up individuals they are.

In one of the few bright spots in my life that fall, I'd managed to get hired as a cashier at the local gas station/convenience store. The manager, Madge, was this fifty-something hard-core biker chick, who had obviously seen some bad shit in her life. She was really cool about letting me scarf food, and she didn't care that I hadn't taken a shower or that everyone thought I was a slut. I guess she must have heard something, because one day in the middle of November, I came in for my shift, and there was a cot set up in the back storeroom, with an army blanket and a pillow.

She told me if I lifted any cigarettes or beer or let any of my friends in back, the deal was off, but so long as I didn't I could stay there. So from then on, I lived at the mini-mart, which thank God was only a mile from my high school.

The second person who did me a real solid was our family doctor, Stuart Brody. He came by the mini-mart one day during my shift, pretending like it was just by chance even though I knew he never bought gas there. He had some story about how a bad flu was going around and he wanted me to come in and get the vaccine. I wasn't going to go since I didn't have any money, but he said the state was paying for it.

Old Stu is a pretty pathetic liar, so I figured he'd heard a rumor and was trying this way to help me out. I would still have said no, but he added that he knew Madge and if I didn't go he'd rat me out to her. No one argued with Madge, so I went to the appointment. And it turned out Dr. Brody was really cool. He asked me if I was sexually active, and when I said yes, insisted on a full round of blood tests. He never tried to tell me to abstain or anything, but just lectured me about protecting myself from STDs and not being afraid to say no. But he also recommended that I get that birth control shot "because condoms sometimes break" and he never charged me a penny.

The final person who really went above and beyond was my English teacher, Mr. Murphy. After the apocalypse, as far as the school went, I'd joined the small group of Brandon bottom-feeders who were marking time before getting knocked up or sent away. With my usual clear thinking, I'd basically decided to keep my already spotless record as a complete fuckup clean of anything that smacked of achievement. During my college counseling meeting, I proudly told Call-Me-Heather that I wasn't even applying to *community college*, which just caused the bitch to smile smugly and sign me up for the required life-skills class for non-college-bound seniors.

But when Mr. Murphy heard about it, he just about had kittens. He stopped me after class and said angrily that he'd just talked to Heather Saunders and he wanted to know why his best student wasn't applying to college.

It was the first time anyone had flat out said they believed in me, that I deserved better, and it felt really, really good.

He was pretty pissed and had a few choice words to say about Heather Saunders, which was probably why I listened to him at all. Long story short, he *made* me apply to college and helped me get the application materials together, even writing a letter explaining why he felt the school had acted unfairly towards me. And almost as important, he lent (read: *gave*) me the money to pay the application fees, which like the pathetic loser I was I couldn't afford.

No surprise he was one of those "don't sell yourself short" types, so he insisted that I include a really top college, and I mean TOP, on the list, along with the various SUNYs, which ended up being one of the truly good things anyone has ever done for me in my short miserable life. BECAUSE, drumroll please, I GOT ACCEPTED!

And he did all this without ever making any creepy offers to ride in his car or sleep in his basement. He was a decent guy—and a really good teacher. It was clear that he guessed that things were pretty rough for me, but luckily he never said anything and he didn't seem too judgmental about the slut part.

It's in Providence, Rhode Island—the college—in case you were wondering.

Fine, it's Brown University! And it's really famous!

Moving on: I was always super careful at the school not to tell people in authority what was happening. My experience with the guidance counselor had taught me that do-gooders in the "helping professions" can actually harm you worse than cops or judges if you don't read from the script they hand you. I honestly had no idea what would happen if people knew I was homeless, but I had visions of being thrown in jail or a halfway house or run out of town. It was hard enough getting by in my hometown where I had access to school (and one free meal a day), a job, and occasional favors from friends without trying to survive on the streets of Albany or Rochester.

So far my life story had read like the PSA about "The Demon Booze! Johnny's Story." I was a living, breathing cautionary tale about the dangers of tequila and teen sex.

And the worst of it is that I haven't even gotten to the bad part.

Chapter 2

So, on to the bad part.

There was one person, a male person, who did some helpful things for me, but who does not deserve a spot in heaven alongside Robert Murphy, Stuart Brody, or Madge, since he most definitely had what might be called an agenda. I'll call him Mr. X.

I'd known X all my life, which is not as creepy as it sounds, since our parents were the kind of half-friends where you eat dinner together a few times a year at the Tennis & Golf Club and go to each other's Christmas open houses. X was around Stephen's age, which isn't *that much* older— maybe nine years.

Even as a kid, I'd always gotten along with him and liked talking to him. I never knew Z to say anything phony or dumb…

Oh, forget about the damned alias! His name was Gareth, okay!

So after Stephen kicked me out of the house, I started running into Gareth pretty often—more often than I had before I was homeless—and he'd always ask me to lunch, basically a sandwich and a soda. (And also, he let me use the private shower in his office, which was infinitely nicer than the Athletic Center showers, and always had really nice, expensive-smelling shampoo.)

Nothing Happened! Not that I was unwilling or anything. I'd always had a kind of mini-crush on him, the kind you have on an incredibly handsome and smart person you're totally and completely in love with but have no hope of ever scoring, so instead you date football players named Tim.

Forget I said that.

I liked him—I admit that—but I also knew he was bad news. In the first place, he's a manipulative bastard. I mean the lunches were nice and all, but Gareth was the only person other than Madge who knew I was living at the mini-mart, and given that he is completely loaded, a sandwich constituted a pretty minimal form of help.

But the other problem with Gareth is that he's a criminal—like the Lex Luthor kind. I think I first figured that out when I was twelve years old. It never made sense that he'd moved back to our town after college—he was too smart and too cool. And he was also making really serious money, enough to buy a couple thousand acres and build a gazillion-dollar, *Architectural Digest* dream house instead of living in a five-bedroom fake colonial like everyone else with any money.

Anyway, in our neck of the wood, illegal meant one of two things: you ran meth labs or you worked for Sol Bransky. And though Gareth had definitely been born without the normal human allotment of scruples, he was *not* a Satanic scumbag, which is the most charitable thing that can be said about meth dealers.

So that left the Branskys, upstate's answer to organized crime. From what I could piece together, the Bransky family had originally built up their fortune smuggling Canadian whisky during Prohibition. Like a lot of those families, the Branskys had tried to distance themselves from their shadier origins by buying real estate and intermarrying with the Adirondack Great Camp crowd, but the rumors never really died down that the current patriarch, Solomon Bransky, was involved in everything from bookmaking at Saratoga Race Course, to cigarette smuggling, to stock manipulation.

I have no idea what Gareth did for Sol Bransky and honestly I didn't want to know. Between being homeless, trying to get into college, and pulling as many shifts as I could get at my glamorous cashier job, I had plenty of shit on my plate. And then there was the whole "gift horse" thing, because people weren't exactly lining up to help me, and Gareth at least wanted to spend time with me.

I mean, I knew something was up. He was a little too familiar with my schedule and what classes I was taking. But he wasn't creepy about it, except that he was older and I was a down-on-her-luck school slut. But he never treated me like a slut, never "accidentally" touched me, or made some lame excuse about getting me a fresh towel so he could check me out while I was in the shower.

So the confirmation that I wasn't imagining that Gareth was hatching some sort of fiendish plot regarding me finally occurred in early April—just after I'd gotten the news that I'd gotten accepted to a *fucking fantastic* college even though I was this Dickensian basket case. And since I'm not an idiot, I had not mentioned this to a single person other than Mr. Murphy.

So we were finishing up the sandwiches, and Gareth says, "By the way, congratulations."

I couldn't help a slight gulp. First, there is no "by the way" with Gareth. Every syllable that comes out of his mouth is calculated. Second, I'd literally just gotten my acceptance letter the day before. I quickly decided to play dumb (like most school sluts, I do a pretty good dizzy female act.) I fluttered my eyelashes and said, "For what?"

He shook his head and said disapprovingly, "*Nat*alie."

So I switched to my obnoxious teen act and said "*Gar*eth."

So he switched to staring me down, and I must say he is really good at that. He sat back in his chair and just watched me until I couldn't stand it anymore. I knew by then that something was up, but I really didn't want to deal with it. A big part of my problem with Gareth is that he is one of the few people in the world who knows how smart I am, and for some reason that puts me at a huge disadvantage with him.

Finally, I looked away and said, "Did Mr. Murphy tell you?"

"No, but I know you got into Brown. How are you planning to pay for it?"

I felt like I was going to cry, which was a bad way for us to start whatever this was. But sitting there in his incredibly nice office, with the antique oriental carpet and the oil landscape paintings on the wall, I couldn't help but see myself the way he was seeing me. Little Orphan Natalie, who knew where to sneak a shower and how to live off of gas station food, but who'd broken into a cold sweat from just looking at the financial aid forms, so she'd *never even sent them in.*

Finally, I gave him my best stare back, since he didn't like my bullshit and I thought his question was bullshit given that he obviously knew the answer, and finally I just shrugged. I'm not sure how to describe it—it was easy to see that the other lunches had been building up to this one. He'd made some plan way back, which was now coming to fruition.

13

He must have seen it in my face, so he said, "We'll cut to the chase, shall we? You've not taken any steps to qualify for financial aid, and you are not planning to ask Stephen for help—do I have this right?" I shrugged—maybe a bit sullenly. "Natalie, drop the angry teen act. Is this right?"

He was right—in a nutshell—which just made me angry. "What the fuck do you want from me, Gareth? I mean, what's up with the lunches? Why am I here?"

"Maybe we should postpone this conversation? We can speak when your attitude is…more constructive?"

"I don't want to postpone it. Were you asking me something you didn't know?"

"I was asking for your benefit. It wasn't clear to me if you fully understand your situation."

"You think I don't know how poor I am?"

"You opted to apply to Brown, Natalie—I presumed because you have some hope of actually attending. And yet if memory serves, you have ten days left before you have to send in your deposit to reserve your hard-won spot. Did you have a plan, or were you just waiting for divine intervention?"

He was right, again. I had no way to pay the deposit, and my solution to that was my usual: I wasn't thinking about it. "I don't fucking know. I didn't even look at the date, since as you seem to know already, I don't have the fucking money—and no, I'm not going to my fucking stepbrother."

14

He hardened. "Natalie, I know this will sound absurd to you, but I don't care for your language. Now, either you will treat this as, say, a college interview, one where you choose not to curse out the person interviewing you, or we will simply postpone. Or not, if you have no interest in hearing me out. I am happy to keep buying you sandwiches. We can even up it to twice a week if you wish."

That hurt. I could feel him backing me into a corner, as if he knew exactly how desperate I was, how little I could afford not to listen to him. "Sorry," was all I said.

He nodded. "I understand this is a painful topic. I have a proposition I'd like to make to you, if you are capable of giving it your careful consideration."

I frowned and said with maximum sarcasm, "Proposition?"

"I see we understand each other."

That was blunt. I could be blunt too. "What are you, some kind of pimp?" It was easier to say it because I didn't want to believe he was serious.

He laughed. "I don't run street-walkers, but I think you would be right for a position with quite specific requirements that would be hard to fill otherwise."

Apparently, all was out on the table, but just to make sure, I asked, "We are talking about prostitution here, aren't we? Sex for money? You want me to be, like, an escort?" I tried to sound defiant, but to be honest, I was biting back the tears.

15

"A bit more involved than an escort." His tone was maddeningly blasé, as if this was what every future college student would naturally plan on.

"Involved? Like your mistress or something."

I put as much contempt into my voice as I could, but in truth I could think of worse things—actually, a lot of worse things—than being his mistress—or girlfriend. I wonder what that says about me?

"I am not paying you to have sex with me," he said pointedly and, to my mind, hypocritically.

"With someone else then?"

"I would prefer to discuss the details someplace more private," he said.

Add manipulative asshole to the list of charges!

"Come home with me now," he continued. "We can have dinner and then if you like, you are welcome to one of the guestrooms, which will enable you to sleep in a proper bed instead of your cot at the gas station. It will give us a chance to explore what I had in mind."

"Explore, huh?" My voice was a bit shrill.

"Explore as in *discuss*. There is nothing in this that should cause you alarm."

I shook my head bitterly. I couldn't believe this was happening. All I could think was that he'd heard the rumors about my afterschool activities and figured a slut like me was up for anything.

He seemed to pick up on the thought and said in that same maddeningly amused tone, "I know better than to believe that kind of high-school gossip. And even if the stories were true, you are utterly

16

wrong if you think I've made some kind of judgment about you. You need money. I have a job I think you would be right for, and I am offering it to you, nothing more."

"Which is to say, I'm desperate so that must mean I'm a fucking whore."

"You *are* desperate, so tone down the hostility. I won't warn you again."

I winced and hunched sullenly in my chair before I finally asked, "How much money?"

"Four years' tuition—all costs, room, board, books—plus a modest allowance for clothes, travel, and incidental expenses."

I sat up, and then I almost got up and walked out—almost. He'd scared me. That was way too much money, a lot more than you'd get "escorting" some middle-age loser to a nightclub and then giving him a blow job—a thousand times! I didn't even want to think what I would have to do to get it, but I figured it would make sleeping with the whole football team seem like a peck on the cheek.

I know I'd turned bright red. I *hated* that I couldn't just walk out and that he knew it.

He said gently, "You should hear me out. In fact, if you come home with me tonight, I will give you enough for the deposit. We will have dinner, talk out what I had in mind. I promise you will be under no obligation. At least that will buy you time to work out some other financing arrangement."

There was something in his tone that made that possibility sound wholly far-fetched, but I tried to shut it out. "No obligation? Just for

17

coming home with you?" He nodded, so I asked suspiciously, "Why would you do that?"

"Obviously, I think I can talk you into my proposal so to me this is a reasonable risk."

"This isn't like some sick pickup line to get me to have sex with you?"

He looked at me as if I were crazy to even think about it, which I thought was a little harsh, but he simply said, "No." When I didn't say anything, he added, "This is a good deal for you. You come home with me, hear out my proposal, and tomorrow I will send in the deposit."

I thought for a moment and then finally asked, "Can I trust you?" I know it doesn't really make sense to ask someone that, but I wanted to hear what he had to say.

Gareth paused for a long time and then said, "Yes."

"That's it? Yes?" I said dubiously.

"You need more?" he said with a slight mocking edge. "Fine. I will never try to cheat you. If I say I will do something, I will. Any agreements you make with me, I will hold you to. I would add that because the power between us is unequal, you will have to trust me. You can. And if we do reach this agreement, I will consider myself responsible for all aspects of your life, financial, physical, and psychological."

I found something in his words a bit sobering, to be honest. On the one hand, having been shoved by Stephen's perfidy into adult-level responsibility for myself and having made a complete hash of it, I couldn't help wondering what it would be like not to have to scramble for daily necessities. On the other, "all aspects of my life" seemed a tad on the comprehensive side. I absolutely believed he would hold me to anything we agreed to, and Gareth was being deliberately pointed here as if to make totally clear that I would be handing over control of my life. I might be a fuckup, but I had been managing on my own for months. I *was* eighteen and about to start college (at least in theory). Wasn't I supposed to be heading in the "greater independence" direction of my incipient adulthood?

Gareth's expression made clear that he knew exactly what my hesitation was. He gave me a smile that made me shiver and then said with totally phony mildness, "Let's go. I'll take you by the mall to pick up some clothes and whatever else you need right away."

Was it possible he didn't care for my skank uniform of ripped, low-rider jeans and cleavage-revealing T-shirt? Say it isn't so!

He stood up then to pack up his briefcase, but I still hesitated. As he went about gathering his papers, he said without looking up, "We both know you are going to say yes. Don't play games with me."

"I have no choice, right? Because I'm desperate?"

"Exactly."

Chapter 3

So he did have a really nice car. It was a BMW, with leather seats, and it just felt expensive, but not ridiculously ostentatious like a Bentley or something. I slumped in the seat for most of the trip to the mall, since it felt safer playing the angry teen than any other possible role—like that of femme fatale whore!

Except for batting down my feet when I tried to put them on the dashboard he seemed in a pretty good mood: like he was more amused than irritated by my one-word answers to his inquiries on stupid adult topics like whether I had homework, but then he had won his point, hadn't he?

I'll admit it was comfortable. Not because the car was expensive, but with him. I guess it always had been. That's why I'd said yes to those lunches, because he was easy to talk to. He got me. He never said anything that struck me as being fake or a flat-out lie, he never bullshitted, or pretended not to know what was going on with me. But he never seemed to feel sorry for me either. That partially pissed me off, since I felt pretty sorry for myself, but it also felt like on some level like he respected me too much—if that makes sense.

At the mall, he bought me five pairs of Gap jeans, the same number of T-shirts, three pairs of sweat pants, two pairs of Converse All Stars, blue and black, socks, boring cotton underwear, normal bras. Not exactly a whore uniform and not the style I wore to maintain my school slut image. I felt like his kid sister.

After the mall, I shucked off the sullenness enough to become more curious about who I was dealing with, so as we drove completely out of the settled area and onto one of those dirt roads that counts as a highway upstate, I got up the nerve to push him on what he did for a living.

"This and that," was his answer, which I thought was a little coy.

"Seriously Gareth, I get that you work for the Branskys, but if it's anything really heinous, then I want you to drive me home."

"Home?" he said, which I thought was just mean.

"Fine. I don't have a home, but if you're a fucking child pornographer…." He shot me one his looks. The criminal who doesn't like swearing! "Sorry, a child pornographer or human trafficker or trade nuclear arms, then I'll keep my job at the gas station and save up for community college. Even desperate people have standards." He was silent, so I added, "*You* used the word trust." I heard my voice crack a little. The fear was surging again, more from what I could imagine than anything I actually suspected.

He looked at me for a second even though it meant he wasn't looking at the road. Then he said, "This is the last time you ask me about any aspect of my business that doesn't directly concern you—no exceptions. As far as your concern goes, there is nothing in what I do that should pose an insuperable objection on *your* part." (I caught the implication—a desperate person's part.)

"Nothing with kids—beyond tenth graders buying pot? Creepy porno stuff?"

"No, absolutely not."

"Meth?"

21

"No," he said firmly.

"No eternal damnation stuff? Blood diamonds? Illegal whaling? Dumping poisons into rivers in India?"

He looked amused again. "I don't dare make guesses about my own salvation, but that's not due to the nature of my business or how I run it."

"The pimp with the heart of gold?"

"I'm not a pimp!"

"You seem to want to be."

Was that a good comeback or what!

"So what's the deal, Gareth?" I continued. "You're not a pimp, then what's this mysterious job you want me for?"

He gave me a sharp glance. "I've laid out the details in a contract," he answered. "It would be simplest to discuss them when we have the document in front of us."

Contract? This was sounding better and better—and *completely* clear and explicit.

"Hello! Gareth!" I snapped. "You implied I was being paid to have sex. Forgive me if I want to know who with?"

"This is your last question," he warned.

"Fine!" Asshole!

"His name is James."

Exponentially bigger asshole!

James—that was it. Talk about conversation killers. We drove the rest of the way to his house in strained silence.

I was jarred out of my profound ponderings on the word "James" by our arrival at his house which was, no exaggeration, *spectacular*. Gareth had built on a seriously nice piece of property, about fifteen miles from anything, and he'd hired a real architect, not some McMansion developer. The guy must have been a complete genius, since he'd successfully designed the ultimate dream house of a cool, rich, smart person. It looked a fusion of a futuristic castle and something by Frank Lloyd Wright.

The house kind of divided. The front door opened into a huge, glass-lined space, that stretched on and on and enclosed the kitchen, dining room and living room. That part of the house was built—cantilevered?—over a mini version of the gorges that upstate is famous for, with a fast-moving stream running underneath. A large, arched opening at the far end opened to a sort of hexagonal vestibule which had stairs going up and down and several doors that led to more traditional rooms off the main space.

Gareth had clearly hired a decorator. I refused to believe that Lex Luthor had time to look at fabric swatches. The furniture was mostly mid-century modern steel and leather stuff, which wasn't my favorite, but it had classy touches like really good Oriental rugs and a Steinway piano.

The place was scary clean, so much that it was really hard to imagine myself staying there, since I was never exactly neat even when I had a home. The kitchen was super high-end and screamed to be admired, so I duly admired it, though it looked like he never used it. Personally, even if I get Bill Gates rich—perhaps when my career as *prostitute* really takes off?—I would never put in an expensive kitchen if I didn't even cook.

23

So basically it was a truly cool house. It wasn't anything like his parents' house, which was just like my parents' house and every other rich family's house in our neck: colonials full of high-end faux antiques from Ethan Allen, expensive glass knick-knacks, and mind-numbingly tasteful watercolors, which were carefully coordinated with the rugs, drapes, and accent pillows—barf.

He didn't offer to show me the bedrooms right then even though I was supposedly staying the night. Instead, he pointed me to a room off the main room that he rather pretentiously called the "library," and which a normal person would call the TV room.

True it had oak shelves full of books along with reading chairs, a sectional, and a large desk without so much as a scrap of paper on it. But it also had one of those enormous fifty-two-inch bachelor TVs, complete with Xbox and a fancy stereo setup, surrounded by a bunch of black leather recliners, which were comfortable but I thought kind of tacky. Again, it looked like he never went in there.

"I have some things to take care of. I prefer that you not wander around my house—ever. Given your suspicions, you should have no trouble coming up with an array of lurid reasons. I assume you are familiar with a little invention called satellite television?"

I gave him my best "fuck-you" eye roll and then countered, "Am I allowed to touch the books? Use the bathroom?" Not that I particularly wanted to read, but it sounded all smart and collegy.

"Help yourself to anything in here, but stay put," he said firmly. "There's a bathroom through there. When I come back, we'll get you settled in one of the guest rooms."

24

I just repressed a quip about not sharing his bed. *Thank God*, because I realized a second later how horrible it would have been if he'd made his own quip. He gave me one of his amused smiles and left.

And then the bastard actually locked the fucking door on me!

Let's just say that panic ensued. Whatever I'd been running on— adrenaline, caffeine, insanity—crashed, and I became starkly aware of my situation. I was locked in Gareth's house, Gareth who had clearly come up with some psycho plan concerning me.

How did I know he wasn't some Hannibal Lecter/Jeffrey Dahmer type? I mean just because his parents were in my parents' country club didn't mean he couldn't be a sex-maniac-pervert-rapist. I already suspected (read: was positive) he was upstate New York's Lex Luthor— *which*, being the college-bound genius that I am, I had blithely informed him of.

I couldn't help jumping up to test the door, which I rattled frantically, until I became more scared by the thought that he might be outside listening for me to do it. I checked the windows next, only to find they opened out into a two-story drop onto some roaring rapids. I also noted that there was no telephone in the room, which, given that it contained a desk, was so improbable as to qualify as creepy bizarre, and made me feel even more like a prisoner.

After ten minutes of running around the room like a lunatic, I sank down into the huge leather sectional—also sort of tacky—and then curled up, trying to settle my stomach.

What can I say? I started sobbing. After all my witty bravado, I was officially scared shitless. Not just of him, but of everything. Of how

25

vulnerable I was; of how impossible it was that I could get out of my situation, not just at that moment, but in general; of what it would do to me mentally if I lost the one truly good opportunity I had, getting into a top college, because of my failure to figure out the right paperwork so I could get the aid that I actually qualified for.

I had no more favors to call in. The stupidest things were really difficult for me—getting to a grocery store or pharmacy, making a long-distance telephone call. And now Gareth, the one person with the power and the will to help me, wanted me to sell my soul to him—or at least my body—and obviously in some manner that went beyond "join my stable of high-class call girls" or he would have already come out and said it!

And it really burned me that I wanted to like him, but he was so ready to take advantage of me.

Chapter 4

I must have fallen asleep. I hadn't turned on any lights, and when I woke up, the room was completely dark except for the light coming through the door, which Gareth had just opened. He didn't look as scary in person as he had in my crazed ravings from earlier—more mildly surprised and annoyed that I had crashed out on the couch like that.

He didn't say anything but just came over to the couch and offered his hand. I let him help me up and *then,* all casual-like, he put his hand on my lower back, supposedly to usher me back to the main room.

I'll admit the touch gave me shivers. Actually it probably qualified as a jolt. As first touches go, it was pretty powerful. I don't think he'd ever touched me there or anywhere before. It also seemed to signal some change between us since the last time I'd seen him—one that most likely went along with his locking me up in a room in his house.

I guess it felt intimate and possessive—or maybe proprietary? Christ. Scary but a little thrilling too. I made a snap decision to play along with him in case he really was a homicidal sex-fiend, but what I was feeling was closer to desire than fear—or maybe fear of desire.

And what do you know, I shivered again. He looked at me as if he were about to ask if I were cold, but then seemed to think better of it, which of course made me blush like some junior high twit, which he also noticed.

I know this because he raised his goddamned eyebrows at me and then looked me over—like blatantly checked out my breasts (which are pretty big, by the way!)—and then gave me an approving half-smile. This caused a rush of blood to various parts of my body, including my face, followed by a gasp/whimper.

Gareth had changed his clothes from the office and now was wearing jeans and an ordinary dark blue oxford shirt, only he'd unbuttoned three buttons, which seemed very Euro and brazen and which just about pushed me over the edge.

I mentioned before that he is really good-looking? Well that wasn't an exaggeration. I personally thought he was the most attractive man I'd ever seen. With a full name like Gareth Boyd you're probably expecting six foot three, red hair, massive muscles—maybe even a kilt and a sexy brogue. You'd be totally off. His dad might have been Scottish but Gareth had mostly inherited his coloring from his mom, who was, get this, *Cuban*, as in major Latin-inflected hotness. He was just over six feet, almost black hair, dark eyes, gorgeous olive skin.

I'm not bad looking by any means, but if he was like a nine and a half out of ten, I'm more in the range of seven and a half, possibly an eight. I have reddish brown (novelists would call it auburn) hair, brown eyes, okay lashes; I have a great smile and I do have freckles, which most guys like. Luckily (or maybe it was unluckily) my body is closer to a nine, thanks to my extremely ogle-worthy boobs (32D) and ass that at least four people have called cute (believably). Otherwise, I'm a not-very-impressive five foot five, have decent legs, a bit of fat on my thighs, but nothing that keeps me from wearing a string bikini—and getting stares!

Anyhow, my great tits notwithstanding, I was about to die of mortification. I was blushing and gasping at him in a way that he clearly

28

knew how to interpret—all because he'd put his hand on the small of my back!

He led me up to the dining room table, which ran along one of the glass walls of the great room. He'd set two places at one end and put out two serving bowls, one with salad and one with pasta and red sauce. I don't know if he made it or bought it and just heated it up, I just know it wasn't Chef Boyardee, which was the only kind of pasta I ate post-Stephen. There was a wine glass at the head spot—presumably his—and a can of Coke and a glass at mine to his left.

He pulled out a chair for me, but before I could sit down, the bastard put his hand to my face and gently flicked my hair. And then planted a light kiss on my lips before taking his seat!

I think I really was on the verge of passing out or bursting into tears or something else equally mature. It seemed insane that such a light touch could have aroused me like that. I know I'd never felt anything like it before—certainly not with some fumbling football players going "up my shirt" or "down my pants" or hitting the various bases.

He was watching me with that same amused expression and then said, "Sit." When I still stood there, he said more firmly, "Now, Natalie." I sank down in the chair in a daze, gaping at him. He obviously had no problem playing around with me, or whatever he was doing, because he proceeded to put his hand on mine. And when I instinctively tried to whisk it away, he equally quickly took my wrist and put both our hands together next to his place setting.

"What are you doing?" I said finally, my voice sounding ridiculously husky.

29

At this, he reached over and placed his hand on the back of my head as if to pull me in to kiss him. I jumped up so quickly I knocked the chair over and then started to back away towards the glass wall. I could feel tears coming to my eyes. Clearly it was my night to do my best impression of a super cool ice maiden.

In the meantime, he'd gotten up from the table, and staring at me carefully and holding his hands out in front of him as if he were warning me not to bolt, he walked towards me until he'd backed me up against the cold glass wall.

He took my hands in his and lightly kissed the knuckles of one—so lightly it was only, like, a smidgen more than just blowing on it—and then turned it over and did the same thing to the underside of my wrist. Then he pushed his body against mine, as he gradually moved my wrists until they were behind my back!

I struggled, but he was *strong* and had no trouble keeping my hands pinned as he moved in to lightly kiss the line of my chin, my neck, my ear. My arousal level flew from warm to near orgasm. I felt a surge of wetness in my underwear. Improbable as it sounds to say of the school slut, I had never felt that before—not even with Tim.

It was all too much—too unexpected, too weird, too fast. To go from fumbling, lame-ass high school boys to brutally hot, career criminal was beyond my mental capacity to absorb.

And much as I wanted him, I was even more scared. I had no idea what he wanted from me. He'd said no sex, hadn't he? Said he'd always do what he promised, right? Was this some sort of marketing ploy to get me to say yes? Or had he just assumed I'd agreed, and this was part of my new duties?

Bottom line: too much. I started to wrench madly and try to pull away, even as I felt his grip tighten on my wrists and his body press harder into mine.

"Quiet, Natalie," he whispered in my ear. "Stop struggling." Though it was phrased as an order, his tone was more…seductive, what we might call his Rico Suave voice, which should have made me laugh, but instead just fueled my panic, not helped by the very noticeable lump in his jeans.

"What the fuck do you want?" I cried at him. "What are you doing?"

"I want you to calm down and stop struggling," he said quietly but pointedly, so pointedly that I couldn't help but obey him.

I swallowed roughly and pressed against the cold glass wall in an effort to bring myself under control. I couldn't stop the shaking, but I managed to stop trying to wrench my wrists away from him.

"Good girl," he said lightly and released my wrists and leaned away.

The second he let go, my legs just seemed to give way. He caught me under the arms and held me up until I was steady enough to stand on my own. By now, tears were streaming down my face. He brushed my cheek lightly, showing me the tears on his hand.

"I didn't expect you to react this way." He was smiling at me, as if the whole thing were funny. In a voice that was closer to normal—i.e. not his Rico Suave seducer voice—he said, "Come back to the table. You should eat something."

I followed him—what else could I do?—and took my seat again. He shook out his napkin and put it on his lap and then opened my Coke and poured it for me and poured himself a glass of red wine.

"Drink some. You look like you're in shock."

I took a sip and finally got up the courage to say, "Don't laugh at me." Even to my ears it sounded inane.

"Sorry, I don't mean to make fun of you, truly Natalie. A few months ago, the whole town was awash with talk that you engaged in orgies with the football team, and yet you practically faint if a man kisses you."

"It wasn't like that. I never had an...an orgy," I sobbed.

I'd thought I was such a sophisticated player, being as I was school slut and all, but when it came to the point, I stumbled over the word like the world's most embarrassed fifth grader.

"Shush. I know."

"Is that why...why you wanted me to...."

"I already told you it wasn't, Natalie," he said, reverting to his bossy tone.

"You also said you didn't want to have sex with me," I said defensively.

"I never said anything so idiotic. I said that I didn't invite you here for sex and that you are not under any obligation to me. I apologize. I think I read your signals...incorrectly?"

His face was almost merry at the thought of my freaking out like some innocent virgin even though everyone claimed I'd had a threesome with some football players.

32

I wanted to tell him to go fuck himself. Seriously, I wanted to kill him. I did like him, but I sure as hell wasn't sending signals, whatever he meant by that. I just felt way out of my depth with him.

In the meantime he was spooning out pasta on my plate. "Eat, Natalie. You need to calm down. This will help."

We didn't talk any more during dinner, and afterwards he cleared the dishes and then showed me into a brown and blue guest room with two twin beds that again gave ample evidence of how good a decorator he'd hired. He'd put the bags from the mall on one of the beds and pointed to some drawers, "suggesting" that I put the clothes away, since he was obviously a neat freak.

He showed me the TV and remote and then opened the bathroom door and pointed to a new toothbrush and toothpaste, shampoo and herbal soap, which made me wonder if he had stuff like that just sitting in some linen closet, to be ready for his many guests? I mean, what straight, single man thinks of things like that? Unless of course he has a lot of female company.

I had a sudden suspicion that he must have a girlfriend, even though the house showed no obvious evidence of one, or even subtle evidence that a woman regularly spent time here. It felt like some masculine sanctuary actually, which might have been why he didn't want me wandering around. Instead of, say, bodies in the basement or suitcases of cash in the closet.

But I had to know about the girlfriend part. I mean I couldn't have him kissing me and me getting like...*heated*, if he had some official

33

girlfriend/fiancée showing up here later tonight. Being a school slut did not make me a ho-bitch.

I chose the direct approach: "Gareth, what's with the herbal soaps?"

"Herbal soaps?" he responded blandly.

"It just seems kind of Martha Stewart to me."

"Is there a point here, Natalie?"

"Yes. The point is do you have a girlfriend?"

He laughed at that, which made me stomp away from him. He moved quickly—like really quickly—and before I'd realized it had grabbed my arm and pushed me against the wall again, James Bond seducer style. And so of course, the damn shaking and blubbering started up again, which was starting to feel a little old.

"Are you worried about that?" he asked in a sultry voice—really sultry. He was lightly brushing his cheek against mine as he said it into my ear. I gasped again, at the same time I felt the shocks between my legs and then some serious wetness.

I guess I was too tired to deal with—wanting him?—even though I think I really did, badly. I pushed him away and shouted, "You really are an asshole."

I meant it, too. I thought he was. I didn't care what my reputation was. I didn't think he was fair. But of course that was the point. He wasn't fair. He'd made it abundantly clear that he was taking advantage of me, because he was rich and, I now realized, a lot older. I'd never felt the age difference so much. I mean he was barely thirty, if that, and really hot, and except for the neatness and the bad language thing, he didn't act "old" as in stodgy.

34

I guess it wasn't so much whether he'd slept with a lot of women, since I never asked him about that, but just that he was completely in control of the situation. He knew how to push my buttons and keep me off-kilter and seemed to enjoy watching me wig out, while I stood there without a clue whether he was just teasing me or he harbored some deep passion or just felt like getting laid by someone he thought was a sure thing. I repeat: NOT FAIR.

He didn't seem angry, despite my "bad" language, like he knew he'd pushed me too far. He kissed my forehead and said, "Get some sleep. We'll talk in the morning," and then went towards the door.

Patronizing asshole.

"Are you going to lock me in again?" I asked, wishing as soon as I'd said it that I hadn't.

He gave me a kind of evil seducer smile. "Yes—and every night. Get used to it."

"It's not like I'm going to rob you, you know."

"My house, my rules. Get some sleep. We'll talk in the morning." And with that he left and locked the fucking door.

Chapter 5

So the next morning over an herb and goat cheese omelet (that's not a joke!), Gareth handed me a document along with a pad of Post-its and a yellow highlighter pen.

"What the fuck is this?" I asked politely.

"Watch the language, Natalie."

"You expect me to read this?" The thing was at least five pages, single-spaced, printed on fucking bonded paper.

"Natalie, fix the attitude. Now. My paying your deposit is contingent on your hearing my offer, which means reading the contract and discussing any problems now, because they will not be renegotiated once you sign."

"All of this so I can have sex with this James guy?" I said, rolling it up into a baton and waving it.

"Lovely as you are," he said taking it from me and spreading it out on the table, "Two hundred thousand dollars would be a bit above market for sex—even the more outré varieties. I prefer to think of it this way: in return for my taking financial responsibility for you, I expect you to concede my authority over other aspects of your life."

"Authority?" I said, more than a bit dubious.

"Yes, Natalie, authority," he said with one of his enigmatic smiles. "And since the amount of money is quite large, I felt justified in demanding a correspondingly large degree of authority. If you'll review pages two through four."

36

I grabbed the thing from him and started reading. "Clothes! Schedule! Hygiene!" I blurted out the headings. "What the fuck!"

"Page four deals with acceptable language, and page five with the penalties you may be subject to for violating my rules."

I flipped to page five, and I felt my face go scarlet. "You can't be serious!"

Gareth grabbed my chin and pulled my face around to look at him. "I am absolutely serious, Natalie. Make no mistake. I will hold you to the letter of this agreement."

"You want me to be, like, your slave," I responded, my voice shaking slightly.

"Slave is a technical term that usually involves a far more complete submission than is being asked of you. You would have no duties besides those outlined on page one, and I am confident you will not find them a hardship. However, if it is clear after a trial period that you and James are truly incompatible, I will release you from your contract along with the first year's tuition as a severance. *But* if you decide to accept, you will become a member of this household, which is not a democracy. Obeying my rules is not optional, nor will I release you merely because you dislike them or feel like rebelling. Given the way you've been living, I suspect there will be a period of adjustment. That's fine, so long as you are clear that if you disobey me, I will punish you. Now I expect you to read every word of that and inform me *now* if you find anything truly objectionable."

"No clothes," I burst out shrilly after skimming the first two pages. "I won't do that, not unless it's dark." Very unslutlike I know, but I hate, hate, being naked in front of someone else.

37

"You won't go nude? Dare I ask?" Gareth sounded neither pitying nor angry—almost amused.

"No you daren't. I won't do it. Non-negotiable."

"Fine, we can work around that." He took a pen and crossed out the offending words. "Keep reading."

I read further and, honestly, I wanted to die of embarrassment. Talk about outré! Only Gareth could have come up with something like this, a bizarro mix of legalese and perversion. The first page was devoted to laying out the sex acts I would have to perform with "James," even including "business hours" (nine a.m. to four p.m.) during which said acts were allowed. The acts themselves were basically what you'd expect—oral/straight sex, with a bunch of kinky extras like handcuffs and blindfolds thrown in, along with something called "light discipline," explained with a helpful note, "see paragraph 17 below."

Along with having sex with James, I was subject to "intimacies excluding sex" defined as "touching, kissing, fondling, handling, etc.," from the household "residents."

"Residents?" I asked.

"Myself, James, and Daniel." Great—another helpfully clear answer.

All of this stuff fell under the heading of "prior consent," which I guess meant that once I signed I couldn't refuse. On the flip side, I was not allowed "intimacies of any kind including casual touch" with any males other than the abovementioned "residents." Another clause is too excruciating to quote, but the point was *no jerking off*—ouch. Luckily for me, the contract specified—*specified!*—that every time I had sex, both parties had to achieve "satisfaction" or "business hours" were over for the day.

I am not making this shit up!

There was also a paragraph on "health concerns." In addition to promising to pay for all needed medical care, the agreement said I had to keep getting the birth control shots. I'd had my shot just the week before so I was good for three months. There was another section on STDs which included its own appendix in the form of a sworn affidavit that all residents' blood work had shown up clear in tests for the last six months—*six months*.

Like how long had he been planning this?

It wasn't too hard to read between the lines: no condoms.

No drugs and alcohol, yada yada—not a surprise and also not a problem, given that a few shots of tequila had pretty much ruined my life.

To be totally honest, none of that seemed that bad. I was getting the picture that Gareth and roomies were into that BDSM stuff, but there was nothing about animals, or me kissing other girls, or even anal sex, which was not on the Natalie agenda, not even for Gareth. (In fact I'd put it at the tippy-top of my NEVER AGAIN list, and no, I am not saying anything more about it!)

The problem was the pages that followed: three pages of "house rules," which I'll call the "slave girl" stuff. They covered everything from brushing my teeth to what clothes I had to wear to what rooms I was allowed use of (the ones I'd already been in.)

He'd even included an entire section on "unacceptable language," which said that I would have to "refrain at all times" from "rude, surly or hostile language, including use of obscenities," with "**<u>No exceptions</u>**" bolded and underlined, and basically to keep quiet when ordered.

All of this was followed by the abovementioned paragraph 17, which required a full page, laying out the punishments I would face if I disobeyed any of these rules. These included kneeling, being restrained and, you guessed it, corporal punishment. I'll spare you what was written there, including the list of implements that could be used on yours truly's *bare ass*, because I found it even more embarrassing than the stuff about jerking off.

There was nothing about me scrubbing floors or doing laundry, so you might say the "slave girl" part consisted simply of me being an obedient tool.

"This is ridiculous," I said at the end.

"How so?"

"You want to control every aspect of my life."

"Exactly," he said with maddening coolness. "I have no doubt that you will find that challenging, but we are talking about a large amount of money."

"I'm not the only person in the history of the world who couldn't pay for college, you know. So far as I know, they don't all become fucking whores and sex slaves."

"It's not just that you don't have the money for college," he said with noticeably more heat. "Thanks to that out-of-control mouth of yours, you've been a half step away from living on the streets for the last seven

40

months. I've seen the places your own judgment takes you, and frankly I'm not impressed."

I winced and went to the window/wall and looked outside. It was one of those cold, rainy, upstate days—more winter than spring and as such, very inspiring. I tried pleading. "You could just give me the money. You're totally loaded. It would be nothing to you."

"And it's everything to you," he said, following me to the window and putting his hands on my shoulders and rubbing! "If I gave you the money, I'd have no influence over you—which is exactly the point."

"Why me? You think I'm like…damaged goods?"

"You certainly consider yourself that, or you wouldn't be in this position, and you wouldn't have come near me."

I spun around. "I had a fucking sandwich with you!"

"No, it was more than that, and you know it. We really need to have this point clear. Here's the problem, Natalie: you were smart enough to get accepted at your top-choice school, but since then you have conducted yourself as if you had no plans of actually going. You guessed about the nature of my business ventures, suspected there was more to the lunches than met the eye, and yet continued to come, even as your situation became more and more precarious. You've seen enough of the world to know that I am not the only person willing to take advantage of an out-of-luck, extremely attractive young woman" (extremely attractive!). "I differ only in that I will make sure that you graduate from Brown. I would add that I've seen this coming for a while."

"So you're saying all this is my fault—everything that's happened to me."

41

"No, far from it. You've been supremely unlucky. But you seem on the fence about whether you are going to allow these misfortunes to define the rest of your life. I understand your reluctance to meet my terms, but I promise that if you do, there will be no more sleeping or working in a gas station. You will go to and finish college." After a minute he added, "I would have made some kind of proposition to you whether you planned on going to college or not. It's both your good and bad fortune that you want to go to such an expensive school. Where more is given, more is expected."

That from the rich-boy pimp gangster.

I couldn't help shooting him a look that probably came off as kind of desperate. For in all those bloody five pages there wasn't a syllable about me and him—as in what our relationship would be.

On the one hand, how important to him could I be if he was planning to whore me out to his roommates? On the other hand, he wouldn't have concocted this villainous scheme and then nursed it for so long, if he had no interest—would he?

Still, it seemed likely that his feelings for me would be of a far more dismissible kind than mine for him, and in any case he had all the power. He could easily go date anyone he wanted while I was stuck clinging to him.

Maybe it sounds ridiculous, but I found these issues even more agonizing than talking to him about spanking and blow jobs.

"What is this going to do to me?" I said trying to shift attention away from the fact that I was the world's most pathetic tool. "You told me to

42

trust you, so pretend for a moment that you're actually my friend and not some pimp."

"I am your friend. So trust me. Listen to what I just said. Having sex with James will not be a problem for you. Obeying and submitting to all of us *will* be a significant challenge, but for the amount of incentive being offered, I think you should be able to bring yourself to kneel, wear the clothes I tell you, be silent when told not to speak, and speak politely the rest of the time, because hardly more is involved than that. And you need to understand that in asking you to take on this role, I am incurring obligations that go beyond the financial. In essence, your well-being in all senses, emotional, psychological and physical, becomes my responsibility. If I see that you are being harmed in any way, humiliated, frightened, degraded, made to feel as if your feelings don't matter, I will intervene, decisively."

"At the moment I'm not a whore. I don't have sex for money."

"No. Instead you do it and get nothing for it and actually pay a heavy price in other ways."

I had no clever answer for this since it was only too true. I couldn't quite bring myself to say yes, since he hadn't explained the part about him and me. I gave him a look that I hoped conveyed what was bothering me—after all he was Mr. Perceptive—and what do you know, he grabbed.

"It will evolve. There's no script here," he said quietly.

"You never said whether you have a girlfriend." I couldn't keep the pain out of my voice. I would be dependent on him—completely—I didn't think I could stand it if I was nothing to him—or just some whore that he laid every now and then when she had a free night.

"I don't, and I will promise not to date other women while we are together. It seems only fair since you will not be permitted to date even when you're at school."

And it turned out *that* was the key argument to get me to say yes, which I did in the form of a shrug.

Gareth nodded and said, "I'm going to take that as a yes. Correct me now if I am mistaken." He made a decent pause and then continued: "If you refer to page six, you'll see that I am offering a four week trial period. That's the only way I think you can give this a fair shot. In consideration for this, I will pay the first semester's tuition in full, today. Does that seem fair to you?" Twenty-seven thousand dollars for four weeks?—yes, you could say that sounded fair. "Natalie?"

"Yes, more than fair."

"I want to be clear: for this to be a representative experience, during the trial period you won't have the power to leave. And I will hold you to this." He looked at me to make sure I understood.

"I get to be your slave girl for a month, I got it," I said in what had to be called a flip tone.

He looked like he didn't like my phrasing or my tone but didn't challenge it. "Fine. Sign here." I signed both copies, and then he did— and that was that. "As of now our arrangement has officially started. Natalie?"

"Ducky—fine—started." You can see from this that I was giving the whole thing my profound consideration.

44

"Good. A month from now, we will make the final decision. If you agree to stay on, you and I will go over and sign the contract, which while not legal, will make things clear between us. If you do sign, you will be committed until you start Brown."

"Wait a moment. As of now? What about school? I still have a month left."

"Actually, I made some arrangements regarding that. You will not be returning to Brandon."

"What the fuck, Gareth?"

Well he'd said that things had started, and start they did. He must have been waiting for it. He was strangely smooth and fast in his movements, because the words were hardly out of my mouth when he was in front of my chair, pulling me up by both hands. A second later, he'd tied a white cotton gag in my mouth. I immediately started to thrash to take it off, which apparently he'd also expected, because in a single movement he had both my wrists behind my back and had put on a pair of metal handcuffs that were covered with some sort of foam to cushion them.

By then I was more than just thrashing. I was in a full-fledged panic, trying to pull away from him, crying, screaming, only of course the sound was completely muffled because I was gagged.

He grabbed my shoulders and pulled me over to the couch. Sitting on one end, with his legs along the seat, he pulled me against him, shoving my legs onto the couch as well. He was really strong. I hadn't realized how strong he was, but he was way stronger than me. And he seemed to know some wrestling moves—probably learned from subduing other crazed whores.

I tried to head butt him, but he'd already put his hand up to my forehead and pulled my head onto his shoulder and kept it there, while he kept the other around my waist, pulling me against him. When I tried to kick, he put his legs over mine, until basically I was completely immobilized. After a few futile attempts to move—and a few feints which didn't fool him—I sank into him, panting and crying, but still pinned and helpless.

"Are you done struggling?" he asked in a surprisingly gentle voice—like I could answer him!

My response was to start thrashing again. I knew I couldn't get away, but I would have given anything to hurt him—hopefully by breaking his fucking nose! But it was useless and, after a moment, the struggle just felt pathetic given that I couldn't move at all. By now, I was sobbing and shuddering, and he started making shushing sounds, like I was a hysterical baby.

"Quiet, Natalie. You need to calm yourself. Take slow, deep breaths through your nose."

There was something lulling in his voice that made me do what he said, even though I was mentally cursing him to hell.

My body relaxed again, and he said, "I warned you, no more of that language. Whenever you use it, you will wear the gag for ten minutes. If I have to handcuff you so you don't take it off, then it will be fifteen minutes. Do you understand? Nod your head."

46

That led to another round of my struggling and sobbing and him shushing me and gently kissing my cheek—like I'd hurt myself instead of being cuffed and gagged by him.

In the same soothing tone he said, "Natalie, I need to reach over for the timer on the coffee table. The fifteen minutes will not start until I set it, so by struggling you are only prolonging the time you are like this. Can I let go of you? If you try to hurt me, I warn you I will punish you further."

I fully relaxed then, for once not being my usual dumb self so I could find out what he meant by "punish further." I nodded as well as I could, with his grip on my head, and he let go and reached over onto the table for a digital timer.

He set it for fifteen minutes even though I'd already been tied up for at least three, not that I could protest.

We settled in again, and he continued with his little effing (could I say that?) pep talk. "The main goal of the next few days will be to accustom you to controlling your behavior to meet expectations and learning to accept those punishments you've earned quietly and without any sullen defiance."

Meet expectations: it sounded like some corporate team-building crap. It seemed to flow pretty naturally from him, which made me wonder how many people he'd subjected to this kind of treatment. He'd put the timer in a visible spot on the edge of the coffee table, and I was horrified to see that less than two minutes had passed.

This whole time he'd been soothing me, petting my hair and my face and then my arms. I started to stiffen again as I felt his hand glide over

47

and rub against my left breast with his knuckles. The traitorous thing promptly went hard, poking up visibly through my new T-shirt. He shifted a little to free his other arm and started up the same treatment on the other breast, which also played traitor. I heard his breathing change a little and felt that telltale poking at my butt as he started to get hard. What do you know! My lying bound and gagged on his lap was exciting him!

Unfortunately, that seemed to be happening to me as well. He kept up with petting my breasts, now using both of his hands at once, moving from featherlight brushes to full-hand massage. The sensation was exquisitely pleasurable at first, to the point of driving me to wiggle my ass into his lap, but after another minute it became unbearable. I tried to shift away since I couldn't tell him to quit it.

He tightened his grip and said in what I would soon learn to recognize as his "command" voice, "No struggling. You will let me touch you when and where I please."

The touching—or possibly the command—sent a palpable all-body shock wave through me, starting not in my breasts, but between my legs, moving up my torso, to my neck and even the muscles on my scalp. It was strong enough to probably qualify as a mini-orgasm, and needless to say, breasts, loins, clitoris all started humming. *They* were all fine with being bound and gagged, so long as they got turned on.

Gareth clearly felt the jolt and knew what it was. He reverted to his soothing voice and said, "Good girl, Natalie."

Lucky me, getting master's praise.

By this point, he was shifting under me, I assume because he was getting uncomfortably hard, which I admit was not doing anything to cool my jets. I shot a glance at the timer. All of five minutes had gone past, only three more from when I last checked. At this rate, he would have me climaxing in his lap—probably by ordering me to, like I was some pathetic masochistic doormat pain junky.

As it happened, any thought of climaxing or me being a good girl turned out to be ridiculously optimistic. Apparently Gareth didn't intend to push things that far, since he toned down the breast petting and didn't move onto greener pastures as it were, which I decided was a good thing, because I would have dropped dead from shame if he found out how wet I was down there.

He kissed my cheek and then sat forward to move me off his lap. When we were sitting next to each other, he examined my face, running his finger along my lips, which were already chapped from being stretched by the gag. The tears had mostly dried up, though I was still drawing shuddering breaths—from crying of course, nothing else.

He nodded and said, "That was good. You let yourself be calmed, which is very important. What we're doing here is basically cognitive behavioral therapy, that is, behavior modification by means of rewards and punishments. Now I want you to walk over to the corner of the room by the fireplace and kneel facing the wall. If you do that, I will take five minutes off your punishment. If you don't I will add five. What will it be, Natalie?"

Unfortunately, this just set me off to the point of qualifying as Natalie DEFCON One. Bottom line, I really hate fucking therapists and for him to spew that shit at me, when I couldn't scream at him to go fuck himself was just too fucking much!

I literally shook with impotent rage. I guess it was lucky that I was gagged, because if I hadn't been I would have let out a string of obscenities that would have made his fucking ears fall off—and probably left me gagged and cuffed for the next week.

He must have been able to tell from my face, because he let out a bit of a sigh and then with that same freaky speed had me lying against him on the couch, my movements completely restrained like before. This time he let go of me for less than a second to reach for the timer to add his fucking five minutes. So now I still had ten minutes left.

Unfuckingbelievable!

I stiffened against him, which was as close as I could come to thrashing, and he apparently decided I needed to ride it out, because he dropped the pep talk—and the sexual stimulation—and just gripped me like I was having a grand mal seizure.

I guess he was right in a way, because I really was out of control. He could have threatened to cut my hand off at that moment, and I don't think I could have stopped, so I suppose it counted as his generosity that he didn't make any threats.

NOT!

He was still a complete Satanic asshole—telling me to kneel in the corner of his fucking living room! That thought started the shaking again, and around we went. And went and went.

When the timer did go off, I was still out of control, which he obviously knew. He took the gag off for less than thirty seconds, just enough time for me to let out some pretty raw "commentary" on his treatment of me, and so back on it went.

He took up his precious timer again, and a second later fifteen minutes was blinking at me in all its red digital glory. This actually happened twice more after that. For a grand total of sixty-five minutes according to the little red timer with me cuffed and gagged for using bad language.

After the second time he had to reset the timer, and he took me over to the corner where there was a special little clamp attached to the wall (more than one as I later learned). He turned me to face the room, pushed me to a sitting position, and then attached the clamp to the handcuffs. I banged my head against the wall, which didn't hurt as much as it should have because it was padded—padded?

He obviously didn't like it, because he said in his favorite voice, "Don't do that again, Natalie, unless you really do want to spend the rest of the day like this."

I slumped against the wall, which was as far as my meek acknowledgement could go. He gave me a kiss on the top of my head, as if recognizing that we would be at this for a good long while, which indeed we would. He of course was not handcuffed to the wall, so he could go get his goddamned Mac PowerBook and start answering emails on the sofa, while I sat there in the corner undergoing my "therapy."

He'd considerately put the timer where I could stare at it, presumably to serve as some kind of motivational tool. It failed pretty miserably. Somehow as we got closer to the end of the fifteen minutes, I found myself going postal again, building up that lovely head of steam so I could explode at him once he pulled the plug.

Just before the timer went off the next time, I saw him go towards the kitchen and come back with a tall glass of ice water, like he knew what was going to happen. The gag was hardly off when the "fucking bastards" started up, though I was crying so hard I was barely coherent.

This time, instead of immediately putting the gag back in place, he covered my mouth with his hand for a second and said, "You need to drink some water. Nod your head if you understand."

I shuddered, but at least his words jogged some small remnant of reason in my mind because I realized that I was incredibly thirsty. Some instinct made me nod, and he took his hand off and let me take a long gulp, wait a second and then another, before putting the gag on again.

He gave me another kiss on the head and even a little hug—like he felt sorry for me, which just caused me to shake again.

He ignored my temper, but looking at my face he must have realized that my lips were getting badly chapped, so he left the room for a moment and came back with some Blistex and smeared it on. Then he reset the timer and returned to the sofa and his emails, not paying that much attention to me, as if he recognized that there would be many hours of this going forward and, like me, he would just have to learn to cope with it.

By now I had pretty much exhausted myself, because my eyes started to lose focus when I tried to stare at the hypnotic red blinking of the timer, and eventually I drifted into a doze.

A while later, I was jostled awake. He was looking at me analytically, I guess to gage my current rage level, which was pretty low at that point. He nodded to himself and released the clamp on the wall and helped me up, though he didn't take the handcuffs or the gag off.

He took me by the arm, cop style, and walked me back to the guest room, I guess realizing that we'd had enough "behavior modification therapy" for today.

In his "stern teacher" voice, which differed somewhat from his "command" voice, he said, "You're going to spend the rest of the day in here. If you break things, I will keep you cuffed to the bed. It is very important that you control your temper, Natalie. No doubt you think today was harsh, but this is what it will be like from now on. The more you lose your temper, the unhappier you will be, I guarantee. Do you understand?"

I nodded even though I hadn't understood a word. Basically I was a half step away from being shell-shocked. He took me over to one of the beds and made me sit down on the edge and put a pillow on my lap.

"I'm going to uncuff you now. Don't take the gag off until I'm out of the room. If you're going to scream, do it into the pillow."

This I did understand and managed to nod without being prompted. He kissed my forehead one last time and nestled my hair while he still could and then, holding up a warning finger, he went behind me to unlock the handcuffs. He managed to make a quick retreat without looking like he was rushing, shut and locked the door, and I assume moved rapidly out of earshot so we didn't have to start the whole ordeal again.

He needn't have to because I was past screaming at that point. I wearily untied the gag and threw it in the direction of the waste paper basket, after which I rolled off the bed and onto the floor, still clutching the pillow, and curled up in a ball in the space between the bed and the wall. After a few minutes, I realized I was cold, pulled the rest of the bedding on top of me, and buried myself under it.

Chapter 6

Next thing I remember was waking up some time during the afternoon, stiff and miserable from sleeping on the floor. I was surprised to find that the blanket and pillows from the other bed had been arranged around me, which meant that Gareth had been checking on me while I was sleeping like the dead.

That supposition was confirmed by the sight of a pitcher of ice water with limes floating in it sitting on the dresser, along with a water glass. I got up to pour myself a glass, wondering if this was some Dom equivalent of an apologetic bouquet of roses, but then I saw a folded piece of note paper, which clarified things.

Natalie, we never finished our conversation earlier. As I began to inform you, I arranged for you to be excused from classes for the rest of the school year on the plea that you had been accepted for an internship at a NYC media company, of which I happen to own a large interest. Charlie Atkins [my principal] *did not show the slightest hesitation in allowing you to accept, nor did he indicate he was surprised that I was the one approaching him—interpret that as you will.*

I arranged this several weeks ago on the assumption that we would be able to reach an agreement. I also arranged for a replacement for you at the gas station, because I assumed you would wish to uphold that basic courtesy to your employers. That is all I have to say. Any yelling about this should take place now, before I return, as I consider the topic closed, and I will not react well to hearing it raised by you.

I am sure my behavior strikes you as high-handed but it is best to be clear: in offering to pay you this large sum of money—which at the moment amounts to $27,000 for four weeks of your life—I consider myself as having purchased the right to make all such decisions for you. This is non-negotiable.

I can't claim that I was surprised by your behavior today, but I was disappointed, though perhaps not for the reasons you think. I have no doubt whatsoever that obeying me will be very difficult for you. It may seem preposterous to you, but my intent at all times is to arrange things so that you can do so without suffering the kind of anguish you experienced today.

I recognize that you were out of control, but I also regard your behavior as consistent with the larger pattern we discussed earlier, that is to say, indicative of the kinds of decisions you make and judgment you show when your own well-being is the one primarily at stake.

I can sense the anger rising already, so I will leave off. I strongly recommend you avail yourself of the bath, which is a whirlpool. The switch is to the left of the sink and bath salts etc. are in the right cabinet. Tomorrow we will review my general expectations as laid out in the contract so that my response does not again catch you off guard.

I will bring you your dinner around 6 p.m. I expect you to behave yourself.

Gareth.

Needless to say I was burning after this and punched the wall and kicked the bed and did some other really mature teen actions, though I

56

didn't make any noise that would bring him back in with handcuffs and gag for more timer therapy.

If I'm being honest, which I suppose I should at least try to be, I would also say I was somewhat sobered by it too. What he said actually made some sense, and I couldn't accuse him of rubbing my face in what was happening or making me feel worse about it.

I mean, I did want the money, right? It was a tidy amount, right? But then I would think about how I was currently locked in my bedroom like a kid on a time-out and how he'd kept me handcuffed and gagged all day (or at least for one twenty-fourth of a day) because I'd used a fucking swear word, and that would set off another round of kicking the bed.

I guess you could say my brain was in a state of tumult. But tantrums are tiring and without him there to get mad at, eventually being left alone in my room to stew resulted in boredom, which resulted in me deciding, in what I hoped was a defiant way, that I would take a bath in his fucking whirlpool bath and use his expensive bath salts—not because he wanted me to, but because *I* fucking wanted to!

I get why he'd recommended it because it was a seriously nice tub, especially for some guest room with twin beds in it. It felt really, really good to stretch out in the hot water, with the little jets purring, and the bubbles tickling my.... I assume you get where I'm going with this.

Basically, I'd been experiencing a fair (read: extremely heavy) amount of sexual stimulation spending the last twenty-four hours with sexy Alpha man there, and having him, like, give me shoulder rubs and fondle my breasts and all.

Upshot: after a few minutes "relaxing," I didn't feel so relaxed. I felt brutally turned on, and though I was disgusted at myself for it, I did find my thoughts moving towards Gareth in a distinctly fantasizing way. I tried to picture Daniel Craig and Eric Bana, but I couldn't seem to sustain the fantasy, and after a few seconds the picture of Gareth the asshole giving me his amused smile, would infiltrate and completely whoop Daniel Craig's James Bond leer. And I guess I should say that the memory of his "command" voice may have played some trivial part in getting me aroused as well.

Anyway, it really didn't take much more than those thoughts to get my thighs, like, really quivering, which along with the bubbles and the vibrations from the whirlpool seemed likely to bring me to a climax without my doing what I actually did do, which was arch back, breasts out of the water like a swimsuit model, put one leg up on the edge of the tub and go at it, one hand massaging my left breast, the other my now throbbing clitoris—I'm sure you know how it works.

I swear the little paragraph in my contract regarding self-abuse was completely out of my thoughts at that moment.

Unfortunately, the real Gareth, not the fantasy, chose this moment to bang on the door, which was a buzzkill to say the least.

"What?" I yelled, "I'm in the tub," miraculously managing to sever the adjective "fucking" from the noun "tub."

"I know you are," he said pointedly from inside the bedroom.

My mental state shot quickly from buzzkill to soul-crushing embarrassment. How the hell would he know that unless he had some hidden camera? Which meant he'd just been getting quite a show, and I now realized I'd just been busted breaking yet another of his rules.

He came into the bathroom, and completely ignoring my blushing attempt to coax the dissolving bubbles over my lithe, naked, nymph-like body, flicked off the whirlpool. "You've had enough."

That sent my thoughts in a different direction, and I roared out, "What the hell is that supposed to mean?" by another miracle reflexively substituting 'hell' for my favorite four-letter word. He looked at me disapprovingly, and I snapped, "Hell is not a bad word." *Bad word*, what was I four?

He said firmly, "I will remind you of paragraph twelve: no masturbating or climaxing without permission, and yes there are cameras in the bedroom too. There are in every room in the house." He made his exit, no doubt preening himself on how charitable he was in getting out of there before I could let loose with more of my opinions.

Needless to say, I was left sputtering both from outrage at what he had just said and the fresh surge of libido that gripped me the second I saw him and was subjected to the "command tone."

I mentally nursed the surge as best I could, to the point of being driven to a bit of underwater writhing, but release was not forthcoming, and the rubbing just made it worse. The failure was enough to bring on wracking cramps, which I'd never felt before, and now discovered were some female equivalent to blue balls.

Of course, there is nothing like being told you can't do something to ensure you think of nothing else for the rest of the day. I should also admit that I indulged pretty regularly in the abovementioned activity—

59

being a healthy girl of eighteen, and not getting much satisfaction that way with the boys I usually made it with.

But Gareth the buzzkiller had happened upon the perfect way to make sure it didn't happen. I didn't give a shit about his little rules, but the thought of going at it while he watched me on a hidden monitor was more of a deterrent than a dive into Lake George in February.

I guess you could say that sums up most of the interesting activities in my "day one in the diary of a sex slave."

I got out of the bath, trying awkwardly to grab a towel and dry myself off without putting on more of a show, and then opening all the closet doors, in the hopes of blocking the cameras while I got dressed.

After I got dressed, I spent about ten minutes trying to find them—that's what James Bond always does, right? But I guess I was not cut out for espionage, because I didn't find a single thing I could confidently identify as a camera.

There was nothing to do after that but surf the ten thousand channels on his TV, until he brought the promised dinner tray with some rotisserie chicken and roasted potatoes, broccoli, Coke, and a large assortment of expensive-looking fruit. We didn't exchange any words, either when he brought it or when he picked it up exactly seventy-five seconds after I finished eating and went back to surfing—just as a little reminder that I was in fact being monitored.

He came back again at eleven thirty and told me to get ready for bed, actually asking if I had everything I needed. He approached the bed as he said it, but didn't try to touch me, which after some of the cable I'd been watching, would have been welcome. He offered to get me some books from the library if I wanted. I took that as some sort of disapproving hint about my watching too much TV, so I said "no" in a way that sounded like "me read? Are you effing nuts?"

It was weird talking as if we were in some ordinary host/houseguest relationship, so weird that I finally said, "I don't care about the contract. You have no right to do this. No one does."

He looked at me for a long moment and then came and sat on the bed—the same bed, not the other one—and said after arranging his thoughts for a minute, "It's not about what I have a right to do, Natalie, but what you have given me power to do."

"So we're back to it's my fault—because I swore. It's not like it's *against the law*."

I made the last part as cutting as possible, WHICH HE DESERVED—I mean what is some bad language next to, like, being a crime lord? He was gently patting the outside of my thigh, staring thoughtfully in that general triangle-between-the-legs direction, but almost distractedly, like he wasn't aware of it.

Then he seemed to recollect himself and moved the patting to my cheek—ON MY FACE. He was looking at me in a more tender, lovey-dovey kind of way than he ever had before, which I admit made me feel awkward and then annoyed, like he was some sort of paternal figure engaged in loving discipline of a wayward female.

"I'm not like some submissive doormat, you know."

He awoke from his little trance and said, "No indeed. I doubt there is anyone who would call your behavior today submissive."

61

"You make fun of me, but you're making a mistake with this. I can't do it. I'm not, like, the right person for this."

He said seriously, "I'm not making fun of you, Natalie. I think doing so would be reprehensible. I don't do this because I think you deserve it, but because I want to and I can. If it makes you feel better, you can think of this as being about my predilections, not yours. I really don't want you to feel guilty for things you can't prevent, though I think you do, which is a large reason why you are here."

"What's that supposed to mean?"

He thought for a moment and then said, "You realize in all the many lunches we had together, you never once failed to make some remark on your "slut" reputation, all witty and self-deprecating of course, and yet you made them to me, someone you had good reason to mistrust."

"Sue me for liking you, Gareth." My voice was pretty shrill as I said it and conveyed more information than I felt like I could afford, not that any of it seemed like news to him, which of course produced some even more revealing tears.

"Shush, that's not what I mean, Natalie. I invited *you*, remember. My point is this: in reality, your behavior at Brandon was not what I would call particularly slutty, and yes I know because I've kept tabs on you. You were a bit free with yourself, but I know you liked, or thought you liked, all the boys you had sex with, so why think of yourself in that way at all? There were, are, quite a few young women at Brandon who have slept with more people than you, and yet they never referred to themselves as 'school slut' or acted in a way that would give them that kind of reputation."

62

"So we are back to the main point that this is my fault."

"The main point is that you should not expect me, or people like me, to act like Bob Murphy [my English teacher]," he said with a touch more heat. "Most people will take you on your own estimation of yourself, and those who are like me will exploit whatever advantages you give us. I want you, and I'd much prefer to have you on my own terms, it's as simple as that. Going forward, Natalie, if you wish to make your own terms, you will have to live your life somewhat differently."

Strange as it sounds, I think he really was trying to be encouraging, in his incredibly weird, psychotic way, but there was something kind of chilling in it—or maybe thrilling, because when he talked about his "terms" I found my breath hitch, like, a tiny bit, and that part of me "down there" started crying out for some attention, which was made a ton worse because of the no-jerking-off rule and because I was not exactly eager to start twisting and rubbing myself on the mattress and sheets to get a little relief with Gareth sitting right there.

I know I was biting my lip, half from being about to cry at what he was saying and half from his having gone back to absently patting my thigh, only now, he'd sort of moved over from outer to inner—which is proof if you ever needed it that a man can be just as big a tease as a woman. The touch was light through my jeans, but electric in the way that all his touches seemed to be, and caused a series of half-voluntary contractions of *those* muscles, which I fervently prayed he didn't notice.

Fortunately, or maybe unfortunately, he seemed to recollect himself. I gathered he'd already decided that more of *that*—petting, heavy

63

breathing, fondling—was not on the agenda tonight, which seemed pretty cruel given the no-jerking-off rule.

"Go brush your teeth and get ready for bed. Lights go out in ten minutes." My temper flared at this, so he said in something closer to his "command" voice, "You need to understand that I *will* bring you to the point of decent compliance, Natalie. I'm positive of it because I have no intention of stopping until I have. Your holding out will buy you a lot of emotional turmoil, but it will not change the basic outcome of this."

And with that, he left, locking the door as usual. You have to admit, it was a pretty good exit line if his goal was to leave someone trembling and whimpering over what his intentions were.

He didn't come back, but it seems he didn't need to. The lights and TV flicked out at what I assume was precisely ten minutes later as measured by a handy digital timer. The fact that he'd had a remote switch installed, along with various hidden cameras, made me wonder about what kind of sex-fiend-psycho his architect was.

I of course was not in bed, as I had disobeyed by dawdling like the naughty girl I was. Standing in the pitch black, fumbling without luck for my nightshirt, I felt a surge of rage at the long list of indignities I was being subjected to. I screamed out at the dark room, "I only have to hold out four effing weeks, and effing does not count as an effing swear word!"

Chapter 7

The next day, he upped the ante—a lot. I don't know if he thought I was ready or realized I never would be, but the behavior modification in the form of a long list of little rules started fast and hard as soon as he came and got me for breakfast.

I'll share some of them with you, since I'm sure you'll find them *hysterically amusing* as I certainly did.

RULE ONE: *The coming-into-the-room protocol*

Evidently, some parts of my behavior indicated that I might be nursing some teensy grudge that would lead me to try to, say, smash Gareth's head in with a table lamp as he came in the room. There's a chance that he reached this conclusion after catching me frantically trying to wrench the lamp off the bedside table, which just so happened to be bolted to the table like in a motel.

So after that the rule was whenever he gave a warning knock, I was supposed to go sit on the bed and grip the headboard behind me—within twenty seconds of the knock or face "punishment" for disobedience.

Right after he told me this and before I could say anything, he put his hand over my mouth and curtly informed me that unless I planned to wear the gag all day I would not argue with him about the validity of any of his rules. I somehow bit my lip and then said snidely, "Can I ask a question?"

I guess he viewed this as progress because he nodded. "Go ahead."

"What if I'm in the bathroom?"

"I'll wait until you're done before I knock." Yet another reminder that he would be monitoring every piss I took.

RULES TWO THROUGH FIVE concerned my morning schedule, which was so incredibly complex it needed rules to make someone like me remember it:

WAKE UP—when he knocked on the door

MAKE BED—neatly, as soon as I was out of it, presumably to spare his tender nerves the sight of a messy bed

TAKE CARE OF NEEDS—I made him spell it out since I figured it would bother him. Take care of needs = go to the bathroom and brush my teeth

TAKE SHOWER—he did feel like he had to spell out what was entailed by "shower": shampoo and condition hair, wash carefully *with soap*, shave legs—EVERY DAY.

In his defense, since I'd been living at the gas station I'd dropped down to about two showers a week, shaving and shampoo strictly optional—like when someone had left the necessary articles in the Athletic Center showers. What do you want? Razors are expensive!

RULE SIX: *Clothes*

If there were no clothes out, I could wear what I wanted, i.e. jeans/sweat pants and a T-shirt which was all I had. If there were clothes on the bed, I was to wear those.

All to be done in less than forty minutes measured by, you guessed it, the digital timer.

He sat on the bed as he went over all of these and then summed up with a little speech. "You will follow these rules exactly, and deviations will result in punishments, starting with you kneeling for five minutes. And if you ever try to hurt me, Natalie, we switch over to corporal punishment, which will be designed to ensure that you *never* try again. Are we clear?"

"This is crap. All of it. I can't do any of this!"

"Make a bed? Take a shower? These activities are so challenging for you?"

"You know what I mean!"

"No, in this case I really don't. We've hardly arrived at any sensitive requests yet, Natalie. You are refusing to shower? To brush your teeth? I have to say I greatly dislike your arguing with me about things you would do in any case, and after today I won't tolerate it."

Read: more time in the corner.

"You want to control every part of me—everything I do."

"Yes, precisely."

"This is bullshit—I'm sorry, I didn't mean…. FUCK! Aargh! Is there any way we can change this rule?"

I really hadn't meant to swear at him. I guess he realized that because he shook his head as if privately amused instead of pissed off, but then seemed to spot a way of converting it to a "teachable moment," because he said, "No—the rule stays. I'll make this compromise, though. You go through your morning routine and get dressed. Then, if you come out and on your own go and kneel in the corner of the living room without my having to cuff you, you will only have to stay for five minutes instead of ten and you don't have to wear the gag. Your choice."

"Forget it!" I said angrily, literally baring my teeth at him.

He wisely chose to make his exit, though as he left the room, he threw out, "To repeat the point that has been made several times already: nine hundred dollars a day should buy me an awful lot of obedience, Natalie."

I told you he was smart, right? Well his little maneuver, 'cause that's what it was, gave me a pretty good taste of how diabolically his mind worked. I mean, was I really going to refuse to brush my teeth? Take a shower?

But the kicker was the "choice" part. If I didn't go kneel, then he would gag me and handcuff me to the wall. But since it was framed as a choice, refusing to kneel left it open to suspicion that I preferred the rough stuff. And by letting me wait until after my shower for the punishment, I had plenty of time to think through said "choices"— which again would make whichever one I ended up with seem like the one I wanted.

But before that happened, I got my first experience with the "clothes rule." When I came out of the shower, lying on the bed was 1. a silk thong, 2. a matching bra, 3. a white button-down shirt (apparently one of his), and 4. draw-string shorts, not Daisy Duke short, but hardly cargos either. None of it qualified as objectionably slutty, and it was nothing I wouldn't have worn myself, but it was certainly more suggestive—and accessible—than my jeans and T-shirts.

68

I felt a flare of anger at the raw indignity of it and threw his stuff on the floor and went to get out some of "my clothes"—i.e. the ones he had bought me—and what do you know, the bureau drawers were locked!

Gareth of course chose this moment to open the door without knocking and said amiably, "You're free to stay in the towel if you prefer, but don't leave the clothes on the floor." He paused to give me a pretty lingering look-over and then finished with, "In that case, I hope you choose the handcuffs."

He left without closing the door, before I could curse him out. I guess the therapy was working, because I somehow restrained myself enough to scream out nothing worse than "argh," lest I be dragged out for punishment in my towel.

As I said, he was demonic. I could either wear the towel or what he picked for me. So I angrily donned the abovementioned "intimate apparel," that I did notice bore labels from "La Perla," which meant the two items, composing a whole six square inches of material, ran a cool two hundred dollars. I put on the shirt and shorts, which were cut pretty loose, in contrast to the thong/bra combo. They did look kind of sexy, and I admit that I did check myself out in the mirror as subtly as I could so he wouldn't catch me.

So now was the test. He'd left the door open, obviously so I would come out once I was dressed. If I didn't walk out on my own, he would drag me out and cuff me etc., so with my face flaming, I took a step out of the door.

He was waiting for it, and I have to say he looked a little flushed himself. He raised his eyebrows in a question mark for me, and when I didn't move, he took out a white length of cloth and took a step towards me. It did the trick. I hightailed it over to the corner. He'd decorated it since the day before, adding a fleece rug, some cushions and a down comforter, which made it feel a little like Jeannie's bottle and made me wonder if I'd be wearing a bikini top and harem pants next.

Once I got to the corner, however, I froze up. My knees just wouldn't bend. I'm not totally sure why. I do know my anxiety level soared and I started shaking and broke into a clammy sweat. At the same time, my breath rate increased like I was hyperventilating. I clutched my forearms to get some sort of grip on myself, but it just didn't work. I was panicking.

I wanted to scream at myself, kick the wall, vent somehow. I didn't even feel angry at him, I just felt desperate. I turned around to see if he was coming towards me with the handcuffs, but he was still standing across the room, watching me.

The moment I met his eye, the tears started, and I sobbed, "I can't do it." It was so pathetic I actually said, "I'm sorry."

I mean, talk about barfing up your *inner feelings!* Of all the tools on the planet, I had to be the most pitiful.

He came over to me, but instead of doing his super cop take-down, he stood behind me, put his hands on my shoulders, and massaged them for a moment, murmuring, "Shush, Natalie, calm," in his most soothing voice.

He kissed my neck, which caused more shakes of a somewhat different kind to run through my body, and I found my knees lulled into bending. Once I was kneeling on the floor, I put my hands against the wall to steady myself. I glanced over and saw that he had picked up a timer and was setting it, which did cause more shaking of the smash-someone's-head-in-with-a-table-lamp variety as opposed to the getting-a-shoulder-massage variety. However, he didn't place it where I could see it, and it occurred to me that he had learned a few lessons himself yesterday.

It was one of the hardest things I've ever had to do—those five minutes—and no, I don't think they were character building, *at all!* They were the most exposed five minutes of my life almost. I knew Gareth was watching me, and who the hell knows what he was thinking, since unlike me, who was this out-of-control wreck, so far as I knew he'd never lost it once in his lousy life.

When the timer finally blinged, I was startled to find he was right behind me. I couldn't look him in the eye. I felt ashamed that I had just knelt there like he wanted without fighting back. He offered me a hand up and when I was standing, he hugged me and kissed the top of my head, acknowledging how hard that had been.

I can say this for Gareth: he had boasted that he wouldn't make fun of me, and that was true. He didn't make me feel stupid for obeying him. He didn't gloat or look smug. He didn't even look particularly pleased. I don't think he felt guilty for what he was putting me through, but he didn't underestimate it either. There was a tension in everything he did, a determination, which made me feel like there was more going on than I understood, but I also felt like it wasn't really about me—or it was, but in some way that I wasn't seeing.

We went over to the dining area where, good host that he was, he had set out breakfast stuff on the sideboard—juices, fruit, a selection of cereals, rolls, and milk in one of those ceramic pitchers from Italy.

Somehow the sight of that milk pitcher enabled me to throw off my angst from my first foray into "submission." It was up there with the herbal soaps, only worse. I mean, what man puts milk in a pitcher instead of just putting out the goddamned carton? And what was that man doing with me, a girl who lived in a gas station, and who if she ever had houseguests would probably toss some Twinkies and Cokes on the table for breakfast with a gleeful "*Bon appétit.*"

It sounds gay, but he didn't give off that vibe at all, at least I didn't think so. After all, if he were gay, would he get all hard from me lying bound and gagged on top of him?

I think he was just complicated, which meant he didn't fit into any easy categories like that. One thing I am sure of was that everything with Gareth—gestures, clothes, the way he put out napkins—was calculated, which of course meant I spent a lot of time doing what I'm doing here, trying to figure him out.

I *assume,* in part because he took his coffee black and didn't eat cereal, that he only put milk in a pitcher because *I* was there. Did that mean he thought of me as his houseguest? Instead of or in addition to being his love slave? Or maybe he was making some point about good manners, trying to drag me back into the upper middle class from the depths of convenience-store skankhood that I had fallen into.

Anyway, he gestured to me to help myself and then poured himself some coffee and took two rolls and sat down. I spent some time mixing

72

the juices together 'til they looked like a cocktail with a name like "Baja sunset." The cereals were all "healthy"—i.e. no Lucky Charms—so I had to make due with some "organic" (read: cardboard) flakes. They were completely disgusting, so I had to put in five heaping spoonfuls of sugar just to make them edible.

Gareth of course was watching all of this and finally, as I reached for my sixth spoonful of sugar, he picked up the sugar bowl and put it on the sideboard.

"What?" I said defensively.

"That's enough sugar."

"It's not like I'm ADHD, you know. If you bought decent cereal, I wouldn't have to put any sugar on at all!"

"I'm not convinced that you're not ADHD seeing as impulsivity and poor judgment are among its symptoms. In any case, Stuart Brody mentioned to me that your diet has been, shall we say, less than balanced. I have no doubt you've been eating nothing but Ding Dongs and Doritos for the past five months. Since I've promised to watch out for your welfare, it stands to reason that will include making sure you eat a healthy diet."

"Are you always like this?" I said, frustrated. I mean, how to make sense of this guy? He clearly was into some pretty out-there sexual stuff, but in other ways—neatness, diet, swearing—I had never met anyone so uptight.

He didn't bite but just said, "Finish your breakfast, Natalie." He picked up his copy of the *Wall Street Journal*, taking bites from his rolls, since he was classy and Euro while I, ugly American that I was, sat there fuming that there was no Captain Crunch, *not* reading the newspaper.

After a moment, though, something occurred to me. "Why would you speak to Dr. Brody about my eating habits?"

"You haven't guessed?" he said without looking up from his paper.

"Did you.... You paid my doctor's bills?"

"Yes, and for the birth control shots." He lowered his paper so he could give me a pointed look, not because he wanted thanks, which he could wait the next thousand years for as far as I was concerned, but to hammer home just how long he'd been planning this out. "It was the best way to make sure you stayed healthy."

"As in disease free?"

"Healthy," he corrected.

"Isn't that against the law? I mean for Dr. Brody to give you my medical records. Did you, like, bribe him?"

I admit I felt disappointed that Dr. Brody hadn't helped me just to be nice to me, but because of Gareth's evil-genius plotting.

He gave me his favorite disapproving look. "Stuart Brody? It's a small town, Natalie. Shortly after you left the house, I mentioned that I would be happy to help out quietly if there were people in town who needed care they couldn't afford—I just needed a bill with a list of procedures. I know Patricia Brody from the board of the clinic, so the next time I saw her I allowed the conversation to come around to you. Believe me, Pat only needed a hint to make sure Stuart kept an eye on you. So you see, nothing sinister."

"In the *Brodys*."

74

He went back to his paper, while I brooded over what he'd just said. I felt like I had just gotten a better picture of him than since this whole thing started. He was someone who sat on boards and helped out neighbors who needed medical care. But don't think for a minute this meant he was some Robin Hood saint. I'm sure he had no problem giving money to charity, but I think his arrangement with me was typical of everything he did, charitable or business. There always some reason—some benefit for him. Usually it was probably an obvious one, like whatever it was gave him power or influence or access. But sometimes it was more personal and twisted, like with me.

I mean he had basically given Dr. Brody a blank check to help out people in town who needed medical care, just so he could get it for me along with my medical records? The whole thing served as yet another reminder that this wasn't about money. There had to be cheaper, faster, easier ways to find a disease-free sex slave.

Unfortunately, that was about the limit of civil conversation for us for the rest of that day and the next. As far as I'm concerned it was one hundred percent Gareth's fault. What happened was, after breakfast he said he wished to discuss what he called his "expectations." Obviously, that in and of itself was a huge provocation, but THEN the bastard said that he "expected" me to KNEEL while we discussed his fucking expectations and not only kneel but keep my eyes lowered and my hands in my lap.

I AM NOT KIDDING!

I showed what must have been a super human level of restraint by confining my reply to a highly polite, "You're out of your mind."

75

To which *he* replied, "Do it now, or I'll put you back in the corner for ten minutes. Moreover, I will not tolerate surly, rude, or hostile remarks from you and will punish them the same way I punish obscene language. Now are you going to kneel like I told you or not?"

Never one to hold back, I came back with a pretty sweet response, that probably did technically fall into the categories of "rude," "hostile," and "surly." I mean who was he kidding? That rule pretty much excluded ninety-nine percent of my speech. But that was the point, because my response immediately earned me ten minutes wearing the gag, and since I started to struggle, he had to handcuff me—add five minutes. I refused to walk over to "my corner," so add another five minutes; plus another ten minutes I'd already gotten for refusing to kneel when he told me—to equal, you got it, thirty minutes.

From that point on, each punishment seemed to incite behavior that would earn me further punishments. The basic problem was that he made it clear that until I willingly did this slave-girl kneeling business— WITH MY FUCKING EYES LOWERED!—I could expect to spend my time kneeling anyway, only handcuffed to the wall. And if I said anything that fell into the various punishable categories, I'd be gagged as well.

So that gives you a pretty good clue as to how I spent those two days with him. THAT'S RIGHT, on my knees, scantily clad in my white oxford shirt and shorts, sexy lingerie peeking out through the gaps. Sounds really erotic, right?

I wish. Actually, I almost do wish that I had been doing what is usually expected from whores on their knees, but there was NOTHING like that AT ALL.

Turns out that first day was an anomaly. If I were being critical—*not that I ever would be*—I would say he was being "withholding," because except for the inevitable manhandling that went along with his handcuffing me, dragging me to the corner, forcing me to my knees, and securing my hands to one of the dozens of clamps, he basically didn't touch me. And since Gareth was apparently the world's leading expert in the efficient restraint of unruly females, the abovementioned acts did not require as much contact as you might think.

For sure, there was none of the teasing, stroking, petting, nestling my hair, or patting my head that had driven me out of my mind the first day. It would have been nice if my libido had gone into hibernation as a result, but no, that would have been too easy. As wildlife metaphors go, "polecat in heat" would probably be closer to the truth, especially if that polecat was, like, unusually frustrated because SHE WASN'T ALLOWED TO JERK OFF!

So basically "my corner" became my new home between the hours of nine thirty a.m. and four o'clock p.m., when he locked me in my room again. That caused some problems when it came to meals. The metrosexual breakfast buffet was almost the last meal I ate at the table with Gareth for a long time, because in his house, eating at a table is a privilege for nice, obedient girls, not foul-mouthed delinquents.

I'll give you a little picture of that first cheerful lunch we shared. So I was comfortably seething in my corner, mulling over the different bones in his body I wanted to break, when Gareth came up holding a tray and announced, "It's lunch time."

He put the tray down just out of reach and went to get a chair and sat down right in front of me. Of course, I immediately decided I wouldn't give him the satisfaction of cooperating so I turned my head away in snarly disdain, since I was still gagged and couldn't scoff verbally.

But consistent with his new, less affectionate methods, he grabbed the hair on top of my head and yanked. "I already made clear I will not tolerate defiance over things you would do anyway. Now when you have been behaving well, you can join me at the table, but if you are being punished, then meals will be served in a less agreeable manner. Are we clear?" When I didn't respond, he yanked my hair again, so I nodded angrily. "I'm going to remove your gag now. Behave yourself, or I promise I will come down very hard on you." (Read: corporal punishment).

I wasn't ready to cross that Rubicon and anyway, I was hungry, so I nodded, hopefully not very meekly. He nodded back and reached behind my head and untied the gag. He immediately held a glass of ice water to my lips for me to drink, guessing I was thirsty which I was—very. Then he picked up the plate off the tray.

"Can't I feed myself?" I protested.

"When you are able to sit out your punishment without being handcuffed," he answered and then forked a bite of curried chicken salad and started to feed me.

We continued like this. When I finished with the chicken salad, he moved on to his favorite "balanced diet" component, a plate of cut-up

78

fruit, giving me an occasional drink from the glass of water or patting my mouth with a napkin if I got any food on myself. Neither of us said a word, him for his usual inscrutable reasons, me because of the worry that plagued me every time I employed language—that I would slip up and utter some outlawed terms.

It was strangely mesmerizing. I found myself fixating on the movement of his hand from the plate to my mouth, maybe because I was pretty hungry—in more ways than one. I should have found it humiliating, being fed like that, but Gareth had ways of doing stuff like this that made those feelings seem beside the point. He never laughed at me, or made me feel stupid, or even like I'd asked for it, which seems remarkable given the kind of shit I pulled over those few days—I mean, he was paying me what amounted to nine hundred dollars a day.

It's hard to admit, but I did feel grateful for him not laughing at me, because if he had, I don't think I could have taken it. The way he treated me roused my hostility, which has a certain power, instead of shame, which just sucks.

It probably served his purposes that he didn't, because once the embarrassment was taken out of the picture, it was easier to appreciate how sensual it was to be fed like that. This was true despite the fact that he didn't do or say anything openly sexual—in fact he was annoyingly businesslike about it.

And since *he* wasn't acting like this was a scene from an adult movie, it wouldn't have been appropriate for *me* to arch my back, breasts out, and stick out my tongue when he fed me a strawberry. However, I did feel a shiver each time he brushed my lips with his fingers, so that by the time we were halfway through the fruit plate, I was basically smoldering.

But I suppose part of his educational program was to allow my frustration to max out, because once the meal was over he got up and took the tray away and then went back to the sofa and his computer and paid no attention to me, while I sat there, handcuffed to the wall, trying not to pant and rub against the floor.

I can also say this for Gareth: no matter how badly I behaved he never made me miss a meal as a punishment. He never even threatened it, maybe due to his "concern" over my "unbalanced diet." That was good, because you might say I have a personal issue when it comes to missing meals—as in, I really, really, really, really hate it. I do have a reason for this.

My rock bottom moment after leaving home came a few weeks after I'd finally used up my invitations to stay with my friends. I was camping out at the library, which up 'til then I'd pretended was really cool and rebellious. But then one night about eleven p.m. I got really hungry—as in out-of-my mind ravenous. The nearest convenience store was about seven miles away, nothing if you have a car, but for me it might as well have been seven hundred miles.

Anyway, it's really painful to talk about, but I ended up fishing an open yogurt container and a half-eaten cookie out of the waste paper basket. I was so hungry I licked out the last dregs of yogurt from the container. I swear they didn't have pencil shavings or fungus or anything else gross on them, but still I sobbed through every bite.

80

Part of me feels ashamed even complaining about it, because the truth is that was about the limit of my experience with going hungry, and obviously it was nothing in the scheme of things. Believe me, *I know* there are people out there who go through infinitely worse, and I really would hate myself if I ever sounded like I was comparing myself to them or getting people to feel sorry for me.

But that episode *for me* basically demolished the last pretense that this was some Boxcar Kids adventure where I was all clever and resourceful, and forced me to face up to the fact that I was a homeless runaway who had to pick food out of garbage cans. It ended the honeymoon, and after that the whole survival thing just felt degrading and miserable. Another result was that I got really paranoid anytime I thought there was even a chance I might get hungry. That's a big reason why I was so ready to camp out at the gas station.

Now you might think after all those months eating mini-mart food I would have OD'd on "Ding Dongs and Doritos" as Gareth put it, but YOU'D BE WRONG.

Given what I've already told you, I'm sure it comes as no surprise that Gareth was into what uptight people like to call "healthy eating." He basically instituted this "no junk food" policy, so my meals were always heavy on items like fresh fruit, steamed vegetables, whole grain bread, and crap like that.

After the "breakfast cereal incident," he cracked down on sugar, so there was no more Coke at meals—I drank milk or ice water—and since I wasn't serving myself food anymore, I had to eat my cardboard cereal flakes *au natural.*

81

I mean, don't get me wrong: he wasn't a vegetarian or anything really wacked out, and he was a half-decent cook. I was able to put my foot down about not eating fish or mushrooms, and I was allowed to have peanut butter and honey (but not peanut butter and Fluff) and the occasional grilled cheese (on whole-grain bread with "real" not "American" cheese).

But he was completely immovable on the sweet cereal issue—ditto Oreos, Doritos, Twinkies, SpaghettiOs, even chocolate chip cookies. He wouldn't even buy the expensive gourmet, no-weird-ingredient kind of chocolate chips, which was completely unfair because he could totally afford them. When I broke down and begged for pizza, he shut me up by saying he would get one if I went and kneeled in my corner, which produced another one of my rude/hostile/surly answers = more time kneeling in my corner.

Truth be told, I probably would have cracked if he had offered up Twinkies or Lucky Charms—I might even have for Fruity Pebbles. But like with the bad language, he was determined to break my junk food addiction, and I would say that determination is probably Gareth's most notable characteristic.

Maybe that was the problem. The fact that he was so determined just fueled my need to thwart him. What I do know is that it was a battle of wills between us, one that even at the time felt like a pointless stalemate. I basically dug in and refused to do anything he wanted. He continued to punish me in that patient way he had, not showing any frustration or anger, but also not indulging in any pep talks or reminders. He clearly had a plan, and if he was worried or surprised at my recalcitrance, he showed no signs.

The main reason I didn't give in sooner was that I genuinely felt out of control. Things just set me off, and before I was able to stop myself I would explode. Once that happened, there was no reminding myself about the money. I just wanted to break things, hurt him, hurt myself—anything to get back at him. And since most of the time I was handcuffed, there was little I could do but break out into what even I will admit qualified as offensive language.

In my cooler moments—usually alone at night after "lights-out"—I was occasionally lucid enough to recognize that he was going to be able to wait me out. It wasn't that I planned on giving in, it's just that he seemed positive that I would, and he was the one who had thought all of this through, who acted like he knew exactly why I was doing what I was doing, whereas I felt utterly lost about both him and myself.

I call it a stalemate, because he didn't try to escalate things—i.e. move to corporal punishment. Even at the time, I sensed that it was his choice not mine, yet another sign that he was working from some sort of Manchurian Candidate, mind-control master-plan.

What I realize now is that he was giving me these days—so I could look back and say I'd fought the good fight, blah, blah, blah. As you can guess, there were reasons he might think I would need this, ones that would shortly become apparent.

Chapter 8

I got the first hint that the change was coming the fourth night, when Gareth came by to say goodnight and helpfully announced, "Tomorrow there's going to be a change."

It sounded ominous, and I immediately sat up. "What change?"

"James is arriving."

That shook me pretty badly, but I still managed a pretty sweet comeback: "Don't you mean John? My first client, awesome!"

I could tell that made him pretty pissed. He said in his "warning" tone, "I don't see how that attitude helps anyone—you least of all."

"I thought you'd be psyched to start up the pimping for real, make back some of that money," I said contemptuously.

I thought he was good at setting me off. Well that set *him* off—really set him off. He grabbed both my arms, pulled me off the bed, and shoved me against the wall, pinning my arms behind my back, and then leaned in, brushing his cheek against mine, and spoke directly into my ear: "I am not your pimp."

He spoke low, not in his Rico Suave voice or even "the command tone," but in a voice that was closer to pure menace—I'll call it "scary voice." It served as a very effective reminder that he was a criminal—as in bona fide, Tony Soprano-caliber criminal. *This*—what we were doing—sometimes felt like a game, a crazy battle of wills with no stakes except pride and a lot sexual frustration. But for once I was forced to remember that for all his intelligence and culture and cool taste in architecture, there was a real world outside, and in that world he was someone who ordered people's legs broken.

Also, that there wasn't a person on earth other than Gareth who knew where I was right now.

But fuck it! Embrace your inner impulsivity! As he loved to remind me, I wasn't exactly distinguished for my good judgment, right? Especially where my own well-being was concerned? So in my most sarcastic tone, I said, "Maybe you'd rather be a client then. How about a hundred for a blow job?"

Dumb, huh? You got that one right. He pulled back enough to look me in the eye, and I almost peed in my pants—I mean that literally. The look really was that scary. I swallowed and tried to push my shoulders back defiantly, but in the present context the gesture looked really pathetic—like in the movies, the guy who keeps blabbing at the bad guy because he's too dumb and arrogant to realize he's about to eat a bullet.

Keeping my hands gripped—quite firmly I might add—with his left hand, he brought his right hand around and pulled my chin lightly so that I was looking directly at him. The gesture said perfectly clearly, "Don't be a fool, Natalie."

My eyes teared up, and I shifted into what could be called a more submissive posture, eyes down, shoulders slumped, etc., and then said almost pleadingly, "You said you wouldn't hurt me—you said I had to trust you."

He didn't respond to this but just stared at me, a pause that was in his favor not mine as far as this encounter went. He reached over and brushed my cheeks with his knuckles. I couldn't help flinching because

85

the way he did it made it seem like a prelude to his backhanding me—or strangling me.

He didn't strangle me—you probably guessed as much. He didn't hit me either but kept staring, studying me, waiting I suppose.

It worked because finally I couldn't stand it and gasped out, "I'm sorry. I didn't mean to make you angry like that." He raised his eyebrows, so I corrected, "I shouldn't have."

I guess that was true. I mean you shouldn't kick a growling Rottweiler. Unfortunately people like me seem to require periodic reminders about stuff like that. Brandon should include advice on not provoking people who might kill you in its life-skills curriculum. I wasn't the only lowlife fuckup in that class who might have benefited.

He gave me a nod in the manner of an emperor who has decided to spare the life of a rebellious slave, which just about captured the current power dynamic between us. I was in full-out wuss mode by now— trembling, whimpering, biting my lips. All my snarly defiance and hostile wit had vamoosed in the biggest way.

He looked satisfied that I finally appreciated the consequences of fucking with him and then moved in and gave me a light kiss on the lips. I raised my face to meet his, lips slightly parted, eyes fluttering. I'm not sure why, except that at that moment I was so scared, I was desperate for any sign that I hadn't blown things with him, made him hate me, want to hurt me.

I feel partially disgusted that I felt that way, but there it is.

He pulled back, like he was surprised, and then moved in to kiss me again. It was still featherlight, but this time I felt his tongue make a sweep. I wasn't expecting it since he never had before. (Ridiculous as it sounds, despite my being his sexually compliant person/sex slave we were only now hitting first base.)

Anyway, usually people taste weird the first time you kiss them—at least that's the case for me. There's this moment of surprise, because in truth each person's kiss and taste is completely distinct and different from every other person's. I guess because we were already so intimate—mentally if not really physically—Gareth's kiss did not feel at all unfamiliar or weird. The taste of his mouth was like an instant high, the kind that turns people into full-fledged junkies the first time they shoot up.

I was still too stunned to kiss back, but I groaned and instinctively rubbed my body against his. He was still holding my wrists behind my back, but he released my right wrist and pulled my left arm up until he was twisting it behind my back painfully. I cried out and tried to pull free, but he used his hold on my arm to force my body against his, and then gripped my hair tightly with his right hand, yanked my head back, and kissed me again.

This time it was rough—brutal even. He smashed our faces together and rammed his tongue into my mouth. I know it sounds clumsy, but it wasn't at all. It was as calculating and deliberate as everything he did, but that didn't mean it wasn't passionate. It was, wildly so, pressing, probing, demanding that I give in to him. And at that moment, I was as far as I'd ever been from resisting. The second he let up enough, I kissed him back, putting my free hand on his chest, pushing back with my tongue, meeting his, losing myself in his taste, his force.

And then I felt it. I was about to have an orgasm. It was on me before I even knew what was happening. We'd only been kissing for about twenty seconds. I groaned and pressed against him. I think he guessed, because he wrapped my hair around his hand to pull it tighter and then broke the kiss just at the last moment, right as my body convulsed.

I cried out, "Oh God, Gareth," not too subtly, and pounded his chest with my fist.

This just from our first-ever real kiss. (Only high-schoolers say *French kiss*, right?)

It was only one jolt, but it was so sharp and strong it was on the edge of painful. It was also the first time I'd ever had an orgasm while in the company of another person. Truthfully, I'd never even been close. Yes, I know it sounds ridiculous that I would go to all the trouble to fool around with enough guys to earn my school slut label and never come once, but those guys had only been interested in getting themselves off, not me. I don't think it even occurred to most of them—and if they ever did think about it, they probably just told themselves (or their buddies) that I had come.

Well I hadn't, until now—right after Gareth scared the shit out of me.

In the meantime, he let go of my hair and smoothed it where my scalp still ached from how hard he'd pulled it. He released my arm and then stood back and let me sink down to the floor. I was dizzy and reeling from the rapid-fire shocks to my system and could feel my body tensing to start crying really hard.

I scooted over towards the corner between the bed and the wall and pulled my knees into my chest and just sat there cowering. This truly was a side of myself that I had never seen. Not one to inspire a lot of pride, certainly, but the rush of emotions was just that—a rush. Exhilarating and terrifying.

I finally was able to get a hold of myself enough to look up at Gareth. He hadn't moved, but as usual was staring at me. I couldn't interpret his reaction. He didn't look mad any more, or smug, or even especially aroused, but he was experiencing some strong emotion. He was even more tensed than usual, like he was balancing between throwing me on the bed, or throwing me out the window.

I was sobbing as quietly as I could, but I couldn't repress a pretty unglamorous hiccup.

That seemed to snap him out of whatever state he was in. He shook his head and then reverted to business as if his initial remark hadn't been interrupted. "He should be here after breakfast."

I was too afraid to say anything, but I risked a pleading look. He didn't soften at all, but said coldly, "You will do whatever he says. Lights out in ten minutes, Natalie. Don't test me again."

It felt a *bit* unfair, since he'd basically just told me he was passing me off to some complete stranger to screw, *and* he'd come close to throttling me, *and* I'd just had my first orgasm with him just from kissing, *and* I still had no idea what had made him so mad.

But either I really do possess some quality resembling intelligence, or the lessons were beginning to sink in, because as soon as he was out of the room, I forced myself to my feet and sobbingly went through an abbreviated routine and was in fact in bed by the time the lights went off.

Chapter 9

The next morning, I managed to make it through the morning routine without getting any punishments, so I was actually sitting at the table for a meal instead of being fed on the floor. Gareth was obviously still pissed. He didn't say an unnecessary word to me as we both served ourselves from the sideboard, and the minute he sat down, he buried himself behind his paper, while I sat there, trying to look sorry and force down my organic flakes without any sugar to disguise the "healthy" taste.

That lasted about five minutes, and finally I couldn't stand it and blurted out, "Are you still angry at me?"

He lowered his paper and said coldly, "Do you want me to be?"

I'd tried to make my question sound contrite, but in my new sobered mode, I didn't flare but simply said, "No." After a pause, I added, "I was scared last night. How worried do I have to be?"

"Everyone has limits, Natalie. Yours take about two minutes to reach. I am usually fairly difficult to provoke. I would advise you not to make a habit of it."

"In other words I should be scared."

He kept reading as he said in the same cold way, "You say that, and yet plenty of men who had been pushed to that state would have struck you last night."

"You know what I mean, Gareth. I have no power over you."

"There are different kinds of power, Natalie. As the past three days should have made apparent, physical force is only one of them and in this case, one that was soundly defeated by your power of resistance."

He sounded bitter. I still didn't get why the "client" thing bothered him, but for the first time I wondered if he might have a point. After all, he *had* sent in the tuition money, I *did* sign his contract.

On the other hand, he'd taken advantage of me. I hadn't had a clue what those terms would entail, while he knew full well how much trouble I was going to have with them.

Finally I said without any of my usual snark, "I don't know what I can say except that I didn't mean to make you that angry. When I'm angry I feel out of control, and I just say things." He didn't respond to that, so I added with a bit of a sniffle, "I don't like being scared of you. I'd say sorry, but it would sound fake."

I thought that was pretty big of me, but he didn't melt and become all lovey-dovey, but said acidly from behind his newspaper, "Don't apologize to me, Natalie. That would be absurd."

After another pause, he apparently finished the article he'd been reading because he folded the paper and put it to the side.

He gave me one of his analytical stares, and then said in what we might call his "disappointed teacher" tone: "Natalie, at the moment, I'm not angry so much as frustrated. James will be here in less than an hour, and things are going to get much more difficult for you quickly. I had hoped this behavior would end on its own—that you would bring it under control. Now it will be done for you. I don't know what I can tell you except that you need to remember going forward that you have

92

already given consent for whatever happens. In a manner of speaking, the entire point of this is that you resign your right to say no. That's what the money is for."

"I don't know how to do what you want. I don't think I can," I said miserably.

"No," he sighed, "I don't think you can either. And from the way you've been acting, I can't help but fear misunderstandings."

"What do you mean?"

"Natalie, over the past three days, you've fought me tooth and nail over just about everything I've asked, but you haven't once asked me to release you from our agreement or let you leave. Well and good. I've tried to be patient and tolerate your need to struggle, which from my perspective is a quite generous concession. *But,* you have been given fair warning about what is coming. I will allow you to fight against James as hard as you want, but for you to accuse him of rape would be extremely destructive to everyone involved. Do you understand the distinction I am making, because it's a crucial one?"

It was hard not to feel shocked when he put it that way. I hadn't asked to leave—I hadn't even thought about it. I couldn't even give him the obvious comeback—"I knew you would say no"—because I didn't want to test him in case he said yes.

It's painful to admit that. I feel ashamed. I should have wanted to, I should have demanded it, but the truth is that the thought of leaving Gareth, of never being close to him again, filled me with far more terror than the thought of anything this James guy might do.

I kind of knew I should be furious about that, and since the announcement about "the change," I'd stewed bitterly about Gareth's handing me over to a stranger. But I couldn't kid myself that ninety percent of that stewing was bullshit. I trusted Gareth enough to know that if he said I wouldn't have a problem with this James guy then I wouldn't. He wasn't going to turn out to be some creep. And it wasn't like I'd been so fussy about the stranger part in the past. I'd had my share of hookups with guys I barely knew at parties or pep rallies.

The real problem was that I wanted Gareth: he knew it, and I would have sworn he wanted me back, so why was he insisting I have sex with his roommate instead of him?

It may seem stupid, but the whole question of rape was so far from my thoughts I wasn't even sure what he meant, but I zoomed in on the implication that I'd been a hypocrite, only pretending to fight, when really I wanted to stay. "You think I've been lying to you? Manipulating you? Claiming that you…while I…"

"Of course not! I know you're sincere. Please give me some credit." He sounded pretty ticked. "But you will forgive me for at least worrying. You won't even kneel when I ask. How are you going to react when James expects you to have sex with him? I don't see any evidence that you think I've backed off from what was spelled out in our contract, which I certainly haven't, but I've also seen no signs that you've tried to prepare yourself. I really don't know what to make of you right now, Natalie, but I am concerned."

I started crying—*quelle surprise!*—but I still managed to stutter out the following highly intelligent remarks: "I don't know how to explain….

When I fight with you...and then you act like you hate me.... I mean, you say I have power, but with you.... When you're mad at me.... I just don't understand you—this—what's happening with us...I mean with *me*. I mean there are people out there who do these things, and I don't know why.... What I mean is, what you want from me...I'm not part of that.... I don't know if.... I'm sorry! I can't say it right."

Impressive, I know, but what else would you expect from an ivy-bound genius such as myself?

Then Gareth did something he'd never done before: he pulled me over to sit on his lap and put his arms around me and just held me. If it was a move, it was a clever one, but I like to think I wasn't—I mean it's not good to be too paranoid.

"Natalie, I told you from the beginning that you have to trust me. It's the only way you will get through this." I flinched. It sounded like a threat, but he seemed to get what bothered me better than I did. "You need to trust me for your own sake, trust that I won't let you be hurt. Without that, this will be much more difficult. But you are not at risk of making me hate you—*I promise.*"

I would have sworn on my mom's grave the look he gave me then went way, *way* beyond not hating me, as if he were trying to tell me he had, like, feelings for me.

But then it was gone so quickly I wondered if I'd just been seeing what I wanted to see.

Gareth shifted back into his "disappointed teacher" tone. "As far as last night goes, yes, I was angry. In my world, it is very dangerous to provoke people like that. You are a woman and I am a man—I am stronger than you. You should appreciate better than most that people lose control. I promised not to hurt you, but that's your only safety, and no promise should negate common sense. You already know I disapprove of how careless you are when your own safety or well-being is at stake. But you don't need to fear my getting angry for any other reason. With James today, I will permit the struggling as long as you understand that you are leaving it to me to decide if matters will continue. If I see any sign that this is more than your usual defiance, if you seem genuinely terrified, I will put a stop to things. Otherwise, I will let them continue. Do you agree? I need to hear you say it."

"Yes," I said before the defiant part of me could start cursing him out. I almost thanked him. I probably should have, pathetic as that sounds. I wanted Gareth to make me. I wanted him to take control. I couldn't seem to consent even though I wanted to stay, even wanted to obey him. And I did recognize he was taking an enormous risk.

"Good," he said and lightly brushed my lips. "I won't abandon you, Natalie. Ever."

Before I could sigh or get all dewy-eyed, though, I heard a male voice say, "Fuck, she really is pretty, Gar, but why do you keep her dressed?" We both looked up at this, to see, you guessed it, "James," the best-looking guy I've ever set eyes on, bar none.

Gareth sighed and shook his head at this and then gently shifted me off his lap. "Natalie, this is James. James, this is Natalie."

"Call me Jamie, Kitten," he said with a smarmy wink.

Kitten?

What. The. Fuck.

Chapter 10

Before I had the chance to plant one in that asshole's nose, Gareth had done his super cop number and had the handcuffs on me and a gag in my mouth.

Jamie—only Gareth would think to call this *dude* James—expressed something of my thoughts when he said, "Fuck it, Gar, is that really necessary?"

Gareth pulled me up and half-led, half-dragged me over to "my corner" and then forced me down facing the room and attached my hands to the clamp in the wall.

"Natalie can't control herself," he said in answer.

"Why is she dressed?" Jamie said.

"Enough, James," he said firmly.

Jamie shrugged and plopped down in one of the chairs, feet on the coffee table. Gareth gave him one of his looks. Jamie played dumb for a moment, but quickly removed them after getting a *more pointed* look from Gareth, which told me a lot of what I needed to know about the power dynamic between them, though that left open the question of the dynamic between Jamie and me.

Turning to me, Gareth said, "Now that James is here, your rules have changed. For the first few days at least, Natalie, there are no punishments. I'll relax the rules on swearing, rudeness, etc. I consider rules on hygiene to be beyond discussion, now and for all time." Another pointed look.

"Mind filling me in?" Jamie said amiably.

"It's not your concern," Gareth answered. "These are your rules, James. All activities will take place in this room. Natalie's room is through there. That is her space and you never go into it. I will be in charge of her meals and care. I'll allow you two sessions with her, morning and afternoon. I already went over what's allowed. I'll just reiterate that if you come, she does as well. If she doesn't, you return her to her room until the next day."

Jamie flashed him a million-dollar smile and said, "You're joking, right? Care for a wager?"

Gareth actually made a wry smile at this, but then immediately became serious again. "For now, she will have to be restrained at all times when she's with you, no exceptions."

"Dude, are restraints really necessary? I promise I'll keep her under control. I wouldn't hurt her," Jamie protested.

"If I were concerned about that, you wouldn't touch her," Gareth said sharply. "*She* needs them. Natalie cannot bring herself to submit. It will be easier for her to accommodate herself to what is required of her if we take any question of struggling or consent out of the equation for her."

Jamie rolled his eyes. "I don't know how you come up with this psycho-shit, Gareth."

"You asked a question, and I gave you an answer. Next time, perhaps you'll find it preferable to do what I ask without arguing with me."

"Jesus, Gareth, chill. Sounds like someone's had a difficult few days." To me he added in the smarmy tone he apparently saved for me, "Have

98

you been giving my buddy a hard time, kitten? Because I know just how to deal with naughty kittens."

I kid you not, that cocksucker actually called me a naughty kitten.

"James, a moment," Gareth said, pointing towards the kitchen.

I could tell he was really pissed. Jamie shrugged like an annoyed teenager, but he immediately got up and followed. It made me wonder. I mean, it took *a lot* for me to make Gareth angry—three days of being as difficult as possible—but best-buddy Jamie here only needed two minutes. I can tell you that their little mini-drama was the strangest thing I've ever seen. I was so caught up with it, I wasn't really thinking too much about the minor fact that I was about to have sex with this guy.

Objectively I have to admit he was seriously hot. It wasn't the same as with Gareth, partly because they were nothing alike. But I'd have a hard time imagining any straight female not being attracted to Jamie. It helped that he was literally better looking than Brad Pitt. He was taller than Gareth—six foot two, maybe—thin without quite qualifying as lanky, with gold-blond hair. But it was his eyes that were the killer—they were blue with long lashes. You heard of bedroom eyes? I had but I'd never seen them—until Jamie. His eyes practically smoldered, like the mere sight of you filled his head with over-the-top erotic fantasies (and by "you" I mean all adult humans with two X chromosomes).

I always have trouble telling how old twenty-somethings are, but I figured him for out of college, but five years younger than Gareth. He dressed like a complete slacker—torn jeans, ratty Screaming Trees concert tee, flip-flops—but within minutes of meeting him I pegged him for a rich kid, and not in the "affluent," five-bedroom colonial kind like mine and Gareth's families—more the Forbes 400, take-the-family-jet-to-the-Saint-Barths-beach-house kind.

I'm not sure why I picked up on that vibe so quickly—probably his hair. He had one of those cool-guy haircuts where you constantly flip your bangs. Only prep-school boys do it that way, the rich ones who look at the world and just know they're going to get whatever they want.

They came back, Jamie looking a bit subdued, evidently because Gareth had just ripped him a new asshole. Gareth was his usual intense self. Jamie looked around and asked, "We start in here?" Gareth nodded his consent. The answer was enough to make Jamie shake off whatever bad feelings he had at being chewed out, and he shot me a look that didn't leave a lot of mystery about what *we* were about to *start*.

It was really happening. Clearly, this was my moment to freak out, and I duly started shaking. But I was also completely helpless.

Jamie was looking at me like a kid whose parents have just unlocked a fully-stocked candy store and told him to "go to it." His eyes were bright with excitement, and he really did look at me hungrily—like I was the most delicious piece of candy he had ever seen, and somehow I could tell he was the type who could eat and eat without filling up. He knelt down and put his hands on my arms and started making shushing sounds. I was panicking, struggling and crying, trying to scream under the gag.

It was enough to give him pause. "You sure she's okay with this?" he asked Gareth.

"I take responsibility for her," Gareth answered.

Jamie shrugged—apparently, that was consent enough for him. He gently rubbed my cheek with his knuckles and said, "You're very beautiful, aren't you."

He continued with the soothing efforts, somehow placing his thighs so he blocked my legs and kept me from kicking his fucking balls. He started to kiss my face, ears, forehead, neck, holding my face gently but firmly so I couldn't head-butt him.

He reached around to untie the gag, but Gareth stopped him, "Leave it." When Jamie started to complain again, Gareth said, "She's not being given the option to refuse, and this will help her accept that."

Again with Gareth's psychotic definition of help. "So basically the program is, 'resistance is futile,'" Jamie said, imitating the Borg cyber-robot voice. He rubbed my face like he felt sorry for me. I narrowed my eyes at him, basically trying to kill him with my mind rays, to which he responded, "Don't be scared, kitten."

Kitten! Scared! Can you believe this motherfucker! I couldn't help looking desperately at Gareth—because of course he was standing right there, *in my line of sight*. Talk about predilections—read *perversions*! He was watching everything, because apparently he's into that—along with digital timers. He gave me a "meaningful" stare—meaning who the hell knows what's in his brain. In the meantime, Jamie started to kiss me down my neck while he unbuttoned my shirt, which caused more panicked flinching on my part.

Jamie, Mr. Sensitive, responded cooingly with, "Shhh, kitten, let me see those beautiful breasts of yours."

101

This guy was really starting to piss me off. He pulled my shirt off to the shoulders, but couldn't take it or my bra off without uncuffing me, so he reached back and released the clamp holding me to the wall. I tried to thrash, but he had hugged my body to his so tightly I couldn't move at all. He lowered me to the floor on my back. My hands were still bound behind me, which was pretty uncomfortable, but he quickly shifted me more to my side, then threw his leg over mine to keep them pinned.

Gareth walked over with the key and unlocked the handcuffs and then they each took one of my hands. Neither had said anything, but their movements were a bit too seamless and coordinated, which really freaked me out. I mean, how often did they do this together? I started to struggle frantically and scream through the gag, but even trying my hardest I couldn't budge my arms at all.

Jamie grinned at this and then pulled the sleeve of my shirt off the arm he was holding, commenting, "Cloth, isn't that kind of vanilla, Gar?"

"James, could you try for one moment to think before you speak?" Gareth bit out, clearly pissed.

Jamie just chuckled and said to me, "You're a spitfire, aren't you? Gareth's little hellcat," patting my head with his free hand. I tried as eloquently as I could to tell him to go fuck himself, to which he replied smugly, "Keep shouting, baby, you're really turning me on." To Gareth, he said, "I can see I'm going to have to keep this one gagged all the time."

Goddamned motherfucking bastard!

I think I would have gone into some kind of insane conniption, but Gareth snapped out, "James, I warned you about this once already. Take her bra off, but then put her shirt back on. You can leave it unbuttoned."

"Christ, Gareth, I didn't say anything!" he protested.

"I was very clear: you will not make things harder for her. Put the shirt back on."

Apparently articles of my clothing served the same function for Jamie that timers and kneeling in the corner did for me—and believe me, it was as WEIRD as it sounds!

Jamie cursed under his breath but pulled the strap of my bra off the arm he'd been holding and then put the sleeve of the shirt back on. He then expertly pinned that arm under his knee and took my other wrist from Gareth and went through the same process. After that, he took the handcuffs back from Gareth and fastened my hands together in front of me and then raised my arms over my head and attached them to a clamp on the floor. He did all of it automatically, as if he didn't have to think about it—like because he did this every day of his life.

Jamie didn't look super built, but he was actually really strong, so strong that my most desperate struggling didn't even seem to register for him. That was not true for Gareth's "punishment," which obviously pissed him off enough that he dropped the friendly patter and became more businesslike, brusquely pulling my shorts and underwear off, shoving a cushion under my hips, stretching my legs out and forcing them apart and pinning them with his knees, without any of the petting and "kittens" he'd used so *seductively* before.

I still felt like I was going out of my mind, but then Gareth paused for a moment with his hand on my chin and gave me another one of his intense stares.

And I have to admit there was something in it that was...compelling? I couldn't stop looking at him, like I was a bird hypnotized by a cobra. I could feel him willing me to stop fighting, and what do you know, my panic started to ease.

I took a deep breath, and I started to feel a different kind of intensity. I had built up so much frustration and desire over the past four days, and I realize now that he had too, because he was looking at me with what I have to call naked desire. I couldn't help remembering the force of his kiss last night, and it made me shudder. He nodded at me and then stood up and moved back to where he was distinctly apart from the main action, though still in my line of sight.

I hadn't been paying attention to Jamie, despite the fact that he was sitting on top of me. While Gareth's and my little visual exchange had been going on, he had taken off his shirt. He noticed the shudder and looked back at Gareth and then at me.

He drew a deep breath, and I could sense something shift for him. He became serious too, like he'd suddenly realized I was a person, not some fantasy sex-kitten. He leaned down until he was lying on top of me, with most of his weight on his arms. He pulled my shirt aside so our chests were pressed together, but instead of going all frat boy over my breasts, he looked at my *face*, gently wiping the tears on my cheek and then kissing my eyelids lightly, all the while subtly shifting his hips to bring us closer.

104

It was a connection I guess, because we both responded. Jamie groaned and his eyes started to glaze, while I instinctively pushed my hips against his. I couldn't help looking at Gareth again. He made an almost imperceptible nod. It worked like a release. I was suddenly as aroused as I think I've ever been. I tried to fight it, but it was like the fighting just made the desire more intense. My arms strained against the clamp on the floor, but the more I pulled, the more my body thrust against Jamie's.

Jamie looked at me wide-eyed, like my reaction had caught him off guard. He groaned again and immediately started to move his body against mine *that way*, kissing my neck, ears much more heatedly.

He moved down next to my breasts and *oh my fucking God* did that feel good. He didn't exactly give off the vibe of "skilled lover," but I never imagined having my breasts touched could feel like that. He blew gently on one and then stroked it with his tongue, while he fingered the other almost as lightly. It was exquisite and excruciating at once. He did it for a minute and then switched, increasing the pressure of his touch just enough.

If I hadn't been gagged, I would have screamed out. My body lurched. I don't know if it was an orgasm or some lesser response. Jamie seemed genuinely staggered by this and slid his hand down between my legs and fingered me lightly, I think to check if I were wet, which I most definitely was.

He shook his head at me and said over his shoulder, "Gareth, your girl is on fire."

That broke the spell slightly, since it reminded me of the fuck-head who had orchestrated this encounter and was *watching* me have sex with his roommate. Of course I started thrashing and fighting again, and I even made some move to head-butt him.

But Jamie just smiled at me and said, "I am going to make you feel so good, kitten. You are going to come so hard for me."

I know it sounds incredibly cheesy and lame, but the way he said it—I don't know—he just had such confidence that it was true, which made me desperate to find out if he'd be as good as he boasted. I shuddered, groaning in my muffled way. He smiled and said "Good girl. Go with it. Don't fight it, kitten," and undid his pants.

He was loose in a second, reached down and positioned himself. And then he took me.

There was no warm-up. He went up on his arms and immediately started thrusting hard and fast. I think I was still fighting him, but there are times when one kind of fighting sort of bleeds into another. With my arms immobilized, all of my responses were channeled into my torso, which was violently arching up to meet him.

I was so out of my mind I had lost all ability to make sense of what was happening, but I heard Jamie cry out with surprise, "Jesus, Gareth, she's close," which just made me more frantic.

Then Gareth said, "Take the gag off." Jamie tried to fumble with the knot and finally gave up and pulled it down.

I managed to scream, "You motherfuckers!" before my ability to launch insults was diverted to semi-articulate moans of the "Oh God" variety.

Jamie reached down and pulled my right leg over his arm and then sped up his rhythm and deepened his thrusts until he was slamming me. We both knew I was past the point of no return.

He said commandingly in a low voice, "Come on, kitten, come for me." I don't know how he did it, but I instantly climaxed, my body convulsing over and over again, while I literally screamed my head off.

At some point in the midst of my orgasm, Jamie came too, yelling, "Baby, yes!" and then collapsed on top of me.

Chapter 11

We just lay there for a while, not that I could move. Jamie was holding me, whispering post-coital compliments. Insanely, after about two minutes he began heating things up again. I think he might have actually humped my leg, when Gareth said firmly, "James, a minute." He must have gone to the kitchen, because he was holding a glass of ice water.

Jamie pouted but rolled off of me, giving me a lewd wink. "I suppose I can wait a minute."

"A few minutes," Gareth said almost fondly.

He brought the water over to me and unclamped my hands and helped me sit up. Then he held the glass for me to drink. For once my hands were bound in front of me, so I tried to take the glass from him, but he shook his head and pushed my hands down. After I had taken a few deep gulps, he had me stand in front of him while he gave me a quick look-over, I guess to make sure I wasn't injured or in shock.

Concluding I was okay, he said quietly, "You should rinse off." He led me back to my room and once we were there, he took off the handcuffs and then went into the bathroom and turned on the shower. I slumped down on the bed still in a daze. Gareth came back and stood there waiting. One of us needed to say something, but what did you say in a situation like this?

Finally he held out his hand and said, "James is waiting."

I felt myself start to shake with rage and jumped up and took a swing at him. Gareth easily caught my arm and twisted it around my back and pulled me in tightly against him.

"Ask to leave," he said savagely. "Ask, Natalie!"

"You fucking bastard," I screamed.

"You can fight me all you want, if that's how we're going to do this, but understand: as long as you stay, I will hold you to our agreement. I will make you obey me. Now either ask to leave, or go and rinse yourself off and then go back into the living room to James."

I shook with sobs, but I didn't say anything. I couldn't say yes, but I couldn't ask to leave. I think this must be what insanity feels like: suddenly the fabric of your brain thins out and starts to shred under competing pressures.

And gripping me in a chokehold, was the king of competing pressures, and he was now kissing me lightly along the line where my shoulder reached my neck, up to the spot under my earlobe. And then there was me: Natalie of the iron will, who had an orgasm during forced sex all of five minutes ago, and was now writhing and groaning under his lightest touch. "You have to trust me," he murmured.

It pissed me off how much I craved him, and I tried to flinch away. "This is fucked! This whole thing is insane."

"I'm sure it seems so," he said, turning me and holding my chin to look at him. Again there was that look in his eyes—like he was trying to tell me something—but it was just too much to hope that it was "I love you." He gently brushed his lips against mine and then said firmly, "No more talk. Delay will only make this worse. Go and rinse off." He led me

109

to the bathroom, and when I just stood there sullenly, he said wryly, "Does this mean you want my help undressing?" I shook my head angrily. "I'll put out some fresh clothes. Ten minutes. If you don't come out on your own, I will drag you."

As usual, Gareth had posed things so that the only tolerable option was obeying him. I ducked in the shower. When I came out, my door was ajar, which chilled any resistance I might have had to putting on my uniform. I had no intention of going out on my own, but my attention was caught by some half-heard words coming from the living room, which I just knew were about me. Curiosity won out. I went and listened discreetly from the doorway of my room.

"She's a sub," Jamie was arguing. "What kind of message does it send to let her get away with this? And anyway it should be my call when she's with me whether I'll permit her clothes."

To which Gareth answered very sharply, "In what way your call? Does this mean you wish to claim her and take responsibility for her?"

"Back off, dude. You know that's not what I meant. I'm just saying, it's obvious you've had a lot of trouble with her, and letting her stay clothed isn't helping."

"To begin with, Natalie does not think of herself as a 'sub.' You are well aware that there is a world of difference between becoming aroused by being dominated and truly wanting to *submit* to another. You say it would help. Help with what? She's not ready. Unless the goal here is to crush her through humiliation, I don't see how it will help. My reading is that being so exposed will exacerbate her feelings of vulnerability to the point of making it impossible for her to find satisfaction."

110

"Jesus Christ, Gareth. Sometimes to hear you talk, I feel like I'm in a bloody seminar. And I promise you, naked or not, I will bring her off."

Again he said that with such confidence, I kind of gasped, even though the idea of being tied up and naked with him was enough to make me break into a cold sweat.

"I'm puzzled sometimes how to respond to you, James. You are happy to bring up psychological reasons to support your position, though how you make these assessments of a person you've never spoken to escapes me. But when I do the same, you become offended. In any case, what am I to make of these persistent challenges to my rights over her?"

"For the last time, I'm not challenging you, Gareth. I don't get why you're being so uptight about this. You're not even sleeping with her. What is she to you?"

"She is my responsibility," he said sharply, getting up. He'd seen me standing in the door. Jamie fisted his hands and walked angrily towards the kitchen.

I couldn't help a small surge of insecurity that I'd already come up short on the sex-slave meter. "Fired already," I said, trying to sound snide. "Do I still get my money?"

I regretted the words as soon as I said them. Besides sounding completely pathetic, the mention of money reminded me that sleeping with Jamie meant I was now officially a whore. Gareth gave me a look that seemed to convey that the idea was ridiculous.

It made me feel grateful to Gareth, stupid as it sounds, both for sticking up for me and for not laying out my hang-ups for Jamie. This was bad enough without him knowing what a freak basket case I was.

111

"Hold out your hands," he said quietly. I felt a slight shudder and obeyed before I could think better of it. He grabbed my right hand and buckled on a padded leather cuff and then buckled on another one to my left hand. The cuffs had rings on them, which he attached with a chain and little padlock. He then pushed me gently to sit on the sofa and sat next to me. He nudged me to turn towards him and lifted my legs to put my feet on the couch. He then buckled more cuffs on my ankles.

"Kneel and wait for him," he commanded. The shudder I felt then was more than slight. My body hummed but my brain must have been semi-catatonic, because I just did what he said.

Jamie came back a minute later, and the second he saw me, he let out a long whistle. "You are so hot, kitten." It took him all of ten seconds to be hard to the point of pulsing, which woke me up from my stupor. The guy had just come fifteen minutes ago, but as I would discover, fifteen minutes for Jamie was equivalent to fifteen hours for most men.

He moved quickly. I was sure he was going to plunge right in, as the saying goes, but he clutched my shoulders and said, "I have to taste you, now."

He really meant it. He sounded ravenous or like an addict in desperate need of a fix. There was none of the playfulness or cheesy compliments like before. I'd almost describe him as feral because he didn't seem totally in control.

He shoved me back to land on some cushions and within a second had my hands clamped over my head and was shoving my thighs apart. When he saw I was struggling, he got a gleam in his eye, which conveyed as clear as a shout there was no escaping what he was about to do, and he was determined to make sure it would be mind-boggling.

I struggled even more then, but he ripped my panties down, grabbed my calves in an iron grip, and next thing my ankles were attached to yet more clamps, as wide apart as he could put them without hurting me. I tried to shove my knees together, but he gently squeezed my thighs and inexorably pushed them back apart, until I was lying utterly exposed. And then he just stared.

High school intimacy, in case you've forgotten, does not happen during the day. It happens at night in the back of a car, on some classroom floor in the school after hours, or on the grass underneath the bleachers at the football field—anywhere you can get a moment of privacy. You're lucky if you get a towel to lie on. If the girl thought ahead she'll be wearing a skirt, but usually both parties' jeans are shoved down to their knees. You are never ever naked, it's always hurried and hushed and guilty. High school guys do not stare at your sex because they're too busy groping it and then shoving into it for your three minutes of not-bliss.

I could not understand why Jamie was so stoked, but he looked like he was in nirvana. He sighed, his eyes glazed, and then whispered, "So gorgeous."

I was officially speechless, which is saying something because for once I wasn't gagged. He took a long languorous lick and groaned, "Heaven." He shoved his hands under my ass to lift me closer, and then he went into a kind of frenzy kissing me there, not even raising his head as he rumbled into my sex something about me being delicious (insane!),

113

and then groaned, "I am going to love making you beg, kitten. I could do this forever."

I'm not totally sure what I screamed, but I think it was "Holy shit!" followed, I am ashamed to admit, by a sobbed, "Please!"

"Again," he said between licks. "Scream my name."

"You motherfucker!" I yelled back, trying to push towards him to get enough pressure so I could come.

He stopped completely and slapped my ass. "Tsk tsk, kitten, none of that. I'm in charge. And from now on you don't come until you scream my name."

He then started circling, deliberately missing the key areas, until I was out of my mind. It was unnerving, because Jamie had an uncanny sense of how hard and how long he could push me to keep me on the edge.

I tried to hold back, I really did, but that just doesn't work with Jamie—or, if I'm going to be honest, with me either. Just the way he ordered me sent a jolt of lust through me, which of course he picked up on. He gave me a knowing smile and said, "You are on fire, kitten. I've never been so turned on in my life. Now be a good girl and obey me."

Again the words caused my whole body to wrench in pleasure, and finally I couldn't stand it. "Please Jamie, please...." I screamed.

"Jamie, please let me come," he instructed.

"You fucking jerk! Jamie, please let me come," I sobbed.

"Good girl, come for me now," he ordered and gave a strong tug at my nub, fingering me at the same time.

"Oh fuck!" I screamed out and shattered into a climax that was almost painful.

There was no time for any rest. Before I could open my eyes, he'd unlocked my ankles, and then he was inside me, thrusting as hard as he could. He didn't kiss me, which was a relief, since I think the intimacy of it might have pushed me into a mental breakdown. Instead, he wrapped his arms around me, crushing his chest to mine, and put his mouth next to my ear, where he teased, "Shall we see if you can come again, kitten?"

"No way! I can't."

He gave me an evil smile, "You can't? Never say that to me, kitten."

"Please Jamie, no," I begged.

Yes I begged! So sue me.

"Get ready, kitten." I was out of my mind by now, overwhelmed by my first and second orgasms during real-live intercourse, and by how completely Jamie could control my responses. He sped up, adjusting his position somehow, and the tension started building yet again. When he was satisfied I was close, he reached down and fondled my clitoris, causing me to spasm.

He smiled triumphantly and warned, "You come when I decide, kitten."

He pulled out then, flipped me over and pulled my hips up 'til I rested on my knees, and then thrust in again. I tried to get up on my hands, but he kept his hand on my back to force my head lower. Then he grabbed both hips and started to pound like a piston until he roared out his own climax.

Chapter 12

So that was indicative of the new regime. Gareth basically made me over to Jamie to have sex with, and the thing with Jamie was that he *really* liked sex—A LOT!

The guy made the biggest horndog at my high school look like a member of the True Love Waits peer support group. He had no job or obligations of any kind that I could tell. No reason why he couldn't spend most of every day in bed—or in our case, on cushions on the living room floor.

He took every minute Gareth allowed him with me and would stare hungrily when Gareth took me back to my room. He had "stamina," as adult film-makers like to say. His recharge time probably averaged ten minutes and except for the first time in the morning, he lasted as long as he wanted. When we weren't having actual sex, he would just rub his hands or his mouth over my body: he could literally spend hours exploring my luscious nubile curves—or my luscious toes? behind my knees? my Achilles tendons? Every square inch was an erogenous zone for Jamie, ripe for fondling, licking, nibbling, sucking, etc.

And of course, since I was always "restrained," there were all sorts of positions to explore. This was a source of inexhaustible entertainment to him. It reminded me a little of a bunch of seven-year-old girls dressing up their little brother or the family cat. Over those first four days, he tried something like two dozen different positions: me on my hands and knees, stomach, back, my hands behind my back, spread-eagled, cuffed at my sides—all easily accomplished thanks to a dozen handy little clamps.

And here's where the kink factor really *factored*, because Gareth kept possession of the keys to the handcuffs. That meant that whenever Jamie wanted to move me around, which was often, he would say something like, "Hey Gar, can we put her hands behind her back?" And Gareth with seemingly endless patience would come over and unlock the miniature lock and together they would move my body into the new position with bizarrely effortless coordination.

Jamie never protested or asked if he could have the key, and in fact, he seemed more than happy for Gareth to share in the fun. He never came out and suggested that they double-team, but he frequently shook his head over Gareth's "uptightness."

Jamie obviously knew him really well, but nothing Gareth did indicated *to m*e that he was weighing joining the party. He had his hands on me repeatedly throughout the day, pulling my body into every kinky position Jamie could come up with, but though it was intimate, his touch was never what I would call sexual. It wasn't unnecessarily rough or tender—it was matter-of-fact.

I think he meant it to be reassuring, which it kind of was, even though it often gave me shivers. That extended to the voyeurism, or whatever that was, since he never left me and Jamie together alone.

Now, no matter how you slice it, sitting in a room all day while two people are having sex is WEIRD and deviant and a bunch of other bad things, and I will go to my grave thinking that! (Though admittedly I was the only one in the house who did.) Jamie for sure had no problem with

117

Gareth watching us, if anything he preferred it, though there was something about it that didn't compute. I mean, I'm no shrink (and thank the maker for *that*!), but I didn't think Jamie was an exhibitionist per se, like he got off on having people watch him, and I didn't think it was a gay thing either, because if there was a man on earth who loved women it was Jamie. It was more connected to Jamie's dependency on Gareth, though why he was like that defied comprehension.

I also can't say that Gareth seemed particularly *into* watching us have sex—like he had arranged this scenario because it got him off. It was hard to say what he felt: he wasn't interested or uninterested. He never acted eager or embarrassed or jealous. He was just intense. Most of the time, he would work at his laptop, checking in on us occasionally, making sure the restraints weren't hurting me, insisting that I drink a glass of water, but otherwise staying out of things. Sometimes he openly watched us, making eye contact with me. He wasn't indifferent certainly, but he seemed intent on influencing my responses rather than satisfying himself.

Jamie didn't mind in the least if I stared at Gareth while we were having sex. Something about him made him seem incapable of ordinary jealousy, and as I said, he was more than happy to share the love. If Gareth was watching, Jamie would invariably direct remarks at him, which was REALLY WEIRD, though after a while it was hard to imagine him not doing that since that would require him to be quiet.

He pretty much blathered continually, before, during, and after sex, completely unperturbed by the fact that I never answered him, even when I wasn't gagged. For a while I found the way he talked mind-boggling given how close he and Gareth were. Let's just say there was not a lot of subtlety: he went on and on about my "gorgeous tits" and "hot pussy" and how he was going to "fuck me so hard." He sounded exactly like a character in a porn movie, and we all know how well-written those are.

It should have been agonizing, but he had a way of carrying off remarks like that, I guess because the porn star lingo was just so incongruous with the slacker act. Unlike Gareth, Jamie didn't take himself very seriously, and there were moments when I thought I saw the hint of a twinkle in his eye, as if he knew how inane or clichéd he sounded, but thought it was funny or at the very least didn't care.

I could tell that Jamie was careful about Gareth's rules—about a million times more careful than I had been. After his early mistakes, he made sure to avoid "belittling" comments that seemed to "make light" of what was happening (though he continued to call me "kitten"). But his verbal caution was clearly because he didn't want to piss Gareth off, not because he was concerned for me. I don't think he had a clue why Gareth was "so fucking uptight" about this.

As far as I was concerned, the fact that Jamie gave a shit about Gareth's rules fell strictly in the category of super bizarro, so much that I spent long hours obsessively trying to make sense of their relationship, without any success. It wasn't just that he was scared that Gareth would shut down the party and take away his new toy, though Gareth definitely would have. The dynamic was too longstanding to have been because of me. I know this because it was mostly unconscious on Jamie's part. (Not Gareth's—nothing was unconscious with him). I wasn't sure if it was fear or habit or some threat Gareth held. Nothing was explained to me and none of it made sense. I mean basically there were these two guys, roughly the same age and background, obviously really close friends, and yet one of them was consistently subordinate to the other.

Jamie was frequently irritated by Gareth's rules and occasionally argued with him, but in dozens of small ways he made it clear that Gareth was in authority, and besides some "oh fuck its" and "whatevers," he didn't seem to have any problem with the power dynamic between them.

For all of that, though—the strange obedience to Gareth, the slacker act, the bottomless supply of vintage concert tees—Jamie had no problem completely dominating me. With him, there was never a question of my consenting or cooperating—no mind games, no behavior modification or timers, or even punishments. He simply forced me to do whatever he wanted. He wasn't harsh or violent, but it was just second nature to him. My consent wasn't even a luxury. As far as I could tell it was not a meaningful concept to him. If he had given it a moment's thought, which I'm not sure he did except when he and Gareth were arguing about me, he probably would have said, "don't worry, she loves it" or "trust me, this is just what she needs" or some other fatuous bullshit.

I almost want to say I didn't exist for him, but that would be misleading because he was completely obsessed with me—or at least with my body. There was often a frenzied quality to his actions that made me think he'd never had a woman made so completely available to him before. I keep coming back to the kid-in-the-candy-store analogy, but he was really like that. He had no inhibitions to speak of, no shame, no embarrassment.

No question, Gareth won this round. Two days with Jamie knocked the fight out of me so thoroughly, it was hard to even remember the part of me that had sat in my corner kicking and cursing out Gareth every time he gave me a second's opening.

It seems strange to say it, because like with Gareth, I spent most of my time with Jamie tied up and gagged, but in every important way, the experiences were diametrically opposed, and it had nothing to with the fact that Jamie had sex with me and Gareth didn't.

There was just no struggling with Jamie. His good-natured obliviousness was more effective than any punishment. "Resistance" really was "futile" because it made no difference to him. I guess you could say he was a little like a human pair of handcuffs—fighting him, crying at him, had about as much effect. He had none of Gareth's need to master my will, to get me to cooperate, and with my will rendered irrelevant, I found that I was powerless to a degree I'd never imagined possible.

He also had none of Gareth's concern for preventing my "anguish," as Gareth put it in that letter that pissed me off so much. I realize now how concerned Gareth was. He always seemed preternaturally aware of my moods, anxieties, motives. This stuff just didn't register for Jamie—like it all happened on a frequency his ears couldn't hear. As I said, he wasn't mean, and he was careful not to make egregiously insensitive remarks that would piss off Gareth, but the extent of his sympathy for what I was feeling could be captured with chipper remarks like, "don't cry, kitten, Jamie will bring you off" followed by a long bout of oral sex.

The complication—humiliation?—for me was that he could "bring me off" pretty much any time he wanted. I should have caught on from his little quip about the "wager," but Gareth's "rule" about my coming was a non-issue from the get-go.

I don't know how to explain this. I mean, of everything that was making me insane during those days, that was the worst by far. How could I stand this guy who was forcing me to have sex—while I was gagged and bound?

I can generate a list of reasons, which sound like bullshit even to me, but here they are anyway. In the first place, I was attracted to Jamie. Not that first time, but after. Obviously he was really good-looking, but that wasn't it. I mean, the two football team jerks who ruined my life were both totally hot too. Conclusion being: no amount of good looks can make up for a guy treating you like a piece of shit. But Jamie never did. And it didn't hurt that he was constantly raving about how gorgeous and sexy I was—and actually sounded sincere while he did it.

Another reason was that he didn't treat me like a whore, which is to say, he never for a second acted like I was there just to get him off. For all his indifference about the consent issue, he cared deeply about how I felt during sex. And that was him, not just because he was trying to follow Gareth's rules. I think he would have been like that with any woman. He *never* acted like my being his paid sex slave, bound and gagged for his use—all those good things—meant that I shouldn't be enjoying it as much as he did.

122

The most obvious factor was that the guy was just plain gifted in bed. You know the cheesy movie line, "He ruined me for anyone else"? Basically that was Jamie. The guys I'd fooled around with hadn't exactly been Casanovas, so I didn't have much basis for comparison, but I'd bet every penny that Gareth promised me that Jamie never willingly left any woman he was with unsatisfied. And I really can't imagine him failing. For all he loved to get off, he wasn't selfish at all in bed. If his partner needed two hours of oral sex to climax, I'm sure he would have happily done it, and he wouldn't have made her feel lame or frigid for it either.

Over those first few days he spent hours figuring out what turned me on, and he obviously wasn't dependent on my telling him anything. He just knew how to read a woman's responses. Once he figured it out, he was ruthless. His eyes would get this heated look, and next he would start murmuring in my ear what he was going to do, and then he would do it: brushing his fingers over my neck, lightly breathing on my breasts, nibbling my thighs, and a minute later I'd be panting and squirming helplessly.

And the restraints didn't hurt things. That's really embarrassing to admit. Jamie was clearly not new to the bondage stuff, but I don't think it was the key for him. He would have been just as happy to have sex without it. Unfortunately, if the restraints weren't *the* key for me, they were pretty key—I liked them, a lot.

I had Jamie to thank—or blame—for that. I realize now that Gareth must have guessed but hadn't forced me to confront it. Almost the opposite: as soon as he realized how much it excited me, he dialed down the erotic element. I was so attracted to him anyway and so mixed up about the whole situation, I didn't recognize my own feelings.

But there was no hiding something like that from Jamie. He was obtuse about a lot of things, but he figured out almost immediately that being restrained—fighting like crazy but being unable to get free, unable to stop him from touching me wherever he wanted—was an insanity-inducing turn-on for me. It made me furious at myself and homicidal towards both of them—not that it did me much good, which of course was the point of the restraints.

Jamie definitely understood how to take advantage of my being completely under his control. He would get this glint in his eye, and he would pretend to check my leather wrist cuffs, and then he would start licking my breast. He was careful about what he said because of Gareth's rule about not rubbing things in my face, but he'd whisper things like "pull as hard as you want, little kitten—I know you like it."

And he knew it excited me when Gareth watched. It made me want to die of shame but I couldn't help that either, and Jamie had that figured out from the beginning. Once again, he was *very* careful that Gareth not hear anything about that, but the third time we had sex, he whispered to me that Gareth was watching. Of course, my traitorous body tensed—at which he gave me a knowing wink. From then on, that was his little private signal that Gareth was watching us, usually followed up by a loud comment to Gareth that "his girl" was especially hot.

I guess you're waiting to hear me say I felt all violated and exploited, but I can't say I did. I wasn't happy—I was completely freaked out and I spent a lot of time crying—but I wasn't miserable either. If I struggled, it was against something other than being there, being with Gareth or having sex with Jamie.

As Gareth pointed out before, I never thought about leaving. And I know that if Gareth had put me in the car and taken me back to the mini-mart, even if he gave me every penny of the money he'd offered, I would have been as miserable as I've ever been in my life. I'm sure you'll think it's a sign of how fucked up I am, and I can't say I disagree. I *knew* I was really fucked up, and I wished all the time that I was different, and from what I can tell, it never did me a fucking bit of good.

Stuff was happening to me that wasn't under my control—I didn't want it, but I didn't not want it either. And don't come at me with all that Stockholm Syndrome bullshit. I mean, I looked it up on Wikipedia and they said those captives, like, fell in love with their captors even though the captors held them at gunpoint and threatened to kill them—and then they had some crap about defense mechanisms and cognitive dissonance, and you already know how I feel about that psycho-bullshit.

Don't get me wrong, Gareth could probably teach the average hostage-taker a thing or two about manipulation and getting under people's skin until they think they're going batshit. If he had once said "I'm totally in love with you" or even just had sex with me, it might have been easier, but he was all into being enigmatic and hard to read because it gave him power.

Judging by his relationship with me and Jamie, power was basically his priority. I wonder sometimes if it was more like a compulsion. He needed to be in control, and unfortunately, control for him meant all sorts of freaky mind games and of course a lot of kinky sexual stuff.

125

But I can't really blame myself for caring about him, when he was almost the only person on the planet who cared about me. And don't even bother trying to convince me that he didn't care because you never will. If he didn't nurse some kind of feeling for me, he wouldn't have courted me for months and months with the sandwiches or gotten a bee up his ass if I ate a Twinkie. That didn't mean he cared about me the way I wanted him to, but at the very least I was important to him, and I can tell you, being important to someone, even if it is in a sick, perverted way, can be a lot better than not being important to anyone.

I'm not claiming any of this was healthy, but I wasn't too healthy before it started either—and for that matter, neither was he. Anyway, I'm hardly the only eighteen-year-old girl who's fallen for the wrong guy.

Chapter 13

The fourth morning after Jamie got there, things were off from the very beginning. In the first place, there was no knock from Gareth to wake me up, no morning protocol, hands gripping the bed—nothing. I woke up on my own a little before ten and spent five minutes lying in bed trying to figure out why the room was so bright and I was so hungry.

There was no obvious explanation and the best I could come up with was that maybe Gareth had called an unannounced vacation day. I went through my usual "hygiene" routine, knowing Gareth would blow a fuse if I didn't. There were no clothes on the bed when I came out of the shower so I put on some sweats and a T-shirt.

I half suspected the door would be locked, but no, it opened just like a normal, non-sex-slave door. I went out into the main room, but there was no Gareth sitting on the sofa with his laptop, then to the kitchen area—still nada—and then towards the front door but there was nothing but a vast emptiness.

This created a mini-existential crisis for me. Since I'd gotten there, I hadn't stepped foot outside, gone anywhere on my own, seen any part of the house except the main room, my bedroom, and the library. Anytime I was alone, I was locked in a room and at all other times I'd been supervised and most often handcuffed as well.

You'd think I'd be stomping at the gate to run wild with my new freedom—or at least to break some of Gareth's dishes, starting with the goddamned Tuscan milk pitcher. But three days of Jamie therapy had done the job. Far from running wild, I was frozen, my anxiety levels soaring off the chart.

It didn't help that I was hungry, which as you already know does bad things to my mind, but I found myself thrown into a complete panic because there was no one there to tell me I could make breakfast. I call it panic, but it wasn't even that I was afraid that Gareth would get angry and punish me if I fixed a bowl of cereal. He wasn't a bully like that, and some part of me knew he would dislike it if I were hungry.

I didn't feel some new urge to be obedient to him, and I probably would have cursed him out just to piss him off if he walked through the door. I was anxious, not scared, which actually was worse. Somehow the week I'd spent there had fucked up my ability to act independently.

I probably would have crumpled up in a ball right there and just starved until Gareth reappeared, but I heard a noise from the library— and helpless wreck that I was, I made a beeline to find someone in power who would give me permission to eat breakfast.

Unfortunately, I wasn't destined to find the source of comforting authority that I apparently now craved. I didn't find Gareth, who I then remembered never seemed to watch TV. I found Jamie slumped in one of the recliners playing Call of Duty on the Xbox.

He looked up when I came in and said with his usual gift for the obvious, "Oh, hey, you're up."

He sat up and took a nervous sip of a beer, apparently not concerned that it was only ten in the morning. He kept glancing between me and the game, as if that might make me disappear so he could go back to blowing bad guys away.

I can't say I blame him: I mean after what had passed over the previous four days, it was hard to act like we were a pair of slightly acquainted houseguests making polite chit-chat in the absence of our host. But the truth was, we'd never been together without Gareth there overseeing the interaction.

In four days, I'd had sex with Jamie more times and in more different positions than most people do in as many months—I'd more than quadrupled my own previous lifetime tally. And yet WE'D NEVER ACTUALLY SPOKEN. At least I hadn't ever spoken to him. He'd talked to me—I already told you about how he blathered continually during sex—but his usual comments on "my red-hot pussy" were clearly inappropriate now, and I somehow doubted there was any etiquette that could smooth over our current predicament.

Since every other time I'd been with him he'd been locking my hands to the floor and pulling my clothes off so he could shove his dick between my legs, I was able to deduce that there was some change in the program today, which my own brilliant reasoning suggested was due to Gareth's absence, leading me to inaugurate the speaking phase of Jamie's and my relationship with the remark: "Where's Gareth?"

He looked slightly panicked at this and said, "Oh, something came up with Sol."

"Sol, you mean Solomon Bransky?" I asked, feeling a stab of alarm. I was getting a vibe off Jamie that this was not good news.

Jamie slapped his leg and said quickly, "Shit, nothing. I mean, it's no big deal, but don't ask me about it," and finished up with another long sip of his beer.

I waited for him to elaborate, but he just sat there looking desperate for me to go, so I finally said, "Is it all right if I get some breakfast?"

Jamie flushed as if he were just remembering that Gareth had told him something about that. "Oh shit, yeah. I guess you're probably hungry. Uh, do you, like, need me to fix you something?"

I couldn't help staring at him. I mean, I know he was a weirdo pervert, but he always seemed to be of normal intelligence. Now I didn't know what to make of him. All signs indicated he was scared shitless, which considering that I'd spent the last four days completely under his control, just didn't compute. If I'd been a braver type, I'd probably have tried to torture him, but as it was, his fear was fueling my own panic.

I said quickly, "I'll just fix myself some cereal." I turned to leave, but then asked, "When is Gareth coming back?"

He actually went pale at this and gulped, "Soon, I hope."

He shook off whatever was bothering him and went back to his game, while I went over to the kitchen area. As I opened various cupboards looking for bowls, I pondered the bizarre fact that Jamie should seem, if anything, more nervous without Gareth there to act as boss than I was, but in the end I was forced to add it to the list of weirdnesses between the two of them that I couldn't figure out.

130

I was able to recover a little of my self-respect when I found the cereal section in the pantry cupboard. It turned out that Gareth, the world's biggest motherfucker, had been holding out on me. For shining like a delicious golden beacon in a sea of tasteless bran was a box of Captain Crunch! I should have guessed, because Jamie didn't exactly telegraph "health food nut"—he probably ordered two Big Macs on his weekly trips to the Golden Arches.

I only wondered that Gareth would permit him to eat junk food on the premises, but obviously there was some bizarro sexual hierarchy in place when it came to diet, because otherwise, all the evidence pointed to the fact that Jamie was as much under Gareth's authority as I was—in some ways even more so.

Anyway, I might have been freaked out without Gareth there to tell me to use a napkin, but I had no problem downing four bowls of those delectable crunchy squares. And the only reason I didn't eat five was I finished the fucking box! It was without competition the most satisfying meal I have ever eaten. If I could have added a bag of Doritos and a blue slushy I would have been in Natalie heaven. But a quick survey of the cupboards didn't reveal any more hidden treasures.

I drew the meal out as long as possible, but you can only spend so much time eating Captain Crunch, and eventually breakfast was over. I went so far as to put the bowl in the sink—next to Jamie's—and figured the house elves could wash up.

After that, I hadn't a clue what to do with myself without my usual routine of sex and handcuffs. The only thing to do in my room was watch TV, which didn't hold much appeal on a warm spring day, so I

131

spent some time sitting at the dining room table, staring out the glass walls. Though I hadn't gone outside since I'd gotten there, I didn't feel any overpowering yearning for the sun, for the world outside this house. I guess that meant I didn't feel like a prisoner.

Instead, school, my job, felt laughably far away. Time here was so fucked up, it took me a minute to figure out that it was Friday. A little after eleven—I'd be halfway through History; then I had A.P. Calculus and afterwards lunch, which I always ate at the cafeteria, since I didn't have a car or money to spare for even a slice of pizza.

After lunch I had my least favorite class, A.P. Chem. Lab, for a mind-numbing two hours. Finish school, walk to the mini-mart so I could start my Friday double shift, sneaking in reading and problem sets between selling candy bars and lotto tickets, finish my shift and then crash out in the back storeroom.

Sitting there, those normal activities felt even more surreal than my wacked-out life at Gareth's.

Surreal—and utterly in the past.

It seemed odd that the events which had thrown my life into such chaos had all taken place over a mere seven days, in the same three rooms, and involved only me and two other people. The scale in time, space and players seemed absurdly modest given the magnitude of the changes that had taken place for me. I had no desire to minimize those changes in my own mind, even though I didn't understand very much about what was happening to me.

But I did know that whatever the change entailed, it was massive and irrevocable. Nothing would ever be the same for me again. The break felt

132

so complete that I could even forgive myself for feeling slightly empty and dispirited that I wasn't handcuffed to the floor having sex with Jamie instead of enjoying a completely free day, but I felt too vague and unsettled to beat myself up.

The only active desire I could form was to go outside, but apparently Gareth's conditioning had finally taken root deep enough that I couldn't bring myself to leave the house without asking for permission, which meant facing Jamie again.

He wasn't happy to have Call of Duty interrupted and said in a sharper tone than I'd ever heard him use before, "What now?"

I hadn't exactly been peppering him with requests, so I felt a little frustrated. Jamie didn't provoke the same level of the defiance that roared to life whenever I was with Gareth, so I didn't tell him to fuck himself, but instead asked, "Can I go outside?"

"Why the fuck are you asking me?" he snapped in a manner that I would have to characterize as hostile, rude, and surly.

"Who am I supposed to ask?" I answered, more confused than annoyed. I mean, I'd spent the past four days either locked in my room or in handcuffs while Jamie forced me to engage in every kinky sex act he could think of. It was obvious that I didn't have even the most basic freedom of movement—run of the house?—use of Gareth's cars? And it wasn't as if Jamie had any qualms about asserting complete control over me. But apparently that control was limited to when Gareth was there.

"Look, I don't give a fuck. Just don't do anything that will piss Gareth off or I'll never hear the end of it, okay?" He struggled for a moment and then apparently to his own surprise managed to produce the

133

following rules: "Like, stay close to the house and don't fall in the fucking stream, or drink the water, or eat any berries and that sort of shit, and don't fucking get lost and for Christ's sake don't hurt yourself or Gareth will rip me a new one—catch my drift?" And with that, he returned to his game, having fulfilled his custodial duties.

I put on my new Converse sneakers—the first time I'd worn shoes in a week—and grabbed a sweatshirt even though it was warm enough that I didn't really need one. It was a beautiful day. The trees and scrub were covered with that early spring yellow haze that in six weeks would be deep green. So for the next few hours I wandered amidst rocks and streams, hill and dale, oak and birch—alone with my thoughts, communing with nature, blah, blah, blah.

In truth I was bored. It was better than watching TV, but that's about all that can be said. I doubt it would surprise you to hear that I am not the world's biggest nature-lover. I mean, I wouldn't shoot Bambi or anything, but the great outdoors was not exactly riveting. I would have liked walking around with Gareth. It was his property, so presumably he'd have something interesting to say about it.

Anyway, I've already said I liked to spend time with him, just talking—or even not talking. But having this "alone time" did little to settle my thoughts except to make clear that as much as I struggled, I couldn't hate what was happening. If I hated it, I wouldn't be eagerly listening for a car to signal that Gareth was home. I didn't like his being away, not knowing when he would come back. I didn't even mind the idea of Jamie as long as Gareth was there. But the idea of going inside and screwing Jamie right this moment seemed outlandish. He felt like a complete stranger and someone I had no interest in.

The weirdest part was that Jamie, who had seemed intent on setting some kind of lifetime record for orgasms reached in a four-day period, didn't seem to have any more interest than I did. There was no escaping that whatever drove the sex between us, great as it was, depended on Gareth.

I was fucked up, Gareth was, the whole thing was fucked up. But what I didn't realize was how fucked up Jamie was.

Chapter 14

I got a glimpse when I went back into the house about five o'clock and discovered Jamie shouting into his cell phone, "What the fuck do you mean, it's been delayed? When is he getting here? You told me six hours—it's been ten.... Dude, I can't do this. I'm freaking out here.... I know you're not telling me... Then why don't you fucking tell me what he said? What if he comes here? You don't know that. Maybe if we go someplace—like someplace public.... No, you don't understand. I can't stay here."

At that point he saw me, and I could literally see the pulse on his neck throbbing.

He hissed at the person on the other line, "Tell Daniel to move his ass. I'm taking her to Rusty's. Don't worry, we'll be back for her bedtime.... Yeah, well fuck you!"

He threw the phone against the wall, smashing it to bits, and let out another string of violent curses. He did his best to shake it off and gave me one of his "dude" smiles, only completely forced. "How was the walk, kitten?" So we were back to the kittens. "Look babe, I'm getting bored here. What do you say we go out for dinner?"

I started to say something to suggest that I didn't think that was such a good idea, when his face hardened and he said in a pretty good imitation of Gareth's scary voice, "You're not arguing with me, are you, kitten?" Something in his face made me gulp. He took the expression as his answer and said, "Good, now go get dressed," and then grabbed my upper arm—just shy of painfully—and directed me towards my bedroom.

His behavior was wacked out enough to scare me. I'd never seen him aggressive like this, but on the phone he'd sounded scared—terrified. It didn't help that he reeked of beer. By now my vibes were screaming that going out was one of those BAD ideas—like in the movies when the teenager announces that she's going for a nighttime swim by herself in the lake.

But since I'm that teenager what did I care? I shrugged off the creepy shadows near the shore and dove right in. Fluttering my eyelashes and giving Jamie my most flattering bimbo smile, I said, "Cool. I haven't been out to dinner in ages. What should I wear? Does it need to be, like, fancy?"

Apparently in this role play, he was the asshole boyfriend, because he said, "Do I look fucking fancy? Just wear something sexy—you can do that, can't you? And don't fucking take too long."

That pissed me off pretty thoroughly, which produced my usual clear thinking and good judgment, because I went in my room and promptly put on the clothes I'd arrived in, which would meet with most frat boys' idea of "sexy": a low-cut, navel-revealing T-shirt—sans bra—along with low-riders and thong. Subtle, right?

Jamie gave me a pretty thorough check-out when I came out, though he was still playing the asshole so he didn't say anything and just turned and walked towards the door without waiting for me. This detracted somewhat from my brief rush of angry satisfaction at the thought that

137

Gareth would shit a brick if he saw what I was wearing. Pissing off someone who isn't around is a pretty meager pleasure.

Jamie's car was a red vintage Porsche, which is to say my initial guess was right: ratty T-shirts notwithstanding, he was a rich kid, just one who was too cool to want to appear rich.

He drove like a total maniac. I made a frantic grab for my seat-belt as soon as we pulled out. He'd been nursing beers all day, and pissed as I was at Jamie, I really didn't want to imagine how Gareth was going to react to his drunk driving with me in the car. And I knew that on a normal day, Jamie would care even more than me what Gareth would think. It was a sign of how thoroughly he had gone off the deep end: right into the abovementioned creepy lake. I just had to hope there wasn't an axe-wielding psycho lurking in the shadows.

I've never been so happy to arrive at a restaurant, though my opinion was modified when I got my first look at "Rusty's," which indeed *wasn't* fancy. From the outside it looked like shack. The blinking neon Bud Lite signs, however, identified it as a bar. The line of motorcycles parked out front identified it as a biker bar.

I couldn't resist a pleading look at Jamie. I mean, I'm all for the occasional walk on the wild side—all-night raves at the New Millennium Disco in Albany—but this place just looked scary, and Jamie was already in a fighting mood.

He caught the look and grabbed my chin and said, "Don't fucking start with me," like I'd been nagging him for the last hour—like I'd ever had a conversation with the douchebag.

I could only wince at his hold, which was hard enough it would probably leave a bruise. There was no escaping it. Jamie was a train wreck, and he'd bought me a first-class ticket for the ride. I turned to open the car door, when he grabbed my arm and said nastily, "Hold on, kitten, before we go in, you'll need this," and pulled out a fucking leather collar and held it towards my neck.

"You're fucking kidding me," I said through my teeth.

He grabbed my hair and pulled my head down onto his lap and proceeded to buckle it around my neck, saying harshly, "You try to go in there without this, kitten, and the men in there will be all over you like flies on shit. This way they'll know you're mine."

"I'm not yours," I said, my voice quavering.

He laughed harshly. "You are tonight."

In case anyone was wondering, this was why I never felt like Gareth was abusive. He'd never shown contempt for my feelings. But Jamie wasn't usually like this either—not even close—and if he were, Gareth wouldn't have left me with him.

Rusty's was your basic upstate biker bar. The floor was covered with sawdust but still managed to be sticky from decades' worth of spilled drinks, piss, puke, and other unidentified fluids. The place reeked of B.O. and stale Miller. Inside it was surprisingly large, with a huge bar that ran most of the length of the building, table seating, a stage and even a small dance area. There was no band at the moment, but a juke box or stereo was blasting Guns 'N Roses.

It already had a decent Friday night crowd, with a more heterogeneous mix of patrons than I'd figured on: yuppie types mixed with bikers mixed with truckers, bar-flies, frat boys. However, the ratio of men to women was about fifteen to one, and the other women looked like what my stepmother used to call "floozies"—skanky biker chicks, older bar lushes, and a few about my age who just looked messed up.

Jamie grabbed my arm—again—and guided me to a table, shoving me in one of the seats, and promptly left for the bar without bothering to ask what I wanted. There was a chalk menu on the wall that showed that the menu options ranged from cocktail nuts all the way to buffalo wings, without even the option of a burger—so much for getting dinner.

I know I had dressed the part, and so it was my fault, but I had to admit that I hated the way the men there were looking at me: like I was some fresh piece of underage meat. For all the bad choices I've made in my life, including but not limited to coming with Jamie tonight and wearing this outfit, I had never actually done something like this: picked up guys at a skanko bar. And despite my activities since I'd gone into business with Gareth, I felt dirty just sitting there.

I looked over at Jamie, but he was continuing his shitty boyfriend act and had settled into a lengthy conversation with the bartender, leaving me to the wolves, who were visibly salivating. I wish it was paranoia on my part, but it wasn't. I knew it was just a matter of time, and what do you know, after watching me sit there alone for four minutes, two guys

140

decided to make their move and came up to the table and without asking just pulled up chairs and sat.

They were about Gareth's age, I guess. One of them was six foot three and completely built. He had a shaved head and tattoos covering every inch of his arms underneath his muscle tee. His face wasn't hideous but it was scarred, both from acne and fights, giving him the general vibe of a bare-knuckle street fighter.

The other wasn't as tall or as obviously strong, but he was definitely more something—pretend classy? rich? If the first guy was Central Casting's idea of a "bouncer/bodyguard," this guy was their pick for the role of "shady nightclub owner." He had a goatee and a diamond earring and was wearing a black silk shirt and black leather pants.

He was pretty good-looking if you're into sleazy types. Normally, I wouldn't say I was, but tonight was a night for REALLY POOR JUDGMENT, so I decided to swim out further into my dark lake and didn't tell them to fuck off, though I'm sure I didn't look too happy.

Nightclub guy ignored my discomfort and said, "So, you are Jamie's new girl."

He had a slight accent that was Russian or something equally comforting. His use of the possessive gave me pause. It could have just meant I was Jamie's girlfriend, but I remembered the collar and began to worry that this was some lifestyle code, as in I belonged to "Jamie"—like he was my master. And if that was the case, what the hell did it mean to these two assholes that Jamie had left me sitting there by myself? I found myself falling back on my usual defense—playing a dizzy bimbo. So I batted my eyelashes and said, "Yeah, me and Jamie, we're, like, totally together. He'll be back in a second."

Unfortunately the guy didn't look fooled and said coldly, "I hope he will."

There was challenge written all over his face, almost like he considered Jamie to be a weaker lion, who didn't have the goods to keep hold of the antelope he'd just taken down, and in this scenario, I had as much say as the abovementioned antelope.

Eying the collar, he said all fake casual, "You're very beautiful, my dear. How long have you and Jamie been together?"

I had no idea what to say. The way he said it made me feel cornered, like whatever answer I gave would give him some advantage. If I lied, he might catch me, if I told the truth, he might think Jamie's hold wasn't very strong. I hedged pathetically and said in the same dizzy tone, "Oh not long, but he's so great, I just get this feeling. I think he might be the one."

At this, Nightclub gave such a sharp look, I couldn't help gulping. "Indeed?" he said. "You sound quite serious."

"We are—*very*," I squeaked, trying to sound confident.

"How fortunate for you," he said with a leer, which I guess he meant to be charming, but which made him look even more like a shark—his teeth were a bit too white and straight. Bouncer didn't even try anything so subtle and instead just surveyed my breasts like he was deciding whether to put down the cash for fifteen minutes out back with me on my knees.

142

I was about to give up and just run for Jamie, when he finally decided to grace us with his presence. He'd moved from beer to Scotch and had remembered to bring a Coke for me, just in case people had missed that he had a jailbait girlfriend. The bastard was visibly wasted, which just made the jackals at the table look more hungry.

Jamie was all smiles and seemed to treat them like long-lost buddies: "Jason, Tyler, how are you guys?"

"Jamie, we have missed you. It's been ages since you came by the club. You were once my best customer. But I see you have an excellent excuse. Who is this luscious piece, Jamie?" the one named Tyler said with maximum sleaze.

"Gentlemen, this is Natalie," Jamie said proudly.

"Charmed," Tyler said, making me want to puke, and then added a bit too casually, "I don't see Gareth here."

"No. You. Don't," Jamie said, raising his scotch in a little toast and then knocking it back.

"He's let you off the leash finally? That calls for a celebration. But your lovely friend needs a drink too," Tyler said, emphasizing the word *friend*. He signaled the waitress and put in an order for a Long Island Iced Tea. Jamie made no objection, but added an order of Buffalo wings and peanuts, as well as another Scotch.

That would have been a good moment for me to speak up, since as you know, alcohol and I are not a good mix. I don't have any excuse. I knew it was a crap decision, but I did it anyway.

When the drinks came, I gulped down half of it, hoping that a light buzz would help me get through this date from hell. To my surprise, it

143

was delicious. Usually I had to force down alcohol, but this tasted just like soda.

Jamie, the human train wreck, said nothing when I ordered a second, but just kept scanning the room nervously, fidgeting exactly like a junky waiting for a hit. And what do you know! Just as the waitress brought another round, he slapped the table and muttered, "Finally." And without saying anything to the rest of us, jumped up in pursuit of someone.

Tyler said drily, "Ah, it seems Jamie's supplier has finally arrived."

Gareth was going to *love* this.

Jamie and the dealer exchanged a few words and then both headed towards the door, presumably to finish the transaction in the parking lot. A moment later a waitress arrived bringing a plate of Buffalo wings and a bowl of peanuts. She paused as if to see who had ordered them, and Tyler motioned towards me, saying "Jamie ordered it."

She slapped both dishes in front of me and picked up Jamie's empty Scotch glass. Though it's a sacrilege in our neck of the woods, Buffalo wings are one of the few junk food dishes I don't like so I pushed the plate towards the center of the table and said, "Help yourself."

Jason looked at Tyler for permission and at Tyler's nod, pulled the plate over and dug in. I nibbled on the peanuts, which were smoked but still managed to taste rancid, washing them down with big gulps of Long Island iced tea number two.

Jason was mostly through the plate of wings when Jamie came back. He was hopped up now, still jumpy but with a pleased look that made it clear he'd successfully scored whatever drugs he needed.

Observing Jason, he said "Fuck, man, you ate my wings." He signaled the waitress a bit too wildly and called out, "More wings and another round for the table."

I was riding a bit too high myself by now and started laughing hysterically as if Jamie had just told the world's funniest joke. Tyler laughed along with us, which should have set off alarm bells. The laugh went on a bit too long and at the end, I realized I had to pee, so I got up, knocking my chair over backwards, which also struck me as extremely funny.

"I just have to pee," I said, surprised at how my words were slurring after only two drinks.

Jamie didn't react, but Tyler stood up quickly and flashed me his million-dollar smile. "Let me help you." The Long-Island-Iced-Tea goggles were in full effect by now, so Tyler was looking less creepy by the minute.

I giggled flirtatiously and said, "Sure." Jamie still said nothing, so Tyler took my arm and led me back towards what was in fact the bathroom.

Even according to my rock-bottom standards, the ladies' room at Rusty's was UNACCEPTABLE. As I opened the door, I was hit by the stink of urine and puke. The room itself was beyond filthy. You can get the measure of how bad it was when I remind you that I'd been living at a gas station for the past five months. The floors were wet and littered with sopping, soiled toilet paper, which was also stuck to the walls; the seats were stained with various body fluids, and the toilets hadn't been flushed—I'll stop here, because if I told you what was floating in there,

145

you'd lose your lunch. I swallowed back my own nausea and tried to breathe through my mouth. I wouldn't have taken a piss in one of those stalls for a thousand bucks—and I'm poor.

I staggered out again and into Tyler's arms. "That's disgusting," I murmured. "Maybe we could go outside."

Don't go into the water, soon-to-be-murdered Teenager Number Two! Don't go into the parking lot with the Russian creepo. Yes, it was my fucking suggestion! But tonight was my night for ace choices.

So I let Tyler lead me out by some back door. I think I did actually pee behind (on) some poor loser's Wrangler. At any rate, the next thing I remember was getting hot and heavy with Tyler on the hood of a Mercedes. The really painful part was that even drunk I knew this was a bad idea, and I wasn't even attracted to him. In fact, I thought he was a repellent sleaze.

But by the time that idea managed finally to make its way into my brain, he already had my shirt up and his mouth on my breast—not my proudest moment. I could feel a cold sweat break out, and I started to feel decidedly sick. I made a weak effort to push Tyler away and get off the car.

Tyler, who wasn't drunk, didn't seem surprised. He helped me down, and then suddenly Jason was there too. "Natalie doesn't feel well," Tyler said smoothly. "She needs a ride home. Perhaps you could tell Jamie."

Jason had gone inside before the words registered enough for me to protest. I could barely stand now and lurched into Tyler's arms. He whispered something as he slipped something in my mouth, like a mint, only of course it wasn't a mint, and a minute later the world went black.

146

Chapter 15

The next thing I remember was waking up naked, on my knees in a strange shower, with my hands bound behind my back—which is not a good feeling, let me tell you.

I was being roughly scrubbed clean by another girl, who was wearing a bathing suit. She went to wash my front and I tried to scream and flinch away from her. She called out something in some Slavic language and immediately another, *quite large* woman, who looked like a prison matron, came and grabbed my hair so I wouldn't move, while the other girl soaped up my breasts, stomach, thighs, and then directed the water to rinse.

They both seemed completely businesslike about what they were doing—this was hardly a porno shower scene—but the water was clearing my head enough to make me realize I was in deep shit.

I tried to shout, but it was as if my voice had disappeared, and I barely gasped out, "Don't fucking touch me."

The two women ignored my protests, but when I tried to shake out of their grip, the woman holding my hair gave me a bruising pinch on the arm. After that I was quiet while they washed my hair with some disgusting fruity smelling shampoo and then pulled me up and led me out of the shower.

I saw then that we were in a large room, like the showers in a school gym. The woman who had been washing me roughly toweled me off and undid my hands. The second my hands were free, I started fighting, but the prison matron slapped my face and pulled me up by the hair until I stopped struggling enough for the younger one to put a baby-doll nightgown on me that barely skimmed my thighs, and nothing else, after which she quickly retied my hands in front of me.

The two women then led me down a seemingly endless hallway that looked creepily similar to any number of corridors at Brandon High, except that it was lit with one of those black lights, which made the nightgown I was wearing take on an indigo neon glow.

As we walked, I could hear music getting louder until we finally left the purple space for a pulsing red one, and I found myself in a porno version of a high school dance. The room looked exactly like a huge gymnasium and was packed with writhing bodies dancing to some sort of bizarro club music.

Between the drug Tyler slipped me before and the choppiness of the strobe light, it was hard to know what exactly I was seeing—whether it was real or only the creations of my own perverted imagination. I saw flashes of naked female bodies, women chained to poles or the walls or kneeling in front of shadowy male figures. A lot of them were wearing cheesy "sexy school girl" outfits, complete with knee socks and micro-mini kilts, panties not included.

As we made our way through the throng of bodies, I saw other girls kneeling facing the walls, hands bound behind their backs, licking or sucking on something. At the far end we reached an area where there were benches with girls bent over them, their asses bare, being paddled by "governess/dominatrix" types, while others stood in line, panties at their feet, I suppose waiting their turns.

148

The two women started to pull me over towards an empty bench and I felt a surge of adrenaline that propelled me from numb confusion to violent frenzy in what seemed like a half-second. I wrenched myself away from them, swinging my bound wrists to clock the small one in the nose and then elbowed the prison matron hard on her (quite matronly) boob.

The two women were so surprised they completely lost hold of me and I bolted towards the nearest door—right into Tyler's arms.

It was probably the worst moment of my life. It took him barely a second to get me subdued. He dragged me through the doors into another corridor. The music was still so loud it was almost impossible to hear, but he barked something in Russian? at the women.

Sometime later, another woman wearing pink hospital scrubs and holding a syringe came over and swabbed a spot on my left arm with some alcohol. I tried to thrash, but Tyler held me in a vice grip while the nurse injected me with something. After that they all relaxed. Obviously they knew what they were doing, because before I could start fighting again, I felt a dizzy numbness sweep over me, which caused me to actually lean against Tyler for support. The bastard kissed me and then hefted me into his arms, copping a feel as he did it.

The whole thing is hard to talk about, actually, and I don't like remembering it so forgive me if I give you the short version. Things went hazy for a while, but when I regained consciousness, I was in a barely-lit room, spread-eagled on a narrow bed, wrists and ankles attached to the corners. I could still hear the music, but it sounded far away.

The door opened and Tyler came in. "I am so happy you could join me at my club, Natalie. 'House of Correction'—clever, no? I'm quite proud of it."

I think he was—is—the sleaziest person in the history of the planet.

"Where's Jamie?" I said, groping feebly for some way out of this.

"I assume he is still passed out at Rusty's. Anyway, I am sure once he sees the footage of us in the parking lot, he will no longer take any interest in you. Jamie has something of a weakness for women like you, but I doubt even he would take kindly to your fucking the owner of the local bondage club. Anyway, certain members of his family will pay quite a lot to make sure he is kept safe."

"Safe? What the fuck are you talking about?" I demanded.

"So you're not a ditz—I didn't think so—just a tramp." He said it sneeringly, as if he weren't the epitome of scum himself. "Do you think you are the first woman to try to entrap the heir to the Vandenberger fortune? Frankly, you are lucky I found you before his family did."

Oh My Fucking God! This was happening because I'd pretended I was dating Jamie? It was like some brutal cosmic joke. I'd heard of the family and even Jamie himself. Everyone in the world had, because his parents had died in a very tabloid-worthy way—suspicious boating accident, rumored to be a murder/suicide—leaving Jamie at age ten the sole heir to about a bajillion dollars. And, I now remembered, his mother was a Bransky.

And now, thanks to Jamie's meltdown, I was tied to a bed while *Tyler* stroked my thighs. I fought against the bonds and shouted, "Get your fucking hands off me."

"Oh, I'm hurt, my dear. And we were having such a pleasant time at Rusty's—many people witnessed it. I'm sure I will have no problem convincing people that you came willingly."

"If you touch me, it's rape, I swear it," I sobbed hysterically. "I don't say yes to this. This is rape!"

"My dear, this is a bondage club. Our customers play out rape scenes every night of the week. I already have the paperwork filled out saying you specially requested this five days ago."

He stood and moved to the front of the bed and started to unzip. I tried to close my eyes and blank my mind, pretend this wasn't happening, but I couldn't look away. It was happening, and I could do nothing to stop it.

I'll say right here: he didn't rape me. It was still an incredibly horrible experience, but it wasn't rape. Frankly, given how horrible it was, I don't know how women get through the real thing. If he had finished, I think he might have killed sex for me for the rest of my life.

But it's over. I got lucky.

At that point I became aware of unusual sounds in the background—shouting in various languages, doors slamming, furniture being smashed. Tyler heard it and quickly zipped up his pants and went outside to investigate.

Some blessed instinct told me the noise was for me, and I shrieked loud enough to shatter my own eardrums. A minute later, the prison matron and Jason burst through the door, followed by a man even larger than Jason, who was holding a gun.

He glanced at me and snarled, "You have fifteen seconds to get her off that bed before I start shooting."

Jason yelled something at the woman in Russian, and she immediately released my hands and feet and pulled me to my feet, before standing back in obvious terror.

"Where are her fucking clothes?" was the next question. Jason barked again, and the woman scurried out as fast as she could.

A moment later, Tyler came in also holding a gun and said furiously, "Daniel, what is this about? How dare you invade my club like this!"

The aforementioned *Daniel* pointed his gun at Tyler and said, "Your club is officially closed. You have until noon tomorrow to empty the place. After that I shoot anyone I find."

"This is outrageous. I am up to date on all payments. How dare Gareth throw out our agreement like this for no reason?"

At this, Daniel cocked the trigger in a way that I can only characterize as intimidating. So far as I could tell he was ready to kill Tyler right then. "No reason?" he said sarcastically. "You were about to rape her."

"This is ridiculous. In the first place, the girl came willingly. Second, you should be thanking me. I hear Solomon has Gareth cleaning up Jamie's messes these days. All I did was take out the trash for you."

"Tyler, you dumb fuck, you made the biggest mistake of your life tonight. That girl isn't Jamie's, she's Gareth's."

"Don't fuck with me, Daniel," Tyler said too calmly. "She was with him—she wore his collar. She gave me some nonsense about how Jamie was 'the one.' She's just a little gold-digger."

152

"Tyler, I don't think you are hearing me. It doesn't matter what *she* said. You touched Gareth's girl."

"This is bullshit," Tyler said through his teeth. "I'm going to Solomon. This is just an excuse to steal my business. Gareth doesn't keep girls, and if he did, it would not be some little whore."

"Go ahead and tell Gareth that. It will save me the trouble of coming back here to kill you. Now, *where are her fucking clothes?*" The woman came in with the clothes I'd been wearing. Daniel rifled through each item before tossing it to me, barking, "Get dressed!"

Once I was dressed, Daniel pushed me face forward against the wall and handcuffed my hands behind my back. Looking like a detective making an arrest, he grabbed my arm and headed towards the door, saying over his shoulder, "Tyler, just so we're clear: I managed to talk him down from killing you tonight, but he specifically told me to tell you: you have forty-eight hours to get out of his territory. If he finds you after that, he'll cut off your balls himself."

Outside there were about ten men, like Daniel dressed in black military-looking clothes, holding what I think were actual AK-47s. Also like Daniel, every single one of them looked like Central Casting's offering for the role of "ex-Delta Force security specialist." It didn't take a Ph.D. in theoretical physics to figure out that this was Gareth's personal army.

Daniel dragged me over to a black Expedition, opened the backseat door of the car and, putting his hand on top of my head, pushed me roughly onto the seat and then reached over and fastened the seat belt. Jamie was there too, also handcuffed, barely conscious. Daniel slammed

153

my door shut and then ripped open the driver's side door, slammed that one shut, and started the engine.

Relieved as I was to have escaped from "The House of Correction" with just a gross same-sex shower and some thigh grazing, Daniel was not exactly a comforting presence. Even though I was being rescued—I hoped—apparently I still needed to be handcuffed. He'd not said a word to me, and I could tell he was doing some kind of breathing exercise to get his rage under control.

He caught me looking at him and said in a tone that I would characterize as *hostile*, "I seem to have arrived in time to stop Tyler, but did anyone actually mess with you? And don't even think about trying to lie to me." His question caught me off guard, and I just blinked at him, not sure what he wanted. He roared out, "Answer the fucking question!"

Next to me, Jamie had been mumbling to himself, but now apparently became roused by the interrogation. "Back the fuck off, Daniel. You're scaring her."

Daniel glanced over his shoulder at him and said furiously, "Jamie, you are in such deep shit right now, you are in no position to ask anything for her. Now answer my fucking question: were you raped?"

"No," I said quickly.

He seemed relieved by that and then said less angrily, "Did anyone touch you—don't try to protect Jamie. I'll find out the truth tomorrow, anyway." Protect Jamie from what? "Answer!" he said, in a tone that made me jump.

"Just some weird Russian women," I said sullenly. He made it sound like it was my fault. "They made me take a shower, and then some nurse gave me a shot. Tyler fondled my thighs, nothing more."

Daniel nodded and then said coolly, "After he had your goddamned breast in his mouth at Rusty's. It looks like you'll survive the night, Jamie. Maybe you'd like to tell me why you decided to attempt suicide tonight?"

At this, Jamie started wailing in a seriously unhinged manner. There was lots about Gareth, and being sorry, and being a fuckup, and deserving whatever they gave him. Then he started manically begging me, "Kitten, I am so sorry—I fucked up so bad, I never fucked up so bad in my life."

It was awful to listen to—embarrassing. Daniel seemed to agree because he snapped out, "Jamie, shut the fuck up, or I swear I will beat you senseless," and then flipped on the car stereo to what I think was Lynyrd Skynyrd or something equally heinous and turned up the volume to max. After that, Jamie sank into drunken mumbling, which luckily I couldn't hear over the blasting abomination that is "country rock."

I sank into a stupor myself and was only roused by Daniel pulling me out of the car in front of Gareth's house. I had no idea what time it was, but it was still dark. Jamie was already outside, looking like he was coming down off the worst trip in junkie history. I thought Daniel would undo the handcuffs, but instead he took each of us by the upper arm and perp-walked us into the house.

His cell rang the moment he shut the door. He pushed both of us to sit against the wall as he answered: "Yeah, we just got here. She's fine… No, she's telling the truth." He paused for what was obviously Gareth on the other line. "They drugged her.... I don't know. I can find out tomorrow.... You already know: he's a fucking mess.... I sent you the parking lot footage, Gareth.... No one's going anywhere; it's under control... I already told you how I was going to deal with him.... Good.... Fine, I'll do it."

He rang off and barked at us, "Don't move." Jamie looked unconscious, and I wasn't much better off. I'd reached my limit—drugged, manhandled, woman-handled, almost raped, definitely molested—I slumped against Jamie and vaguely remember being carried somewhere—not my room—given some sweet liquid to drink, placed on a toilet and told to pee and then put in a strange bed.

Chapter 16

When I woke, I found that one hand was cuffed to the frame of a small cot that had been set up in a room that didn't appear to have any windows. Some part of me was aware that bad shit had gone down the night before, but I pushed away any memories and focused on the present.

There was a weak light, enough for me to see that Jamie was passed out on an identical cot three feet away, with one hand also cuffed to the bed frame. I sat up slightly and saw that Daniel was sitting in one of the living room chairs close to a table lamp he'd placed on the floor.

He got up and unclipped my hand and without a word led me to an adjoining bathroom—which was a good thing, since I now realized I had to pee, which I did, about a gallon.

I had a horrible taste in my mouth and fumbled around for a toothbrush and to my surprise saw mine. I brushed my teeth, and before I came out, Daniel handed me some clothes through the door. I pulled off my filthy clothes from the night before and put on my usual button-down shirt and La Perla underwear, though I vaguely registered that Daniel hadn't given me any shorts. Once I came out, he motioned that I should sit on the bed and gave me a bottle of some citrusy sports drink.

"How's your stomach?" he said gruffly. "Headache?" I shook my head. I felt terrible, but it was more a whole-body queasiness than anything specific. "Once we're done down here, I'll take you back to your room. You'll both need a lot of sleep over the next few days. Stay hydrated, that's important." He didn't elaborate on what had to be "done down here," and I was in no mood to ask, but Jamie was stirring. Daniel gave him a hard look and then said sharply to me, "Don't speak to him."

"Why the fuck not?" I responded automatically.

Daniel bristled and snapped, "You really are a piece of work, aren't you. Hands against the fucking wall!"

Not one to wait for meek compliance, which wasn't exactly imminent, Daniel grabbed my elbow, whipped me around and placed both my hands on the wall, holding me in place in a way that made it impossible to move at all. He forced a folded piece of cloth in my mouth and then secured it with another tied around my head.

I already told you the guy screamed *Special Forces*. He was six foot three, thirtyish, and built like a missile-proof Humvee. He was good-looking in a Delta Force kind of way, which isn't my favorite: his hair was so short there was no telling what color it was, he had a strong chin and piercing eyes that kind of reminded me of Gareth's.

At least he seemed intelligent, but he looked like he hadn't laughed in the last fifteen years—due to having one of his AK-47s jammed up his ass. I could easily imagine him as head of security for Gareth's "business interests," but I couldn't see him buddying up with Jamie, although something about the vibe last night told me they had known each other for years.

Anyway, GI Joe cuffed my hands behind my back and then, for good measure, blindfolded me. Despite my valiant efforts to dig in, he had no difficulty getting my feet to go where he wanted them to. He unlocked a door and then pushed me into a different room. There was some quality in the coolness that made it clear the room was underground and it was tiled. If I'd not known it was impossible, I would have guessed we were in a hospital room. Daniel sat me down against a wall and clamped my hands down, easily catching my feet as I tried to kick him.

He snorted, "Do you always do this? Because it's a huge fucking waste of energy—for both of us."

The next thing, I could feel something being buckled around my ankles and a moment later, both were fastened together and then to the floor so that I could barely move them an inch in any direction.

"Comfortable, right?" he said as if pissed that I made him do that.

I tried to scream and struggle, but I was completely immobilized—which I now realized was something quite different than merely wearing handcuffs.

He pulled off the blindfold and threw it away and then left the room again, locking the door. The room was bigger than the one we'd slept in. There was only a single weak bulb hanging from the ceiling, enough light to see that I'd guessed right about the tiles. There was also a drain on the floor and I could just make out a stainless steel sink against the wall. Talk about Jeffrey Dahmer: the room was completely creepy.

Daniel came back again three minutes later, this time pulling Jamie along. Jamie was wearing his usual jeans but no shirt, and his hands were bound behind his back, though he was *not* blindfolded or gagged, because the second he saw me, he shouted furiously, "What the fuck is she doing here—no way Gareth told you to bring her here."

159

"My call, Jamie. And from your reaction, clearly the right one," Daniel said coolly.

Jamie struggled to pull away from him and had about as much luck with that as I did, despite being close to Daniel's size. "You fucking prick! I told you it was my fault. She had nothing to do with it. You have no right to bring her into this."

"Well, I think she needs to see this, and what I think goes." He pulled Jamie over to a spot deeper in the room and turned him so that Jamie was facing away from him. "No fucking games, Jamie. You earned this and you know it."

Jamie gave a slight nod and stood quietly while Daniel uncuffed his hands and rebound them in front and then attached them to something above his head. Daniel walked over towards the wall and fiddled with something, which turned out to lower Jamie's arms until his hands were even with his face.

Then he walked over and released my hands and feet from the clamps. My ankles were still tied together, so instead of making me walk he just picked me up by the waist and carried me to where Jamie was standing and made me stand in front of him, close enough for our bodies to touch. He then uncuffed my hands and as with Jamie immediately rebound them in front of me and then pulled them up and fastened them to whatever was holding Jamie's hands. I was of course struggling this whole time. We were so close that I was banging into Jamie, more from terror than anything else.

Jamie hissed something at Daniel, but then started to speak in a low tone right in my ear, "Shush, kitten. Stop struggling. He's not going to

160

touch you, I promise. Kitten, it's okay," and then to Daniel, "She's scared—she can't control it when she's like this."

Daniel came around behind me and crushed me against Jamie until I couldn't move and said very sharply, "Natalie, listen to my voice. Stop thrashing now!" I must say there was something about that masterful tone of his—my whole body shuddered and I stopped moving. "Good." He pulled back slightly and put his hands on my shoulders. I immediately tightened, but he said directly in my ear, "You will relax your shoulders and your neck. Otherwise you will hurt yourself or Jamie."

I felt the panic dissipate slightly. He continued to massage my shoulders and then said, "Lean your head against him. Good. Now listen carefully, there is a bar just above your head—you need to grip it. Do not let go, or you will injure your wrists."

Again there must have been something hypnotic in his voice, because I actually obeyed and reached up and gripped the metal bar that Jamie was also holding. I soon understood why, because Daniel immediately went to the wall, and whatever we were holding onto rose until Jamie's arms were taut, and I was almost hanging by my arms off the ground. Daniel quickly slipped something underneath my feet and unbound my ankles, but I still could only stand on my toes.

I know I was shaking and crying; Jamie kept murmuring soothing words into my ear, his lips practically against my ear. "I'm sorry you have to see this, kitten. Don't be scared. He's not going to touch you. You don't need to be scared of him." He kissed my forehead and then laughed a little. "Your rubbing me like that's making me horny as hell, kitten. I wonder if Daniel will let me take you afterwards."

161

Daniel snorted from deep in the room and said, "You won't be in any shape for that, Jamie."

I couldn't help flinching, and Jamie said quickly, "Kitten listen, I knew this was coming. It's the way we do things. I know you don't understand, just trust me. Daniel's an expert at this, and he's fair. When it starts keep your eyes closed. Can you do that for me, kitten?"

I now saw why, because Daniel had come towards us carrying a leather whip, one that wouldn't have been out of place in a movie about Roman gladiators or the Inquisition. In real life, it was terrifying, enough to make me start thrashing again.

Jamie sounded almost desperate as he whispered, "Quiet, kitten, just close your eyes, rest your head on me. Please, kitten." To Daniel he said angrily, "She's going to hurt herself."

But Daniel was already wrapping something around both of our waists, like a narrow belt which he pulled as tightly as he could until our bodies were crushed together. He also lifted the apparatus that held our hands another inch so that I could barely touch one toe at a time to the floor. Without the floor, I had no more leverage to move. Being tied so tightly to Jamie took some of the strain off my arms.

Daniel then stood back and said almost formally, "Jamie, the terms of your agreement with Gareth specifically prohibit drugs and alcohol. Last night you violated those terms numerous times."

"I did," Jamie said tensely.

"You understand that because of your actions, Natalie was almost raped, that she was in fact abused and subjected to extreme distress."

"Yes."

162

"Do you accept my right to punish you?"

"Yes."

Daniel came close again, this time holding some sort of rubber stick. Jamie started to shake his head, but Daniel said firmly, "Don't fuck around, Jamie. You know the drill."

"I won't be able to talk. You have to help her if she gets in trouble."

"Gareth charged me with her care," Daniel said pointedly, which caused Jamie to blanch miserably, I guess remembering the job he'd done.

He nodded and opened his mouth and then bit down on the stick. As he walked around us, Daniel said in a low voice, "Don't make it worse for him," which as much as anything forced me to calm down.

My face was pressed into Jamie's chest, so I couldn't see what was happening anyway, but I could sense the movement behind him and it was easy to guess when Daniel said, "Twenty-five strokes."

Jamie braced himself and, coward that I am, I closed my eyes. Just the sound of the leather flying through the air was terrifying enough, but it was nothing to the sick snap as the whip hit Jamie's back. I know he was trying to control his response, but he still let out a grunt of pain.

Daniel said, "One," there was a slight pause and then I heard the sound again: two, three, and so on.

From then on, it was a surreal nightmare, as bad in its way as the House of Correction. By the time Daniel had reached seven, Jamie was shaking. With each stroke I could feel his body tighten with the pain. I sobbed as quietly as I could.

163

After thirteen strokes, Daniel came over and undid the gag and made me drink some water. He then offered some to Jamie, who managed to whisper, "I know it's fucked up, kitten, but it makes it easier having you here."

That weirdly made me feel a tiny bit better. I pressed my cheek against him and rubbed a bit, and he kissed my hair—it made it feel a little like a Jamie Bond movie. Now that I was calmer Daniel lowered us down again, enough for me to put the balls of my feel on the ground and left the gag off. But the break was done. Daniel put the bit back in Jamie's mouth, and the whole thing started again.

By twenty strokes, Jamie was barely conscious, but I could still feel him flinch with each stroke. Finally, after what felt like an hour had passed, Daniel said hoarsely, "Twenty-five. It's over."

He had to force Jamie to open his mouth to take the bit out. Jamie was shuddering, but managed to take some of the liquid Daniel pressed on him. Daniel released the belt that held us together and lowered our arms, which made both of us stagger.

Jamie groaned in pain at the movement and, clearly steeling himself, looked over his shoulder at his back. He let out a hiss, and his face went dangerously white. I gasped out, "Jamie!"

Daniel ever alert, quickly unlocked his handcuffs, but Jamie hissed almost hysterically, "Don't let her see." It was like he was getting delirious, and I suddenly worried he might go into shock.

Daniel quickly tied something over my eyes. I could hear him murmuring to Jamie, "It's done. Look—she's fine, I promise you. I need

164

to take care of you first. Stay with me, Jamie." The door opened and I was alone.

I'd been worried enough about Jamie—with good reason—but in truth, I wasn't doing too well either. Now that it was over, I started shaking and going cold too. The full thrust of what had happened came back to me.

Even as I mentally railed against Daniel as a sadistic psycho, I was remembering what had caused all this. Because of whatever crisis Jamie was having, he'd left me to Tyler's mercy. I would have been raped—really and truly. I suddenly remembered the feeling of Tyler's fingers on my thighs, and it was enough to make me puke out the Gatorade all over the floor.

I don't know whether it was his GI Joe super senses or maybe just a monitor, but Daniel instantly burst through the door. He ripped off the blindfold, checked my eyes and face, and then released my arms and lowered me to the floor, pushing my head between my legs. A second later, he wrapped a soft blanket over me. "What happened?" he barked out. "Are you feeling faint?"

"I'm fine," I cried in a strange keening tone that sounded like a wounded animal—or maybe an asylum inmate. I kept repeating it over and over, but I wasn't fine. A moment later, I tipped over onto the floor and started sobbing hysterically. Daniel hefted me into his arms and raced two doors down the cement-lined corridor, back to the room with the cots. Jamie was curled up on one under about ten blankets, shaking. Daniel lowered me gently onto the other cot and disappeared for a moment, only to return with a pile of blankets. It didn't help, and I started wailing, "I'm sorry, I'm sorry!"

I'm sure it was a fun morning for Daniel between me and Jamie. After crying like it was the end of the world, I started hyperventilating and then retching again. I apologized like mad, but no amount of commands and pleas from Daniel could get me under control.

At some point, I heard him on the phone. "I'm up to my fucking neck here." When I realized it was Gareth, like a crazed tool I screamed, "Tell him I'm sorry."

"You heard that?... She's a mess.... Ten minutes.... Tyler doped her or I'd give her something myself."

Then suddenly, Jamie of all people commanded, "Natalie, to me! Now!"

Somehow his use of my name got through. I got to my feet and staggered the two feet over to his cot. Jamie reached for my wrist and pulled me down onto the cot against him. Then he just put his arms around me. "Shh, Natalie, calm." I was still gasping and shuddering, but the fit of hysterics started to die down.

Somewhere at the edge of consciousness, I heard Daniel say, "Wait a minute.... No, she's calming down. Jamie did it, crazy fuck. Maybe this wasn't such a crackpot experiment after all."

I started to feel sleepy and turned so my back was to Jamie. He pulled me close and nestled the top of my head. It being Jamie, I felt his hands move until one was holding my left breast and one was between my legs, but by then I was too exhausted to care.

Chapter 17

Daniel must have carried me up to my room, because that's where I was when I woke up. The shades were down, but it was obviously the middle of the day. I assume he was monitoring me, because he came in right away carrying a tray, which he put on the table next to the bed. It had an array of sick-person food on it: ginger ale, crackers, chicken soup, applesauce, etc. It had been ages since I'd eaten but my stomach recoiled at the thought of so much as a saltine.

He saw my response and said firmly, "Start with the ginger ale. You need to eat." I took a sip and blanched, but bit a corner off one of the saltines in the hopes that he'd leave, but he just stood there, watching me, looking uncomfortable. Finally he began what sounded like a rehearsed speech. "Gareth feels that the events last night arguably constitute a failure on his part to meet the terms of your contract with him, specifically the section promising to protect you from harm. He feels obligated to offer to release you and would let you keep the money he's already paid."

"I don't understand."

He mumbled, "Fuck it," and then said, "Because of Jamie's fuckup, Gareth feels he should at least offer to let you out of your agreement with him."

"He wants me to leave?" I said, I have to admit, tearfully.

"No, he wants you to stay, but Gareth takes his obligations seriously. He feels he should offer."

"I don't want to leave," I answered a bit too quickly.

Daniel nodded and then said, "You should be clear on something. He is not offering to change the terms of your agreement. If you live in this house, you follow his rules, which include submitting to your share of the punishment for last night's fiasco."

"You're...gonna...me?" I couldn't even say the words.

"Your punishment is Gareth's concern. He'd never whip a woman, but you will have to satisfy him for your part. He saw the footage of you going at it with Tyler Fucking Zoltov, and he's not happy." Daniel gave me a cool stare as I swallowed this tidbit.

Finally I said, "He promised not to hurt me."

"He keeps his promises. Whatever he does will be within the terms of your agreement of him, which was true for Jamie too, for what it's worth. Now what is your answer?"

"I have nowhere to go," I whispered. Daniel just kept staring, so I added, "And I don't want to...to go."

He nodded and said, "Eat. I'll be back in half an hour."

I was tired again despite all the sleep, but I made an effort to nibble on the various offerings. I couldn't help feeling unsettled by Gareth's offer. On the one hand, I was impressed that he'd be scrupulous enough to offer to let me off, but there was also no mistaking my stark relief when Daniel said Gareth didn't want me to go. The mere thought that Gareth wanted out made me feel sick. And yes, I know: I'm a pathetic tool.

I wondered that he hadn't spoken to me himself, but then I realized that was another part of the scrupulousness. Daniel hadn't been audience to my epic struggle of the past week. It would have been humiliating to have to confess that I really wanted to stay after all the crap I'd pulled.

More than anything else, it made me feel strangely grateful to Gareth. But he was careful that way. He didn't rub things in or gloat, which I think is a big part of why I did want to stay. In comparison, Tim, that asshole from the football team, made me feel like a whore and an idiot for trusting him; he'd had no problem humiliating me in front of the whole town.

Daniel returned as promised after half an hour. He glanced at the tray and looked like he was on the brink of insisting that I eat more, but then thought better of it. He went into the bathroom, and I could hear the water running for the bath.

He came back and picked up the tray. "Take a bath—it will help. You are both going to need a few days to recover."

"Can I see Jamie?"

He seemed surprised by that. "Do you want to?" I must have looked surprised in turn, because he said, "I figured once you'd had the chance to think about it, you'd show the bastard the door."

I blinked at that. I mean, Jamie had screwed me royally, but I didn't have enough energy to feel angry with him, and anyway after what he'd gone through last night, I couldn't deny that he'd paid, big time. I just shrugged and Daniel said,

"I'll tell him."

169

As he left, I called out, "Tell Gareth from me, I hope he had a fucking good reason for leaving. Quote those exact words."

Daniel shook his head, "Tell him yourself. He'll be back tomorrow, and then it will be your turn."

Chapter 18

My turn came late afternoon the following day. Apparently Jamie and me were under some sort of house arrest, because I spent all of that day and the most of the next locked in my room watching TV, occasionally interrupted by terse exchanges with Daniel, who brought in a tray for meals.

I was just starting a rerun of "Buffy" when Daniel came in without knocking. He didn't say anything but pulled me off the bed, flipped me over, and handcuffed my hands behind my back and then blindfolded me. I of course started cursing him out, which he tolerated about as well as Gareth did, shoving a cloth in my mouth and tying another around my head. He then walked me out and down the stairs, somehow managing to keep my feet moving despite my struggles. Down two flights, he unlocked a door, and pushed me in.

Once the door was closed, he took off the blindfold. We were in the same room he'd used to punish Jamie. Jamie was there, dressed in his usual jeans and favorite Screaming Trees concert tee. He was pale and moved carefully, but overall he looked better than I would have guessed.

Daniel pushed me roughly into his arms. Jamie gave me one of his heated smiles and immediately started to grope me. He saw that I was terrified and affectionately brushed my face with his thumb.

"Poor kitten, don't be scared. It won't be that bad, I promise. I wish I could stay and help you like you helped me." He literally put his hand down my pants, cooing, "I missed you, kitten. If we had time right now...." He was rock-hard as usual and basically started to make out, kissing my neck and rubbing our pelvises together.

"Jamie, stop acting like a fucking loon," Daniel barked, echoing something of my own thoughts. Scared as I was, some part of me was beginning to grasp that Jamie's puzzle was missing a few key pieces.

Still, he was genuinely trying to make me feel better and kissed my forehead and kept offering reassurances, punctuated with lots of "kittens" and nuzzling of my breasts.

After another minute, Daniel said sharply, "Cut that shit out now and bring her over here," more angry with Jamie than me.

Jamie gave me another kiss and then dragged me over to a padded bench complete with straps for wrists and ankles. I struggled frantically, but Jamie forced me to bend at the waist until I was lying face down, keeping his hand on my back so I couldn't get up, all the while whispering in my ear, "I know you're scared, but you'll be fine, kitten. Gareth would never hurt you. You know this."

Daniel uncuffed my hands and took my right arm, pulled it over the side towards the floor and bound it with something, and then fastened my left hand on the other side. After they were both secure, he pulled them until they were stretched tight. He then moved around behind me and brusquely pulled my sweats and underwear off.

Jamie said eagerly, "Wait, I have a surprise for Gareth." I felt him rubbing his hands over my legs, and then he started to put something on my right foot, which turned out to be a white thigh-high stocking. After his usual amount of fondling, including kisses to my inner thighs, he managed to get both it and the left one on, at which he gushed, "Kitten, I wish you could see how sexy you look right now. Gareth's a lucky bastard. I would kill to redden that ass."

Daniel angrily pushed him out of the way and snarled, "Jamie, would you shut the fuck up?" He then grabbed my right ankle and pulled it to the side, attaching it to a padded cuff followed by the other, until my feet were bound about two feet apart.

I must say, Daniel was all business, carefully checking each bond, testing the straps, adjusting my body to his satisfaction with about the same level of interest he might show if he were tuning a bicycle—less probably. It somehow mitigated a lot of the humiliation I might otherwise have felt at being splayed out like that.

Jamie, of course, showed no such discretion, instead engaging in his usual complimentary patter while copping as many feels as he could. But I was used to him, and some part of me felt soothed when he said with his usual insouciance, "Oh, kitten, what I would give to fuck you right now. I would give you the orgasm of your life."

But I also wasn't surprised when Daniel snapped out in disgust, "Jamie, the shit that comes out of your mouth…. For once in your fucking life, would you just listen to yourself?"

But from what I could tell, Daniel's comments made about as much of an impression on Jamie as Gareth's. Daniel pushed a flat cushion under my hips, and after testing the various straps again, loosened my arms so he could position two small bolsters so my breasts wouldn't be crushed into the table. After that, he tightened my arms again and then attached another strap over my back, just under my arms, and pulled it so

173

tightly, I literally couldn't move my torso a centimeter. Except for my head, which I could lift enough to turn, I was completely immobilized. That done, he knelt down so we were face to face and untied the gag. My lips were already dry, so he put some balm on them and gave me a sip of water through a straw. After that, he replaced the blindfold.

Jamie kissed my forehead and said, "You'll be fine, kitten, promise," and they both left the room.

A very long, terrifying minute later, the door opened, and I heard Gareth's voice say, "Natalie."

Chapter 19

Before I had a chance to answer him, he had put the gag back on me. I flinched and tried to struggle, but it was impossible to move. I was too stunned to make sense of much, but I think I might have been close to hyperventilating when his cool hands moved lightly up and down my back and then started to press down gently and release in a slow, even pattern. "Listen to my voice. Take deep breaths. Follow the rhythm I am creating with my hands." There was enough iron in his tone to get through even my fucked-up brain.

When my breathing had slowed, he came around and undid the blindfold and pulled up a chair so he could sit where we could see each other easily. "We've had a lot of games, you and I, this past week. Unfortunately, the other night we moved beyond games. I have tolerated an awful lot of defiance and disobedience from you, but I will not tolerate you letting Tyler touch you, so now I'm going to punish you. You should understand, Natalie, that I am not doing this because I have some moral right, but because I always hold people to the agreements they make with me, and I don't make agreements with people unless I can do that."

He was gently rubbing my cheek as he said this, but his eyes were almost glittering, and I could feel his rage. I sensed that it was under control, though, which kept me from a complete wig-out. Standing up, he went over towards the other side of the room and picked something up and walked behind me.

175

"I am going to give you twenty blows with a paddle; there will be a five minute break and then, assuming certain suppositions I have made prove correct, which I strongly believe they will, I'm going to give you another twenty with my hand. I know you're scared so I won't drag this out: you'll feel my hand on your back and two seconds later a blow, and then I will continue until the twenty are over."

He was true to his word: I felt his hand on my lower back and then a sharp smack from the paddle.

And Oh My God did it sting! He didn't fucking hold back. It was enough to rouse me from the stunned state I was in. I started to struggle frantically, but there was no going anywhere. Gareth landed one after another, alternating cheeks. He kept his hand on my back the whole time, pressing down gently. Somewhere in the background I could hear him calmly calling out the count.

By the time he'd reached seven, the pain was becoming unbearable, except of course, I had no choice but to bear it.

By the seventeenth, I started to pull desperately, hard enough to endanger my wrists. "Stop pulling now," Gareth said in his sharpest command tone, "or I will give you another five strokes."

And what do you know, he'd finally found a threat that worked, because I stopped instantly. He grunted approval and then dealt out the final three—smack, smack, smack—each more painful than the last.

Done with round one, he put his hands on my ass—more analytically than sexually—I think to make sure I wasn't hurt. He came back towards my head and pulled out his beloved little digital timer and set it for five minutes. Then he untied the gag. I let out a choking gasp, followed by shuddering sobs.

He held a straw to my lips and said firmly, "drink." I took a long sip of water, and then he replaced the gag. "You should know this about me, Natalie: I do not enjoy giving women pain for its own sake. But I will do what I need to bring you to submit to me." He stood up and leaned over my back, brushing my neck with his mouth, blowing lightly on my ears. Then he said in his softest voice, "And now for my supposition. I know the pain is hard to deal with, but I think part of the reason we have been having so many difficulties is this."

I felt his fingers lightly flick between my legs—and immediately felt a surge of moisture. I cried out half from anger, half from pleasure, as he slowly stroked me.

"If I can't bring you to a climax before the timer rings, we will stop. If I can, I will give you the rest of your punishment." I wanted to scream and struggled more furiously than ever, but Gareth kept up his soothing pep talk. "Desire is very complex, Natalie. Acts we reject as shameful, that offend and anger us, can also arouse us like nothing else. I don't think you desire pain per se, so much as fear and punish yourself for those things you do desire."

As he spoke, he was slowly increasing the pressure. I was out of my mind with rage at the punishment—and at having to listen to his fucking psycho-babble—but I could feel the orgasm building inexorably. Just before it hit, he pulled down the gag and said, "You have permission to speak," which was timely, because I started screaming: my first orgasm under his hand and without competition the most intense of my life. It

177

went on forever, each jolt causing my body to seize as if it had just received a blow.

Gareth drew it out as long as possible, but even still, when my faculties returned to their non-orgasmic state and I glimpsed the timer, I saw that there was more than a minute left—and I still had my twenty blows.

I started sobbing at this. He kissed my forehead and then put the blindfold on, but this time left the gag off.

The next thing I heard his voice from behind me, saying, "I will not punish you for things you say when you are receiving blows or during orgasm. This will be the same as before; you'll feel my hand, and then I'll start."

Some part of me desperately wanted to stay quiet—like a CIA agent in a movie—and not give him the satisfaction of hearing me beg. That lasted until the second slap, at which point I started screaming my head off. The orgasm had already addled my brain, and now having the blindfold on seemed to interfere with my sanity to the point that nothing coherent enough to constitute speech actually came out of my mouth.

Twenty doesn't seem like it would be that many. All I can say is, give it a try—for me, five felt unbearable. I was screaming hard enough that by the end I'd lost my voice. I also had a new respect for the way Jamie had endured his whipping without screaming, but between the pain, anger, and humiliation, I was hopeless.

Finally I heard him say, "Done." He pulled off the blindfold and knelt so our faces were barely an inch apart: "Natalie, you have given satisfaction for your actions Friday night."

I managed to croak out, "Fuck you, Gareth."

He kissed my lips gently, and then he was gone.

Daniel and Jamie came back right away. Daniel released the different straps and eased me up from the bench, holding me so I didn't fall. A soft blanket was wrapped around me and suddenly I was swept up into Jamie's arms. He must have still been in serious pain, but he didn't show it as he carried me out of the room, down the hall to the room with the cots. He settled down into the chair Daniel had occupied. He was cuddling me and rubbing my back, but for once he wasn't being all smarmy and seductive.

I was crying so hard I was choking. "I hate him, I hate him."

"You know that's not true," Jamie whispered soothingly.

"He's a fucking bastard."

"That is definitely true." He sounded exhausted, but calm and very un-Jamie. What Daniel had put him through—it was a hundred times worse than what Gareth had done to me. He should have been bitter, furious, but he was at peace with it.

I shuddered at what had gone down, and then I started thinking about my part in it: the Long Island ice teas, the parking lot at Rusty's, making out with Tyler, letting him touch me. I knew at the time it was wrong. I knew it. Not because of my bloody agreement with Gareth, but because even completely wasted I knew the guy was a creep. My vaunted vibes were working perfectly, and they were screaming at me that I wasn't safe with him. But because I was pissed at Gareth and Jamie and freaked about all the things that had been happening to me, I ignored my instincts.

179

And then I thought about Gareth's face, his words. He was truly furious, and not because he was jealous. He hated that I'd done something so grossly stupid and irresponsible that I put myself at grave risk of real, irrevocable harm.

This wasn't like the other times, making out with Tim and Will or even ignoring the school deposit. Gareth knew I was capable of stuff like this, and he'd tried to warn me.

Suddenly I caught a glimpse of this side of myself: I'd been thinking of myself as poor little Natalie with the evil stepbrother; but now I was seeing fucked-up Natalie, who played along when people tried to help her, only to hurl insults at them when she screwed up and blew opportunities. That person disgusted me.

The sobs intensified, and I tried to curl up into a ball. "Oh God, he's so mad. I really screwed up…he's not going to forgive me. How could he?"

Jamie had the nerve to chuckle. "You're raving, kitten. It happens after a punishment, but you know you're talking bullshit. Of course he forgives you. What Tyler did was not your fault. You know that."

"Gareth's so mad," I shuddered.

"You scared him. He knew bad shit was going down, and he was trapped and couldn't do anything. And he's mad about having to punish you. That's not really his thing."

"Then why does he do it?"

"Maybe it's your thing," he said, brushing his hand over my ass.

"That's sick!"

"Yeah, it is." We were both quiet for a few minutes, when he added, "It's sort of a theory he has. He beats you so you don't beat yourself up. So you move past it—like catharsis or something."

"Does it work?" I asked after a moment.

"Let me know if you ever figure it out. For what it's worth, you coming on that bench was the hottest thing I have ever seen."

"You watched!" I sputtered.

"Oh yeah," he groaned, adjusting himself. "I almost wish I hadn't. We still have to wait another...," he checked his watch, "fifteen and a half hours. I just hope my balls don't explode before then."

He let his eyes drift closed, pulling me closer, his hand slipping under the blanket to grip my sex.

Eventually this truly strange interlude was interrupted by Daniel's return. "On your feet," he ordered.

I was too drained and overwhelmed to disobey or protest when he turned me around and reached for my hands to cuff them behind my back.

"What?" I sputtered.

"Rules," he said curtly.

Jamie stood and caressed my cheek and then bent down to kiss me on the mouth—he'd never done that before. "Sleep well, kitten," he said as Daniel tied a blindfold over my eyes and, without further ado, slung me over his shoulder and carried me upstairs.

181

Chapter 20

The next morning began the next phase of my life as house sex-slave, only instead of Gareth, apparently I was now under Daniel's dominion. It was Daniel who woke me up that morning with a barked, "Up!"

"Where's Gareth?" I asked drowsily, before I remembered that I was too angry at him to care where the hell that fucker was.

Daniel did not deign to answer this, but simply dragged me out of bed. "I said up!"

"What's your problem?" I demanded, trying to shake out of his grip. That got me a hard slap on my ass. "What the fuck?" I yelled. I couldn't help warily rubbing my butt. Even through my sweat pants, his swat on top of Gareth's punishment *hurt*.

"The problem is I don't like mouthy subs!" he barked.

I winced at that. Don't ask me why!

Surprisingly, Daniel's eyes narrowed observantly before he growled and pushed me towards the bathroom. "If you can't speak respectfully, then keep your pie hole shut!" he warned.

I stomped off, stung that Daniel had already decided I sucked as a sex slave. But when I got in the shower—yeeow! The agony of the hot water hitting my abused ass quickly scorched off any remaining regret.

Were there truly women who put up with this shit? Liked it? Thinking of the previous night's horrors, I concluded they must be certifiable—if they existed at all.

Unfortunately, the sensation of water sluicing over my sex bore enough resemblance to Gareth's fingers ghosting over the same area to suddenly make my knees weak. I thought about Daniel's meaty hand crashing down on my....

Fuck!

I gripped the wall to steady myself, my sex throbbing mercilessly in some female equivalent of a morning boner. Suffice it to say, by the end of the shower, I was rubbing my thighs together desperately.

To add insult to my manifold injuries (as well as blood to the boner), my "uniform" was lying out on the bed when I came out—sans shorts! Not only would that make it that much easier for Daniel to spank me, but my outfit would show off my reddened ass for all and sundry.

I knew without being told that that had not been Daniel's call. Was Gareth sending little texts dictating my daily outfit?

I did manage to halt any more thigh rubbing just as Daniel threw open the door looking like a marine storming an enemy stronghold. He turned up his lip in a less than flattering scowl at the sight of me in my slave girl outfit and tossed four leather cuffs on the bed. "Turn around!" he ordered.

I was seriously sick of this guy's attitude, and before I could stop myself, snapped, "Fuck you!"

Daniel responded by shoving me on the bed, ripping down my panties, and giving me four slaps on my still sore ass. He ignored my struggles and my screams that he was a "fucking bastard" while he buckled on the cuffs and then locked them behind my back.

When I ignored his order to be quiet, he shoved a cloth in my mouth and demanded furiously, "What the fuck is wrong with you?" He buckled on the ankle cuffs and then helped me to sit up. "Point of advice, Natalie, straight from the CIA program on surviving interrogation: don't gratuitously piss off people who have you at their mercy. When you do hurl insults, make sure you gain some advantage by doing it."

It wasn't what I was expecting to hear, and it did cool my rage by a degree or two, though I was still frantically fighting him—at least mentally. He pulled my panties back up and pushed me to sit on the bed.

He sighed and rubbed his face and finally said with dripping sarcasm, "Gareth has had to leave again to attend to his *matter*, and he left me in charge of you and Jamie." He made it sound like the worst babysitting job in history. "So basically, you're back with Jamie today." I couldn't help a tiny shiver. Jamie had just gone three days without sex. In a drier tone, Daniel added, "I told Jamie to keep the sex to four times today, but if you get sore, tell me."

He sounded like he meant it, and I nodded. I think four was my limit, but we both knew it wasn't Jamie's. "Good. I'm sure he won't object to getting some in before breakfast, so I will leave you two love birds to it."

Daniel had a gift for understatement. Far from objecting, Jamie was in his feral mode. He was instantly on me, his hands everywhere as he dragged me over to my—our—corner. Once I was kneeling, he glanced at Daniel, who was on hand, unlocking my hands.

As with Gareth, they worked together seamlessly as each took a hand and bound them over my head without having to say a word. Jamie

184

shoved two cushions under my hips, ripped down my underwear, and then pulled my legs over his shoulders.

As he did this, he said dreamily, "I wish you could see yourself like this, kitten. That gorgeous pussy of yours is dripping for me."

That raised a snort from across the room. Apparently Daniel had less tolerance for Jamie's poetic effusions than Gareth. Jamie was unperturbed as usual, but lowered his head between my legs. And as usual, he lived up to his promises. He brought me to a bone-shattering orgasm and then moved up to have sex, managing impressive control after this unprecedented period of abstinence, because (as he pointed out several times) he wasn't going to come until I climaxed again.

Once it was over, we just lay there panting for a few minutes, when he started to get hard again. I knew what was coming, and I started to pull against the restraints and register what protest I could. Jamie paid about as much attention as he usually did, which is to say, he began his encouraging patter, kissing my breasts, fingering me, which was generally enough to get me ready for sex again, even when I'd had enough.

But to my surprise, Daniel was willing to take a more active role managing matters between Jamie and me—or perhaps this was a new protocol because of the disastrous Friday night. Whatever it was, he snapped out, "She's had enough. It's time for breakfast. Untie her. We're all going to eat at the table."

Since in the past Gareth had always fed me breakfast in my corner, my hands bound, we both registered some surprise at this—mine silent of course, Jamie's more verbal: "Dude, that's not how Gareth did it."

185

"I don't give a fuck *how Gareth did it*," Daniel said in a heavily sarcastic mimic. "He's not here, I am. This isn't a prison. We're going to eat at the fucking table like normal fucking people. Now untie her or you're done for the day!" The final bit was roared out.

Jamie bowed to the inevitable and reached over to unclamp my hands and untie the gag, muttering complaints the way he used to when Gareth ordered him to do something equally incomprehensible.

So there we were, going over to the dining room table, Daniel grimly determined, me modestly trying to pull my shirt down to hide my ass, Jamie rubbing his hair and hopping around, once again perplexed by the awkwardness of engaging in conversation with his love slave.

It was impossible not to notice the difference between Daniel's breakfast and Gareth's: there was no set table, no cut-up fruit, no Tuscan milk pitcher. Instead cups, bowls, and spoons were stacked at the head of the table next to the box of loathsome cardboard flakes and the milk carton.

Jamie gave voice to my disappointment by bursting out, "Is this all there is?"

"Yes, this is all there is. You waiting for me to make you a fucking goat cheese omelet or something?" Daniel hit back, clearly annoyed that his efforts at playing the gracious host were being judged inadequate. I couldn't help laughing. "What the fuck's up with you?" he barked. I shrugged apologetically and covered my mouth to stifle the giggles. That got his ire up, and he snapped out in a perfect command tone, "I asked you a question. You need another spanking?"

"Man, you spanked her!" Jamie cried, sounding bummed that he hadn't been invited to watch.

"Never interrupt me when I'm speaking to her!" Daniel turned to me and took my chin. "Look at me when I speak to you. I asked you a question."

I couldn't help shivering. There was no defying Daniel when he was like this. I say this without shame. He was huge and he looked like he knew twenty-two ways to kill a man with just his index finger. I squeaked out, "Sorry. It's just that Gareth made me eat one of those."

"Man, Gareth with the food," Daniel groaned. Obviously he and I were on a page when it came to offenses like goat cheese.

Jamie rolled his eyes and said, "Man, the army ruined you. It's goat cheese." It was a good guess that when he wasn't gorging on Captain Crunch, Jamie had spent his life eating things like goat cheese omelets—probably prepared by his family's chef in their Chateau in Provence.

I couldn't help hazarding, "No one got more Captain Crunch?"

"You're the culprit!" Jamie said. "I had to keep it hidden in my car. You finished the whole box."

"Yeah, well, I went four days eating those flakes—WITH NO SUGAR!"

Both Jamie and Daniel were properly struck by my state of culinary martyrdom. Daniel blanched and Jamie said feelingly, "Dude, that's just wrong."

Meanwhile, army type that he was, Daniel had had enough of the pointless hand-wringing. "Jamie, you're on breakfast duty starting now. You can go to Friederich's and get a dozen."

187

Honestly, I almost swooned. Friederich's is the best donut place in, like, the whole of New York State. They make them fresh every hour. I couldn't remember the last time I'd had one, and just the thought of biting into a warm, yeasty, custard-filled donut—I probably would have knelt and done the whole slave girl thing on the spot.

It must have shown on my face, because they both stared at me, and I murmured, "Gareth made me eat this, like, healthy diet."

Daniel shook his head and said decisively, "Well that changes today. Better make it two dozen, Jamie. What kinds do you like?"

"Glazed, custard, crullers. Oh my God, thank you!" Friederich's donuts! I couldn't help jumping up and hugging him, though the moment I saw his face, I pulled back and muttered, "Sorry."

Jamie of course wanted in on the action and said with a pout, "What about me, kitten? I'm going to get them for you!"

So I gave him a kiss on the cheek—which of course gave him the opportunity to pull me in and reach under my panties to cop a feel, which with Jamie meant full finger penetration. I admit I was a little wet, lingering effects of Daniel's use of the command tone. Jamie's eyes glazed over and, donuts forgotten, he started tugging at my clothing.

Fortunately for my sanity, said donuts being on the line, Daniel intervened and said, "Cut that shit out, Jamie, and get us some fucking breakfast."

Jamie sighed but dutifully left. Daniel glanced at me and said curtly, "You'd better put some proper clothes on." Which pretty much caused my gratitude to evaporate.

"I don't choose what I wear, you know!"

188

"Where the fuck did Gareth find you?" he said as he grabbed my arm and directed me back to my room.

I couldn't help turning red at this. Apparently, I wasn't the love slave he'd been hoping for. Not that I cared, AT ALL. But I said sullenly, "He found me at the fucking mini-mart."

"It shows."

Chapter 21

Jamie got back from Friederich's forty-five minutes later. Daniel immediately shot down his suggestion that he feed me in the corner, slave style. Thank God, because knowing Jamie, the "meal" would probably have consisted of him smearing food on my breasts so he could lick it off. Jamie had eaten on the road and made himself scarce while Daniel and I sat at the table and went to work on the remaining twenty donuts.

I say without shame that I had seven. Gareth could go choke on his healthy diet.

Of course, as soon as I was finished it was back to my corner, where I spent the next few hours serving as Jamie's sex toy. But it was clear that Daniel had gotten a bug up his ass, as Jamie put it, because towards three, Daniel suddenly barked that I wasn't going to "spend all fucking day" in the house on a nice day. I was pretty pissed because he made it sound like I was some lazy couch potato slumped in front of a TV instead of spending the day tied up servicing his friend. Jamie immediately started up with his usual protest, "When Gareth was here…."

"For the last fucking time, when Gareth's not here, my opinion is the only one that counts. For better or worse, this is her home. She's not going to live like she's in prison."

"She doesn't. Dude, you haven't been here. She's fine with it."

"That's not the fucking point, Jamie. She needs a normal life."

"Stop acting like I'm treating her badly. What happened before—it hasn't been like that. She's cool with it."

"Well if she is, maybe she shouldn't be."

I can't say I liked the sound of that—or the fact that they were both discussing me while I was sitting right there.

"What the fuck is that supposed to mean?" Jamie stood up and got into Daniel's face. I'd only known him a few days, but even I knew that was something you didn't do with Daniel. "You're acting like I'm mistreating her. I'm not. I swear I'd never hurt her." He punctuated this comment with a sharp poke to Daniel's abdomen, which got the reaction I at least was expecting. A second later, Daniel had Jamie in a chokehold, his arm twisted behind his back.

Jamie was very strong, but like the other night, he was no match for Daniel. The whole thing was sexy as hell to watch, to be honest. He struggled hard, but Daniel just pulled his arm back more and said, "Are you done?"

"What the fuck, Daniel? Don't pull this Delta Force crap on me."

I was relieved that he didn't sound scared at all. I still thought they acted like brothers, though I knew Jamie was an only child. Also, Daniel had none of Jamie's rich-boy vibe, quite the opposite. But I would have bet my total net worth (all seven dollars) that they'd grown up together. Maybe Daniel was like Sabrina in that movie—the chauffeur's son, who grew up above the garage somewhere on Jamie's Newport estate.

"For the twentieth time, it was the Rangers, fuckwit. Now your opinions have been duly noted, and my answer is I don't give a fuck. I'm in charge here. Now are you done arguing with me?"

191

Jamie didn't say anything, but Daniel released him anyway. Jamie gave him a very un-Jamie look—determined and combative. Daniel just snorted and then came over to me and unlocked the handcuffs.

"Put some proper clothes on," he barked in his favorite drill sergeant's tone. "We're taking a walk." Then he said all casual to Jamie, "You come too."

It was almost an order—almost but not quite. Jamie just scoffed, "Thanks but no, I'll skip the forced march." He added in a tone that made me want to crawl under the bed, "I'll see you tomorrow, Kitten," where the "see" basically meant, "make you scream for mercy." And then he walked out the front door, and a second later I heard a car, presumably his Porsche, start up.

Daniel and I just stood there awkwardly, until finally he barked, "What the fuck are you standing there for?"

"Walk?"

"Yes, walk, princess."

Princess! I'm not kidding. I didn't think there could be a more obnoxious nickname than kitten, but I was wrong. But I wasn't precisely in the mood to have Daniel smack my ass, so I put on my sweats and the shoes Gareth had bought me and came out to the great room before Daniel had to drag me.

AND THEN, we spent the next *hour and a half* walking at a heart-attack-inducing pace down Gareth's driveway. When I tried to complain, Daniel snapped something about how he was through with my sitting around on my ass all day, and from now on we would take an exercise walk every day, "And if you don't shut the fuck up, I'll schedule it for six a.m."

I couldn't help snapping back, "You know, this is worse than the health food!" That wasn't true, but it was close. Other than dance, I hate anything that resembles exercise.

To my shock Daniel came back with, "Well I'm beginning to think Gareth had the right idea, because you obviously need someone to whip your ass into shape."

I managed to squelch a quip about how he'd been doing a lot of that, lest he decide to do some ass whipping right there on the driveway, and just fumed silently.

At one point, I got a pebble in my shoe and had to stop and knock it out, which caused Daniel to snap out, "Why the fuck did you wear those shoes for a walk? They don't give any goddamn support."

"Gareth bought them for me. It's that or flip-flops."

After we got home, I took a shower and then figured I'd spend the rest of the day locked in my room as usual. But apparently that didn't mesh with Daniel's campaign for "normalcy." Just as I was settling in front of the TV, he threw open the door and snapped, "You're not hiding in here by yourself. Besides, we need to get you some proper shoes. All Stars might be hip for running around the mall with your girlfriends, but they're worse than useless for hiking."

Running around the mall with my girlfriends? Where did this jerkwad get off? I may not have grown up all *man of the people*, but I'd been working—and hello!—*living* at a gas station for the past five months. And who said anything about fucking hiking?

193

To my surprise, Daniel dragged me into the library where he'd set up an Apple laptop on the desk. Jamie was nowhere to be seen. He made me pull up a chair, and then we went online to some "outdoors" store that specialized in survival gear like crossbows and tents with a cold rating that had to be measured on the Kelvin scale, with a smattering of normal things like hiking boots. He showed me the various options, then droned on about different technical specifications, and finally picked the ones *he* thought were best.

When I saw the price, I couldn't believe it. "They're three hundred and fifty dollars."

"That's what decent hiking boots cost."

"Couldn't we just look on L.L. Bean or something?"

"No," Daniel said simply, as he added something like seven pairs of high-tech socks, which cost fifteen bucks a pair—socks!

I admit I almost cried that he would spend that kind of money on a pair of goddamn hiking boots and some socks—as if I even liked hiking. Not! It had been so long since I'd been able to afford anything that didn't fall under the category of "life-sustaining," and at that moment I had seven dollars plus the clothes Gareth had bought me. The whole thing was pathetic, but there it is.

But Daniel wasn't Gareth's friend for nothing. I guess he picked up on the Natalie pity party. He made his usual harrumph, but then said, "Your wardrobe is a joke. It's about time you bought some decent clothes."

I couldn't help being surprised. It was the first time Daniel had said something to me that could vaguely be construed as nice. "Like what?" I asked.

"How the hell should I know?" he said impatiently. "I'll call Gareth, and we'll decide on a budget. For now just put shit in the cart, and if I approve I'll buy them. We'll treat this computer as yours. You can use it in here."

That caused me to light up. An actual computer, actual internet. I couldn't believe it: for the last eight months I'd been forced to use the stone-aged school computers, and those were only for writing papers.

So I spent the next hour surfing trying to buy clothes, but it was pretty disappointing to be honest. So much for all those hours daydreaming about what I would buy if I had money. Here was my big "Pretty Woman" moment, and I was paralyzed. There were too many choices, and without knowing how much I should spend.... I don't know, I couldn't do it.

After a while I got fed up and sort of snuck over to iTunes, which is a site where I would have no problem spending three hundred and fifty dollars. I really like music, and if I say so myself, I have fantastically good taste. But it had been months since I'd been able to listen to anything except the mini-mart boom box, that is to say unspeakably bad "Light FM." There were times when I kind of sympathized with those people who commit homicide to get an iPod. Mine had died about a week after I left home, leaving me musically high and dry. I swear it felt like every kid in my school had one except me—some had, like, three or four. I probably could have scored someone's old one, but since I didn't have

195

my computer and couldn't load it with my music instead of the Taylor Swift/One Direction garbage everyone else listened to, there never seemed to be any point.

So I spent the next two hours playing around, listening to samples, dreaming about what I'd buy. I was so caught up, I didn't notice until Daniel was four feet away. I quickly clicked over to the Abercrombie site but I probably looked guilty of something.

"Let's see the damage," Daniel said snidely, probably expecting to blow his top over a ten thousand dollar bill. But when he saw that my purchases amounted to one twenty-nine dollar T-shirt (which is a lot for a T-shirt!) he got mad for the opposite reason. "What the fuck is this? You were supposed to pick out some clothes."

"I did," I said defensively. "I picked out a shirt."

"Well what the fuck have you been doing for the last two hours?"

"Nothing."

He looked at me all suspicious like I'd been posting on Jihadist sites or watching porn and, pulling the computer away, did some move which showed him the sites I'd visited, all music sites. I shot him an "I told you so" look.

He stared at me like I was a freakazoid from outer space and said, "ITunes?"

"Sorry, I just didn't know what clothes to get, and I never get to go on iTunes."

Daniel shook his head in surprise but then reverted to his usual tone, "Dinner is ready. Hope you're okay with pizza, princess." Like he was daring me to complain.

196

Complain! "Thank God! No steamed broccoli," I said, shooting him my best Miss America smile, which just made him snort.

There were two large, grease-soaked boxes sitting on the elegant dining room table, the pepperoni aroma polluting Gareth's nutritious enclave with its artery-clogging deliciousness. No Tuscan milk pitchers for Daniel—or plates for that matter. He'd just left out the paper plates and plastic forks that came with the pizza. We exchanged a glance, both thinking the same thing: eating pizza from a box in a formal dining room, even a hip, modernist one, is just lame. Daniel's nose twitched a few times, and finally he grabbed the boxes and nodded at the library. "Fuck it. The Red Sox are playing."

"Won't Gareth pitch a fit?"

Daniel laughed darkly. "Cat's away. But don't even think about getting grease on the furniture, or you won't be able to sit down for a week."

Chapter 22

So that set the pattern for the next few days. Dealing with Daniel wasn't as horrible as it first seemed. On the one hand, he made no secret that he thought I was incredibly annoying as well as the world's worst submissive, and by "no secret," I mean he ripped down my underwear and smacked my ass brutally hard any time I mouthed off or disobeyed him.

But there were occasional conspiratorial moments like with the pizza, almost like we were sharing a rueful laugh at our predicament: both subjects of the same autocratic lord, who successfully ruled us even while he was absentee. I disobeyed pretty often, which probably means deep down I didn't hate it.

(Don't say it—I don't want to hear it!)

I guess there's a certain satisfaction and even comfort in being able to get a reaction out of someone, even though Daniel showed no sexual interest in me whatsoever. Any mention of my being spanked made Jamie's eyes glaze over with lust, but Daniel just looked annoyed. His lack of interest actually made the "discipline" easier to stomach. Maybe, *probably*, that was part of Gareth's plan.

Judging from Jamie's and my punishments, I assume BDSM was Daniel's "thing." No question, like Gareth and Jamie, he expected me to submit to him. He continued to assist Jamie tying me up—apparently Gareth had ordered that I was still to be restrained during sex even though I wasn't really fighting it anymore. But Daniel always treated both the spanking and the bondage like a job, that is to say, an unpleasant and tedious task required by a demanding but generous employer, like he was a Ph.D. in applied math being paid thousands of dollars to teach his advisor's ten-year-old son long division.

Really the biggest change that emerged over the next few days was that Daniel seemed to decide that I needed what he called a "normal life." Apparently that meant some sort of wholesome white-picket-fencitude, with Sunday dinners and minivans. There were several problems with this. In the first place, the idea itself was preposterous. No amount of Special Forces training was going to turn a paid love slave into Jan Fucking Brady.

The more serious problem, though, was that Jamie would have none of it. I would have assumed from the whole post-Rusty's business that Daniel would have won any conflicts between them. It was obvious Gareth had put him in charge, he was as strong as the proverbial bull, and he presumably had a dozen AK-47s in his room to back up any point he cared to make. But as some jerk-off in my eighth-grade geometry class once said to me, the problem with assuming is it makes an "ass out of you and me"— or in this case, just me, because Jamie wasn't the complete slacker pushover he pretended to be either.

The following day, Daniel reasserted his new rule that we eat at the table like "normal fucking people"—that is to say, before we got down to all the sex and bondage. He again pressured Jamie to join us, holding out as temptation Eggo waffles, real Aunt Jemima syrup, and, *get ready for it*: Reddi-wip! Pure heaven, right?

199

No such luck. Jamie was a no-show, which put Daniel in a foul mood, especially when Jamie materialized literally the moment I was done eating. (Almost as if he had been monitoring me on the hidden camera!?) He gave me a pointed look and said, "I'm ready for you, kitten. Now. Danny?"

"Don't fuck around, Jamie," Daniel said warningly.

"You do your part and let me do mine. I know how to take care of her," Jamie said in a tone I'd never heard him use before.

Some challenge passed between them, which Jamie for once won, presumably because he'd just called Gareth, who'd backed him.

Anyway, I'd barely had time to jump to my feet and yell "What the fuck?" when both of them were on me. Jamie grabbed me around the waist and lifted me off the ground, while Daniel cuffed my hands in front of me and shoved a cloth into my mouth.

"Thank you," Jamie said sarcastically and carried me caveman style over to our cushioned sex-cave in the corner of the living room. He must have sensed I was nervous, because he murmured, "That wasn't about you, kitten. Daniel's always had a stick up his ass." He moved half on top of me, brushing my face with the fingertips of his free hand, carefully watching me. "I understand," he murmured soothingly. "I know what you like."

He had an expression that I'd come to recognize, and I defy any woman in existence not to run for her life when she sees it. It was the one that said, I know your darkest fantasies, and in about sixty seconds I am going to make you scream for me. He slowly undid the gag, his eyes glittering.

200

I knew what he was doing and couldn't help whimpering, "Jamie, please!" But he just shook his head. No mercy. That alone was enough to drive me out of my mind, as Jamie well knew. I wrenched away, screaming, "Fuck you."

For once he hadn't attached my hands to the clamp, so I tried to use them to break his nose. He caught them easily and pinned them over my head, smiling knowingly as my eyes glazed, and my body took over, squirming like a shameless little beggar for his touch.

"Good girl, that's right. Go with it." This was Jamie at his most evil: he loved to throw it in my face that nothing turned me on as much as when he dominated me.

"Mother fucker." I struggled again, but if there was one thing Jamie understood, it was my responses. He pinned my legs with his knee and gave me velvet kisses on my eyelids and forehead, and along my chin to my ears.

My next move was to try to resist. I closed my eyes and lay there stiffly, but Jamie said softly, "You're fighting me, kitten." And then he set to work just with his voice and his fingertips, without taking off any of my clothes, and within minutes I was arching under his touch and finally convulsing in a series of wrenching orgasms.

He let go of my hands and I couldn't help curling up in his arms, sobbing and shaking. "Shh, there's my girl," he said soothingly, pulling me in tightly. He held me for a long time, kissing along my hairline and massaging my back, until I was quiet in his arms, and then he started to heat things up again.

I felt him get hard, which inspired my pelvis into some slutty wiggling despite my brain's angry orders to fucking quit it, and he cooed, "Are you ready for me, kitten?" knowing full well that I would be desperate at this point. He pulled my panties off and flipped me on my stomach, pulled me up on my knees, and pressed my chest down to the floor. He was iron-hard and rubbed against me teasingly. "Beg me, kitten. Tell me what you want."

I couldn't help myself. "Please Jamie, please!"

"There's my girl." And he thrust in hard, making me scream. Daniel couldn't have been blind to his point: where it mattered, Jamie was in control.

The whole thing created a confusing dissonance. For all his affection and intimacy, Jamie fiercely resisted anything that would "normalize" our relationship. For everything we'd been through together, we'd only had one actual conversation, right after Gareth punished me. Even when I wasn't gagged, he never let me forget who was in control and if I resisted him even a tiny bit, he punished me ruthlessly with his special brand of sensual torture.

Jamie's attitude didn't surprise me, at least not within the context of an overall wacked-out situation. I'm sure some of it was selfishness on his part. After all, he'd had this (*supremely hot*, nubile) female made over to him to do what he wanted with. Who would give that up? To have an actual conversation after "office hours" would be the first step in a slippery slope to having to treat me like a girlfriend instead of a sex slave. He must have known that the peculiar dynamic between us couldn't last.

He was screwed up, not dumb. Hence, he was fully determined to take advantage of it as long as he could.

But it wasn't just for his own sake either. He was also acting on what he sensed from me. I was grateful to Daniel for wanting me to feel like this was my home, but part of me didn't want to lose what I had with Jamie either. There was a certain comfort in the way Gareth had set up matters. Being bound and gagged really did mean I could just relax and enjoy it. I didn't have to consent, so I didn't have to feel guilty for liking it so much. Given how tuned in Jamie was to me, I wasn't surprised he would figure this out.

But apparently that was exactly the problem for Daniel. The next afternoon, Jamie and I were lazing on the floor after yet another vigorous bout of lovemaking. He was fondling me as he always did, taking advantage of the fact that my hands were still clipped above my head.

"Look at you," he teased. "Could my kitten already be ready for another orgasm?" I whimpered, which he ignored like he always did. "You don't know what you're missing here, Danny. I swear to God this girl is always ready to go."

Daniel made an unflattering snort from the other side of the room.

"What you're doing isn't healthy, dude," Jamie said, in what was clearly the continuation of an earlier conversation. "What's it been, like three months? Did you at least go to the club while you were in Miami? I'm not fucking with you, this is the best I've ever had. Let's go together—like old times." (Pervert alert!)

I was so floored by the idea that Jamie, king of sex himself, thought I was the best, THE BEST, he'd ever had, that I didn't instantly react to

203

his suggestion. He'd hinted to Gareth plenty of times, but in all honesty that was Gareth. But Daniel?

No one was asking me, and I'm not sure what I would have said if they had. I wasn't required by my "contract" to have sex with anyone but Jamie, but I can't say I hated Daniel. I didn't *want* him exactly, but I didn't dislike that he had his hands on and off me throughout the day.

I was *not* too pleased with Daniel's response, which was a barked, "Stop talking like a fucking loon."

I mean, *come on.* The guy treated the very idea of having sex with me as equivalent in enjoyment potential to a third tour in Afghanistan.

Jamie was unperturbed. He started in about how beautiful and responsive I was, how good I felt, how hot the sex was—all with me right there, mind you. Daniel was getting more and more annoyed, but he flipped out when Jamie said, "She's all compliant now. Just what you're into. You've already tied her up a dozen times."

Daniel exploded, "Don't even think about comparing what I do to this... this...." He flicked his hand at us. Clearly there wasn't an epithet low enough. "You two are some freak experiment of Gareth's to see if he can rehabilitate a pair of fucked-up kids. This goes against everything I believe. Consent is not some nicety. It's at the heart of everything I do— at every stage. I don't care how fucked up or poor or desperate she is. And don't kid yourself. A million dollars or a million mind-blowing orgasms can't change that."

I started crying. Daniel's comment forced into stark relief everything that was screwed up about this—and about me for liking it. There was no hiding behind Gareth or the contract. I was a whore and worse, a tool.

204

Jamie pulled me over into his arms, absently shushing me. "Good going, genius," he sneered at Daniel. "Did it ever occur to you that not everyone gets to live in your black and white little world? The two of us may be fucked up, but at least we're not too afraid to feel a little pleasure. I'm not going to let you wreck that with your superior judgments. But if you got off your high horse for half a minute, you might start to think maybe Gareth was right, maybe she is what you need, but then the world wouldn't be all black and white, would it?"

I was shocked at how fierce Jamie sounded. It was so unlike his usual slacker act. He gripped my chin and kissed me deeply on the mouth which he almost never did. At that second he felt like my hero, which was too fucking perverse, since he was effectively defending my right to be his love slave with no say at all.

Daniel watched us like he was trying to figure out what species of insect we were. Finally he seemed to give up and barked, "Out! Let me talk to her."

Jamie started to protest, "What the fuck?"

Instead of arguing, Daniel just picked me up and, ignoring Jamie's protests, carried me to my room and dumped me on the bed, slamming the door closed behind him.

"Was that real or bullshit? And keep your answers to me polite," Daniel asked me, in a manner I found both hostile and surly.

"I don't know what you're talking about," I snarled, politely leaving out the word "fucking."

Apparently that wasn't enough for Daniel, because he grabbed my arm and gave me three sharp swats on my ass. "When I say polite, I mean polite. Are we clear? Answer me, 'yes, Daniel.'"

"Yes, Daniel," I said sullenly, rubbing my ass.

He let me go and then seemed to revert to his grumpy mode. "What's the deal with you and Jamie?"

"I'm not trying to be rude," I said warily. "I'm just not sure what you're asking me."

"Are you okay with him—with what's happening between you?"

"He's okay, I guess. He's never mean or anything."

I couldn't help feeling nervous. In the past when Gareth asked me something like that, it felt like a trap. Daniel seemed pretty straightforward, but how the hell did I know?

Finally, I tried again. "You think I should have left, taken Gareth's offer, that I shouldn't be okay with being, like, a whore." I was shooting for hip/irreverent, but I think I actually hit needy/bitter.

"Where the fuck do you get that idea?"

"You said I shouldn't be okay with…this." I employed Daniel's wavy hand motion as a helpful translation for the word, "this."

"That's not what I meant," Daniel said impatiently.

"Sure," I snapped back. "I *love* having sex constantly while I'm bound and gagged, being as I am the world's biggest tool."

It sounded pathetic, I know, but I couldn't get away from the idea that he was judging me. The truth was I did like Jamie, but I hated the idea that Daniel thought I was some doormat who didn't care how people treated me.

206

"You're a pain in the fucking ass, which pretty much rules out your being a tool," he said with his usual irritation.

There was no winning with him. "Fine," I said angrily. "I'm not a tool. I'm a whore. I'm paid to have sex with him. Is that better? Why would my feelings even matter?"

He actually grabbed my chin and pulled my face around. When I wouldn't look at him, he said in his version of the command tone, "You look at me when I speak to you."

There was no disobeying Daniel's command tone, but I looked at him pretty defiantly—I hoped—though I was blinking. My eyes itched!

"I don't want to hear that talk out of you again, are we clear?" I shrugged a half-yes. "If anyone is to blame, it's Gareth. For whatever psycho reason, he thought this was a good idea, and if you haven't already, you should understand now. Gareth usually gets what he wants. He would have found a way to make it happen. No one here thinks you're a whore, least of all Gareth. If you're okay with Jamie then that solves a lot of problems."

"I do like him," I said finally. "He cares about how I feel. He never makes me feel like I'm doing something low." I risked a look at him to see if he looked disgusted, but he looked relieved.

"Maybe Gareth knew what he was doing," Daniel said thoughtfully. "I told him, I'm not okay with you being forced. I don't care how much money he offered you. Jamie's not your problem."

I appreciated that he thought that. And was willing to say it. Gareth had basically bulldozed through every hesitation I might have felt, but the truth was I didn't feel abused, and I liked having sex with Jamie, but I did wonder. "What's up with him?"

Daniel wasn't Gareth's friend for nothing. He got the subtext—that I knew Jamie was fucked up in more than the usual way. He shrugged and then said, "What isn't up with him? I'm going to punt this one to Gareth. It's his call."

I wasn't surprised so I didn't argue, but there had been certain signs. "He wouldn't hurt me, would he? Like if we were alone? Why am I always, you know, tied up?"

I trusted Gareth, sort of, and for some mysterious reason I completely trusted Daniel, but I really would be a tool if I didn't at least ask.

"That's not it. Gareth would never risk that, especially not with you. I can't answer that. Let's just say he does better like this. If you're okay with it, then we shouldn't rock the boat."

I don't know what it was about Daniel, because he was pretty much an asshole to me, but he really made me feel better—almost like I was doing them a favor by taking on Jamie.

"Where is Gareth? Why'd he leave?"

Daniel opened his mouth to answer, but then shook his head. "There's been some fallout from the shit with Tyler. It's better if he keeps his distance for now."

"What do you mean?"

"Let's just say that the less attention there is on you the better."

I think that was the first time I really met Daniel's eye, and I wasn't too happy about what I saw there. Whatever risk he'd assessed was no

208

joke. He must have read my fear, because he grabbed my chin and said firmly, "I'm not going to let anything happen to you, Cat."

I nodded and murmured, "All right."

Daniel shook off whatever was bothering him. "Good. With Gareth away, this is my call. You have to obey his rules, but as far as I'm concerned you live here, so this is your home, and it's not okay that you spend all your time tied up or locked in a room. You and Jamie are going to need to get used to dealing with each other."

"This wasn't exactly my choice, you know."

"And I'm not saying it was," he shot back. "Your new hiking boots are in the closet. Get dressed, and if you don't want another spanking you will get your ass outside in the next ten minutes."

I decided not to point out to Daniel that his idea of living like "normal fucking people" included his spanking me any time I disobeyed him.

I changed my clothes in a major huff, too pissed to notice until after I'd laced up a hundred and seventy-five dollar boot that Daniel had called me Cat—as in a nickname? I couldn't quite believe it, especially since he couldn't be bothered to speak to me except to bark orders during the whole of our walk, which had now been upgraded into a punishing two-hour hike, including something he called a "rock scramble," which was as horrific as it sounds.

Unfortunately I couldn't completely hate his filthy guts, because after I showered and went into the library, I booted up the computer and saw that he had set up an account for me on iTunes with a five hundred dollar credit for me to buy music. I almost lost it right there, in the sense of sobbing like a complete basket case. It was the happiest I could remember being since before—well, since before my life turned to shit.

Chapter 23

Whatever contentment I felt though, I knew change was coming. The vibes, they don't lie.

Gareth was still AWOL. I assumed Daniel spoke to him every day and Jamie every now and then, but he had no contact at all with me. I was too chicken to ask where he was and when he was coming back. I'm positive it was paranoia on my part, but I couldn't help agonizing about the extended silence. The last time I'd seen Gareth, I'd been tied to a bench so he could whale on my ass. Was he still angry? Was he having second thoughts about allowing me into his life? After all, in addition to royally fucking up, I'd been as difficult as humanly possible. Obviously, I wasn't the sweetly obliging submissive he'd been hoping for. Maybe he was out looking for a better one!

As I said, complete and total paranoia.

Friday rolled around, the one-week anniversary of Jamie's and my last train wreck. I wasn't really thinking about that, though I was definitely on edge. We all were. I assumed it was due to the pouring rain, which is dumb when you think about it since it's not like rain in April is a rare occurrence in upstate New York.

By some miracle, after Jamie and I finished our "business hours," Daniel allowed me to whine my way out of our exercise walk. That right there probably should have warned me that the apocalypse was imminent. I ducked into my room for a quick shower and then headed for the library, eager to continue running down my princely iTunes credit. Unfortunately, thanks to Daniel's fixation on turning us into the Brady Bunch, who should I find hard at work playing Call of Duty but Jamie, the man of a thousand moods.

He was obviously there under protest and let me know it by shooting me a phony smile and a casual "Oh, hey there," like I was some vaguely remembered classmate from middle school. I thought about going back to my room: I recognized this side of Jamie. This was the Jamie who'd dragged me to Rusty's. I'll call him "douchebag Jamie." But I detested looking like a coward and anyway, Daniel would probably just drag me back in again.

I gave an awkward wave and forced myself to take a seat at the desk in front of the laptop, but my enthusiasm for buying music had vaporized. I didn't have head-phones, and tool that I was, I couldn't bring myself to play the samples with Jamie listening. For a while, I made do with buying tracks I'd owned in my previous life but which thanks to Stephen I couldn't get off my old computer, until Daniel ducked his head in twenty minutes later. "Pizza okay for dinner?" he asked. Like he gave a shit about our opinion. He was obviously checking how the "together time" was going.

We both shrugged assents, and then Daniel barked out in his command tone, "Tonight, you will pick out some clothes."

That caused the panic to surge. I wasn't scared of Daniel getting angry, or at least not primarily, because I was finding that except for the spankings he was more bark than bite. The panic was more existential, like the day I couldn't bring myself to make breakfast. It was this inchoate sense of being a total incompetent, like my months living hand-to-mouth had somehow taken a deeper toll than I'd realized. I really tried, but after a few minutes I was close to tears and banged my hand on the desk. "Fuck!"

"Easy, babe," Jamie said, getting up from his recliner. "What's the prob?"

Babe? Prob? I swallowed down what I wanted to say—something rude, surly and hostile—and answered stiffly, "Daniel wants me to buy clothes."

"Don't have kittens. It's just some clothes."

Everything about his attitude severely ratcheted up the tension. Jamie was truly the last person I wanted to share my mental hang-ups with. As I've said before, he could be extremely tuned in to my moods, but that is a world away from being sympathetic. I didn't need to hear from the poor little rich boy there that I was overreacting.

"Let's check out Neiman Marcus," he said with a smarmy wink, pulling the laptop over.

"Neiman Marcus? Are you high?" Forget fifteen dollars for some socks. The *bikinis* there cost seven hundred.

"Chill, babe. I'll pay for it. I'm logging you into my account. Buy anything you want. Throw in a necklace—make-up gift for the other night."

I went scarlet at this. "No," I ground out and then grabbed the computer away from him and slammed it shut.

"Easy, babe. Don't wig." He put his hands up like I was some crazed bitch.

213

And so I promptly did "wig," as in going postal, Natalie DEFCON One. "Fuck you," I yelled, shoving him. "I don't want your fucking money."

"It's just a necklace!" he protested. "Don't have a cow."

Our yelling brought Daniel into the room. "What the fuck?" he roared. "I can't leave you two alone for twenty fucking minutes."

For once, Daniel's anger only fueled mine. "Call Gareth! Now! Tell him I want it added to my contract that if Richie Rich here *EVER* offers me money again it's over. I'll walk back to the mini-mart if I have to."

I moved towards the door. "You want to get me something, Jamie? To make up for that night—for Tyler's splaying me out, feeling me up? For two women washing my breasts? Give me your 'Screaming Trees' shirt."

The bastard actually looked horrified. It was just like I'd guessed. Money was nothing to him, but ask for his favorite shirt and suddenly he's not so eager. (And in fairness it was a really sweet design and genuine shirts for that band are almost impossible to get.)

I ran out of the library into my room, slamming my door so hard the windows rattled. For about a minute it felt really good. Weirdly, given all the shit Jamie had pulled, I'd never gotten really angry at him before, whereas I'd fantasized nightly about dismembering Gareth and Daniel.

But after that glorious minute, the anger started to cool, and I felt a wave of nauseous misery. I think I'd pretended that Jamie was somehow into me, but his comment, the coolness of it, made it clear that he really did think the *money* made us even.

Gareth talked like that, but it was different with him. The money was about leverage for him. He was buying influence over my life, not sex. And he encouraged me to view the money as a way to offset my shame about submitting to him. Daniel went even further and acted like I was doing everyone a favor. But now it was being shoved in my face that Jamie thought he could buy me.

It was the first time I'd felt used, and the thought made me sick.

Not surprisingly, Daniel came in without knocking a few minutes later. "If you're done with your little tantrum, maybe you'd like to explain what that was about."

"I know what you all think."

"*You* know what *I* think," Daniel scoffed.

"I know who he is. I'm surprised you're not wetting your pants afraid I'll sue or something."

I was just spouting off, so I wasn't prepared for Daniel's reaction. He grabbed my wrists and pulled me to my feet. "Are you making some kind of threat?"

"No!"

"Because talk like that gets people killed."

"Who's making the threats now? Well fuck you! I meant what I said. If that little bastard offers me money again, it's over. I want it in my contract. Tell Gareth that!" I screamed, crossing the line into semi-hysteria. "I can't believe this. Gareth hires me to be Jamie's sex toy, and now you're gonna off me? Tyler wasn't fucking kidding."

"Tyler!" Daniel barked out. He grabbed me by the shoulders and shook me hard. "What the fuck did he say to you?"

215

"I don't know," I wailed. "He was all on about how Jamie's family knows about me and he was doing me a favor—like they would have had me killed or something. Well fuck you and fuck Gareth for bringing me here."

Flabbergasted would be too mild a word for Daniel's expression. It doused my meltdown instantly. I mean, given the shit he'd probably seen and done, Daniel getting that upset could not be good. He turned to leave the room, but had his cell out by the time he shut and locked the door.

About a half hour later, he came in with one of those large, flat department store boxes and said, "Get dressed in this. We need to go out."

"What's going on?" I demanded, but again he'd left and locked the door. The box was sitting there on the bed, staring at me. It looked... well, it looked seriously expensive. It took me a silly amount of time, but I finally nudged the top off.

I nearly fell on the floor. Inside was a dress, a Dior dress, no price tag. It was a vintage sixties style cocktail dress, simply cut with a boat neck, three-quarter sleeves, belted waist, and slightly A-line skirt in a gorgeous (and extremely flattering!) shade of shimmering blue-green. Not too old or too young looking, it was sexy without being sleazy, and the most beautiful thing I'd ever seen in my life.

And Gareth was the only man on the planet who would have picked it out for me.

Given the hissy fit I'd just thrown over Jamie offering to buy me a necklace, you might expect that I'd throw it all on the floor.

216

Call me a gold-digging hypocrite, but I didn't. Gareth wasn't Jamie. If he'd meant the dress as an apology, he would have said so. He'd bought it because it was beautiful and because he thought it suited me. But it had not been sitting in my closet, and it was only brought out for an event he'd ordered me to attend.

I don't know when he'd bought it, but I just knew it wasn't in the last three days. Gareth was sensitive about the money issue. He'd bought a small fortune's worth of La Perla underwear, but that was part of the job. When Gareth took me shopping for clothes for my own use, we went to the Gap.

It was scary sometimes how well he knew me, scary because when I thought about it, I felt a deep ache in my gut—my heart. It was impossible to imagine anyone ever knowing me as well as Gareth did, and I couldn't help loving him for it.

At the bottom of the box were two cloth bags: one had a pair of black patent-leather Coach flats and in the other was a matching clutch bag.

The dress fit perfectly—no surprise, this being Gareth. I put on a pair of black silk thigh-highs underneath. I quickly arranged my hair and put on some mascara and lip stick, which was the only makeup I ever wore.

I looked…fabulous.

Daniel knocked and then opened the door. He'd changed into a dark suit with a sober tie, and I'll say it here: he looked blazingly hot. As with my clothes, I could sense Gareth's hand in the whole outfit. The suit was perfectly tailored and obviously expensive, and Daniel just struck me as a guy who given a choice would buy his suits at Men's Wearhouse.

Regardless of how amazing he looked, even a three thousand dollar suit couldn't camouflage that everything about him screamed "bodyguard." Perhaps it was the earbud and slight bulge from the holstered "piece" he was carrying.

He didn't look too happy, which cooled my excitement. Far from complimenting my awesome fabulousness, he opened with, "I don't want any shit." He was holding a long velvet jewelry box. He didn't bother handing it to me, but just opened it and took out a double strand of pearls.

Now, I don't really consider myself a pearls type of girl even though like most of my friends, I'd gotten the "Princess Pearls" earring and necklace set for my thirteenth birthday. My stepmother was one of those women who go around saying things like "You can never go wrong with pearls." She never took hers off, and I'm sure she would have liked knowing that she would die in them.

Still, the neckline of the dress looked bare without a necklace, and pearls certainly went with the whole retro "Mad Men" look. But Daniel was being a bit too cagey. I understood why when I caught a glimpse of the clasp. It was a cluster of diamonds shaped as a flower, with a yellow stone in the middle—one of those minor details that turn a fifteen hundred dollar necklace into a fifty thousand dollar investment piece.

"I can't wear that…" I started to protest, but Daniel snapped, "I don't have time to argue. Consider them a loan."

He looked really tense, so I didn't argue when he stood behind me and put them around my neck.

I couldn't help shivering when his fingers brushed the back of my neck as he turned the clasp, which to my endless humiliation made me turn beet red. Daniel's eyes narrowed and finally after a too-long pause, he said, "Stay close to Jamie. Don't go anywhere by yourself."

He really meant it. Something was happening, something that made Daniel edgy, and anything that made Daniel edgy deserved respect. I'd had enough of stupid risks and said sincerely, "I promise." Daniel looked relieved and gestured to the door.

When I came out, I was shocked to see Jamie dressed the way he must have with his family. It was just khakis and a navy blazer over a pink Polo shirt. The outfit probably cost less than Daniel's dress shirt, but it didn't matter. Jamie could wear torn jeans and flip flops, and he'd still look like he was heir to millions.

He was staring at me in that way he had, which went a ways in mollifying my disappointment at Daniel's complete indifference to my appearance. For once he didn't have any smarmy comments, but gave me a wry smile and held out a plastic grocery bag. I was half afraid to take it, but Daniel tapped his watch warningly, so I reached for it. Jamie had used a shoelace for a bow, but it was knotted so tight, I couldn't get it untied and finally tore through the bag. Out fell four T-shirts: the Screaming Trees concert tee, a vintage Clash, a Duran Duran, which was another favorite shirt of his, and finally a vintage Cure (from the *Boys Don't Cry* tour—a truly sweet design), which I'd never seen him wear. It

219

was my favorite band—ever for all time. When I looked at him, he said almost shyly, "I looked on your computer to see what you'd bought."

I couldn't think of anything to say except maybe "I love you," and since that was out, I just went up on my toes and kissed his cheek.

He clasped my hand tightly. "Are we okay?"

"Yes."

Daniel rolled his eyes at our display of mawkishness—or perhaps our music taste—and grunted, "Now that we have *that* out of the way, can we get a fucking move on?"

"Do you swear this much in front of Gareth?" I asked.

He grabbed my arm and gave me a swat through the dress, causing Jamie's eyes to glaze.

I guess that would be a yes.

Chapter 24

Jamie and I got into the back of the Expedition. To my surprise, another guy was driving, whom Daniel introduced as Carlos. Carlos was pretty much a Latino Daniel—strong, tough, massive.

Hello, special ops.

As we pulled out, Daniel opened the window and tapped the roof, and another set of headlights appeared behind us.

We'd barely driven two minutes when Daniel's phone buzzed. Daniel touched his earbud and handed the phone to Jamie. "Go ahead," Daniel said. They both listened—it had to be Gareth. Daniel grunted occasional responses, but Jamie just nodded.

After about four minutes, Jamie murmured, "Okay," and gave the phone back to Daniel. He leaned back against the seat, looking sick, exhausted.

"You okay with this?" Daniel asked him.

Jamie only swallowed, but then reached for my hand and gripped it almost painfully. His palm was clammy, and he had a thin sheen of sweat over his lip.

Daniel turned to face me: "Here's the score. You've been together for two months, you met skiing in Lake Placid, you're 'serious.'" He made air quotes. "You do a sweep, talk to as many people as you can, hit the dance floor for a few dances, then make your exit. Natalie, tonight you are Miss Perfect Girlfriend, lovely, sweet, and *silent*. Whatever the

221

two of you do, do not separate. I mean glued at the hip. If one of you needs to take a piss, the other waits by the door. Carlos will stay close, but we're not taking any chances."

Jamie nodded absently and just hunched back against the seat, his eyes closed, his grip hard enough to make my fingers go numb. I squeezed back, hoping to make him feel better. I desperately wanted to know what was happening, but I didn't need to hear it from Daniel that Gareth had ordered that I be kept out of the loop.

About twenty minutes later, we drove through a massive wrought iron gate. In the distance was a white-pillared mansion that looked like Tara in *Gone with the Wind*. I knew where we were: the Algonquin Hunt & Polo Club. I'd never been there since the place was way out of my parents' social league, but everyone knew it was The Swanky Place around here. I'd always scoffed at the very idea of our shit town having a Polo club, but I suppose the local Thurston Howells were entitled to their snobby, elitist hubs of obsolete pretentiousness just like Manhattan or Palm Beach. Needless to say, despite the name, no Native American (or person of any color but lily, or rather *WASPy* white) had ever passed its doors as anything other than a busboy.

Daniel must have noticed my lack of enthusiasm for the venue. He caught my eye and gave some visual equivalent of a command: *play along*. He mouthed, "Lovely, sweet and *silent.*" I nodded. I might not know what was happening, but I knew Gareth, and he would never have sent me to a place like this if it hadn't been important.

It was still pouring, so we drove up under the front awning. Uniformed valets were immediately on hand to open the door. Jamie, who one minute ago had looked like Louis XVI on his way to the *Place de la Concorde*, made a miraculous recovery and was all smiles as he helped me out of the car. Daniel stayed to tip the valets and make arrangements for our tail, while Jamie, Carlos, and I made our way up the white marble steps into the largely deserted front hall.

People always think these havens for the super rich look like Versailles but the truth is closer to Grey Gardens. The decor might have merited a full spread in an issue of *House and Garden* in the year 1962—the drapes, the furniture and wallpaper were all perfectly preserved and eons out of date. I bet half the members had a great aunt living in a house decorated just like this. It even smelled like a great aunt: a mixture of mothballs, lemon cleaner, wood smoke, and snobbery.

Our first stop was the coat check even though neither of us was checking a coat. But the moment Jamie came close, the old guy manning it burst out, "Jamie!"

"Sam," Jamie said heartily, shaking his hand. "How are you doing in this rain—leg's not mistreating you?"

I swear there were tears in the man's eyes. "Can't complain, can't complain. And you! You look wonderful, son." Translation: I expected you to be close to death.

"Thanks," Jamie beamed. "Sam, this is Natalie." The segue left no doubt that I was the reason Jamie "looked wonderful." Sam shook my hand, his eyes practically popping out of his head. I smiled warmly, trying to look like the kind of sweetie-pie good girl who rescues lost guys from self-destruction.

223

The exchange with Sam basically set the tone for the next hour. As we moved through the club, we had the same conversation over and over again. It was some sort of engagement party: I didn't catch the groom's name, but the bride-to-be was named Philippa. The crowd was on the old side for an engagement party, making me guess that it was for parents' friends, not the couple's. Most of the men were dressed in conservative suits, but I noticed a smattering of tall, studly twenty-something guys dressed in polo shirts like Jamie. Relying on my ace detective skills, I deduced that they were all polo players.

(Seriously—*polo*—like he was Prince fucking William!)

The women favored old school Chanel suits and cocktail dresses or, and this is not a joke, actual plaid kilts. Even the girls my age wore matronly, horsey-themed Longchamp or Hermes scarves around their necks. Though I know I can't take credit for it, my dress was the classiest outfit there—by a furlong.

Jamie was obviously beloved. He knew every person there, whether guest or employee. They all greeted him fondly and familiarly, but every last one of them conveyed in words or expression that he hadn't been there in ages. There was just enough awkward tiptoeing to indicate that they were avoiding any reference to why he'd been gone—exactly as if he'd been in rehab or a mental hospital. Everyone wanted to know when he'd be rejoining the polo team. Again from the tone, it was obvious he was considered an extremely good player. He gave vague answers that encouraged without actually promising anything.

Only the sweat on his hand gave away that this party was ripping him in two.

Given Daniel's instructions that I keep my mouth shut, I decided to pretend I was Audrey Hepburn in *My Fair Lady*. If a flower girl can pass as a princess, why not a mini-mart cashier? I figured demure and "shy-Di" were out, so I focused on looking serene and entitled. I smiled pleasantly and answered questions when asked, but otherwise made no effort to make conversation.

I recognized a few of the more memorable (read: *hot*) guys from the gas station. Even billionaire brats have to buy their own gas when they're in their sports cars, and contrary to popular opinion, they'd ogled my breasts when they paid for their Snickers bars same as the Teamsters. None of them had stooped so low as to try to pick me up, so I figured I was in no danger of being recognized.

As we worked the room, I began to see there was a method to the madness. I might have been instructed to behave like arm candy, but at each different stop, Jamie made introductions, giving my full name, along with the fact that I was attending Brown in the fall. He never let go of my hand and added frequent, seemingly absent-minded kisses to my temple or our joined hands.

Apparently that made enough of a change from his usual MO to arouse notice. I could practically see the mental gears turning as people registered first the Dior and then the necklace, inevitably followed by a glance at my left hand to check if there was an engagement ring. After about the fifth introduction, I could feel that people were talking about us, though this crowd was too old-money for anything blatant.

Between Jamie's clammy hands and Carlos's unobtrusive menace lurking in the background, I couldn't help feeling deeply uneasy. For

225

once I didn't want to speculate about why Gareth had staged this little appearance for us, not that I could help it. Two things had lodged in my mind: first, every last word and gesture of Jamie's had been carefully calibrated to leave the impression that we were either currently or about to get engaged; and second that Jamie would never have done it if Gareth hadn't ordered him to. The idea that Gareth was even contemplating marrying me off to Jamie made me want to jump off the Twin Bridges.

After we'd worked the crowd for forty-five minutes, Jamie grabbed us each a Coke from the bar and led me to the ball room where the Lester Lanin Band was churning out foxtrots and waltzes. As we stood at the edge of the dance floor watching the dancers, he brought my hand to his lips and murmured into my knuckles, "Jesus, you should get an Academy Award. That was perfect, kitten."

"Sex slave to debutante—all it takes is a dress and some pearls," I quipped.

"None of that, Natalie" he said, squeezing my hand.

His use of my name was enough to bring tears to my eyes. Neither of us could afford to indulge any real feelings right now so I shifted tacks. "Soooooo, polo?"

He had the grace to look embarrassed but then gave me his trademark Jamie smile and said smugly, "You would not believe the number of women dying to fuck polo players."

"Isn't that precious?" He laughed loudly and kissed my forehead. We watched the dancers, who weren't bad, considering. They weren't trying for any competitive ballroom prizes, but even the guests our age could move around the floor, product of a lifetime of country club dances and debutante balls.

Finally I said without turning towards him, "Are you guys going to tell me what's going on?"

He barked a laugh. "Not if I want to keep my balls. Welcome to life with Gareth. Get used to it." The final part was said with a profound sense of resignation. It echoed the way Daniel sometimes talked, and I knew they both meant it. Gareth had said that first day that his household was not a democracy. In fact, it was a dictatorship of varying degrees of benevolence. It soothed my pride a bit to see that Daniel and Jamie were as thoroughly subject to his dominion as I was.

"You up for this?" he asked gesturing towards the floor. The band was starting up the next number.

"Are you?" I countered coyly. I had no doubt he could dance. He moved like he could and the foxtrot aroused no fears in him like it would most males of our generation.

He spun me out, and I wasn't wrong. Jamie is a truly fantastic dancer. It helps that he's so ridiculously attractive, but his dancing was everything it should be in a great amateur: graceful, playful, adaptable, not afraid to ham it up. He had a good strong lead too, with the kind of skill that makes his partner look just as graceful.

But of course, I wasn't just any partner. I mentioned I was hard-core into ballet, right? In fact, until I'd hit puberty and bloomed into my current bodacious physique, I'd been aiming to go pro. My teacher, Rodrigo, had done everything he could to get me to switch to competitive ballroom, since wearing a 32D bra is not considered a

227

disadvantage for doing Salsa, but my stepmom had nixed it on the grounds that ballroom is low class. It had been a couple years since I'd been in a ballroom, but there are some things you just don't forget.

Bottom line: you don't see couples like us every day.

Despite all the stress of the evening, of the past few weeks, the minutes we floated around the dance floor were magical. I think I fell in love with Jamie a little bit that night. I didn't feel the same obsessive yearning for him that I did for Gareth, but part of me wondered if I'd ever really know Gareth, if he'd ever open up to me.

I'd seen the best and worst of Jamie—of that I was positive. This was him at his best, I decided. Absurd I know: Jamie was at his best when he was playing the billionaire polo player? But he was no snob. He knew what kind of place this was, but he'd still treated every person there from Sam the coat check guy to the bride's mother with the same warm charm that came off as completely sincere. And it was sincere in the sense that he genuinely cared about how they felt. He had his lapses into gross douchebaggery like earlier that evening, but what guy doesn't?

There was a poignancy to the whole scene too. Jamie didn't belong here anymore. Seeing him in what should be his natural habitat gave the measure of how very far he'd fallen. Jamie was a deeply fucked up guy. I don't think it was all loss—not at all. But whatever had happened to him had been bad enough that he was never going back to the guy who'd hung out at this club between polo matches.

As the dance came to a close, Jamie spun me around into a dip and then raised my hand to his lips. He knew what he was about: his warm gaze telegraphed "love of my life" to anyone watching—meaning

228

everyone in the room. For my ear only, he murmured, "Your dancing, Nat.... I really don't have words. It's beautiful."

I'd never in my life received a compliment that felt so good. It was exhilarating—and miserably short-lived.

As we applauded the band, Carlos came and whispered something in Jamie's ear. Jamie's hand registered the jolt of surprise, though his expression remained as smiling and easy as ever. Carlos had been shadowing us the whole time—and that's what it felt like. It was weirdly easy to forget he was there. So far as I could tell, Jamie was the only one there with a bodyguard, though no one seemed to regard that as unusual.

We walked off the floor and then down a wide hallway with rather tired Chinoiserie wall-paper in a very sixties shade of silver green, until we reached a mahogany paneled library, complete with big game trophies and furniture upholstered in hideously garish Royal Stewart tartan. There was a fire burning in a large stone hearth—not unwelcome on a rainy April night. Daniel was sitting in an armchair, opposite a distinguished looking older gent whom I'd met earlier—father of the bride, Walter something. He stood up with a tight smile and shook Jamie's hand, but gave me a look that indicated he thought I was a déclassé parvenu. The gorgeous dress Gareth had given me was nothing more than a rose stuck in a pile of shit to disguise the stink.

That didn't feel very good, to be honest.

My face burned. I'd behaved myself at his little girl's special party, when I'd really wanted to go all Occupy Wall Street on him.

"Gareth is out of his mind," he said finally. "You honestly think that Solomon is going to agree to this?" gesturing towards me, the piece of

229

garbage polluting his precious club. Jamie put his arm around me and gripped my shoulder hard.

"Be careful, Walter," Daniel said. "You don't want Gareth as your enemy."

"So we should just sit back while Gareth seizes control of the Vandenberger fortune?"

"Is that what that lowlife Zoltov told you?" Daniel sneered.

"It's obvious," Walter snapped.

Jamie started to laugh, and I swear, I'd never heard anything so bleak.

Walter turned on him. "You think this is funny, son? You should have been a senator, even governor. You still could."

"You're as delusional as the old man," Daniel said firmly.

"Look at him. He's better now," Walter countered.

"And who have we to thank for that?" Daniel said sarcastically. "Fuck this. Have it your way, Walt. But just so we're clear. Gareth created an insurance policy for himself. If Solomon attempts to void his agreement or makes any kind of hostile move here, a series of deliveries will go out both electronically and by messenger to the U.S. Attorney in Albany and Eric Johnson at Treasury. I know what's in the package, and I would give you less than thirty-six hours before the indictments start getting handed down. Gareth doesn't pull punches with people who betray him. He will decimate you. So I hope you've paid for the caterer up front, because otherwise you'll be having Phillipa's wedding reception at Applebee's. Gareth knows what he is about, and they will find and freeze every last dime. Think about that before you get behind this vendetta of the old man's."

"You really hate him," Walter said, divided between surprise and disgust. "Or is it just that you know where your bread is buttered?"

"I know who my friends are, Walter." Daniel rose and nodded at Carlos who'd lurked in the background.

Walter sipped his Scotch, looking bitter. "Be careful, Daniel. He's crazy enough to bring all of us down just for spite."

Daniel smirked and then herded Jamie and me together, down the corridor and out a back door where Carlos had brought the Expedition around. By now it was raining cats and dogs—and probably polo ponies—but of course there was no awning here at the servants' entrance. Jamie didn't hesitate to whip off his coat and hold it over me as we made a dash for the car.

I prayed I'd gotten there without ruining my dress. If we were all going to die tonight, it would be some consolation if I looked fabulous.

This time, Daniel took the driver's seat and motioned to Carlos to join the mysterious backup vehicle. I collapsed on the seat, feeling overwhelmed and exhausted. "You did good, both of you," Daniel said. "Perfect. Put your seat belts on." He tore out the service driveway of the Algonquin Hunt & Polo Club, a place I dearly hoped I'd never see again.

Jamie had his hands over his face. "I need a fucking drink."

"You'll get through this, Jamie. I promise," Daniel said. "I'm not going to let anything happen."

But we'd only driven for a few minutes when there was a double flash of bright lights behind us. Daniel gripped his earpiece and muttered, "Fuck."

Daniel smashed the steering wheel with his hand and began slowing the car down.

"Danny, no!" Jamie sounded terrified, which was really helping my nerves, I can tell you.

"I won't let anything happen to you," he said, taking his gun from the holster. "And get down!" When we just gaped at him, he roared, "On the fucking floor. Now." Jamie grabbed me and shoved me off the seat onto the floor of the backseat, drastically reducing the life expectancy of my dress, and then lay over me, his arms bunched over my head protectively. Daniel pulled over to the side of the road and got out of the car. Jamie rested his forehead on mine, and gently kissed my eyelids. I think that was the first time we'd ever been in physical contact without him being hard.

I have no idea how long it was before Daniel came back to the car. He pulled out onto the road again. "You can get up."

Jamie lifted off me and then helped me up, pulling me in until I was practically sitting on top of him. "They want a meeting at the house," Daniel said.

"We're going?" Jamie sounded horrified.

"They've got Gareth," Daniel said grimly, making my stomach plunge.

"Oh my God," Jamie practically wailed. "This is my fault, if we hadn't...."

"Just lose that idea right now," Daniel shouted him down. "Trust me. Walter was full of shit. This isn't about you, it's about Gareth. You are looking at a classic Charlie Foxtrot. The old man's making a power play,

232

pure and simple. If anyone's to blame, it's me. I let on to Tyler just how angry Gareth was about the other night. He added two and two and went straight to the old man with the news. He knew Sol would be frothing at the mouth once he heard about Natalie. Gareth's finally got a weak spot and he can't fucking help himself."

"You have to kill him, Danny."

"Enough of that," Daniel growled. "You know nothing, you heard nothing, you couldn't possibly speculate—end of story. You will let me and Gareth handle him."

Jamie groaned. "I should tell him, just get it over with."

"I swear to God, Jamie, if you ever say that again, I will beat the living shit out of you. Now shut the fuck up! I thought Johnny might try something like this. It's handled."

We drove in tense silence until I felt the rumble of the wheels going over Gareth's driveway. "Neither of you say or do anything unless I tell you to."

Daniel got out of the car again, his gun in his hand. Jamie pushed me down on his lap, which I did not find comforting in the least.

"Evening, Daniel," a deep voice said.

"Kidnapping, Johnny?" Daniel said angrily. "What are we, the fucking Sopranos now? Are you trying to start a goddamned war?"

"Sol wanted a meeting," Johnny answered. He did have a pretty heavy Brooklyn accent.

"Can't an old man pay a visit to his grandsons?" a new voice called out.

"An old man can pick up a goddamn phone," Daniel answered.

"Rude SOB! Where's Jamie? Where's my grandson?" the second voice said, sounding exactly like a grumpy old man. It had to be Solomon Bransky. Jamie flinched—he was terrified of his grandfather.

There were some more sounds that I couldn't make out, and then the car door opened. To my shock it was Gareth. As usual it was impossible to read his expression. He nodded to Jamie, who pulled me up. Gareth helped me out of the car and then gripped the back of my neck and pulled me in to kiss my forehead. "Let's go inside, shall we?"

I was trying very hard not to lose my shit. Using my super spy powers of deduction, I was getting that Solomon Bransky had decided I was leverage against Gareth. Our very conspicuous appearance at the Algonquin Hunt Club had ensured that about four hundred people now believed I was Jamie Vandenberger's fiancée—i.e. if I showed up dead, questions would be asked.

Daniel moved in front of us, blocking me from getting a clear view, but I could tell there were a bunch of men standing around the driveway, though I saw no signs of Carlos and the mysterious occupants of the "other car."

"You first," Daniel ordered, tossing someone a set of keys, and then backed up his invite by raising his handgun. Gareth just waited, his hand still gripping my neck.

After a minute our group moved. I was sandwiched between Gareth and Jamie, with Daniel in front, so close it was hard to walk without bumping into him.

"Jamie, take Natalie downstairs," Daniel said.

"No!" Sol Bransky snapped. "I want to see this girl who's been causing so much trouble. Bring her in here."

Daniel moved quickly, backing me into a wall with his body pushed against me, his gun raised threateningly.

"What, are you fucking her, too?" Sol sneered.

"Solomon," Gareth warned in a voice so chilling, Daniel actually flinched.

"You bastards are the ones with the guns out," the old man cried. "I'm not going to open fire with my grandsons in the room."

"Grandson," Daniel said under his breath.

"Jamie, don't you have a word for your grandfather?" Bransky demanded.

Gareth nodded at him, and Jamie moved into the room. "Grandfather," he said, sounding bizarrely calm.

Daniel made some motion at Gareth and suddenly there was a flurry of moving red dots, which quickly fixed on Johnny and Solomon Bransky. I knew from the movies they had something to do with assault rifles and targeting and basically the imminent explosion of heads.

"Not playing games, are you Gareth?" the old man chuckled.

"It was my call," Daniel snarled. "After the shit you pulled last Friday, I decided it was time to bring in some backup."

Why was I the only one here scared shitless?

"You made your point. Everyone out but Johnny. Daniel, put away your gun. Now let's see this girl."

Daniel stepped forward. Gareth put his hand on my neck again and moved us deeper into the great room. Sitting in an armchair was Sol

235

Bransky. I admit he was a bit of a let-down. He was really frail and old, and seriously could have been any old geezer at any home in the state. I was more impressed by the massive guy standing behind him, Johnny, who screamed "enforcer," and who really did look like he was moonlighting from *The Sopranos*.

I stood there looking down at the floor while he examined me. It made my skin crawl. If Walter had looked at me like I was garbage, Sol Bransky looked at me like he wanted a lap dance. In other words he might be a criminal mastermind, but he was still a complete creep.

"So this is the girl you paraded around the Hunt Club as Jamie's fiancée? A tramp you picked up off the street to service the three of you!"

To my shock, Daniel's gun was out, pointed at Bransky: "Just keep that up, old man!"

The enforcer guy, Johnny, pulled his gun and aimed it at me. "Think about what you're doing, Daniel."

Jamie moved in front of me. "Jamie, what are you doing?" the old man shouted, utterly outraged.

"Boss?" Johnny said nervously.

"Put your gun down, you moron," Sol shouted. "You did this," he yelled at Gareth. "You said you'd help him. You've let this little whore entrap him!"

"You should be on your knees in gratitude, old man," Daniel burst out. "Thanks to Gareth he's clean and alive. And thanks to Natalie, he's sane."

"He's not clean. He was drunk and high on Friday night."

236

"And now you're going to throw that at us? We both told you he couldn't be left alone…"

Bransky and Daniel began shouting at each other in that way only family members ever do. Here was my final clue on how he and Jamie were connected—not that I gave a shit about it at that moment.

Sol turned on Gareth. "You let that little gold-digger seduce him. You were supposed to protect him!"

"I have," Gareth said in his scary voice. "I can give you no better protection than marrying him to someone I control."

And with those words, Gareth managed to allay all of my fears about having a real gun pointed at me. Of course, he did that by ripping out my heart and freezing my intestines.

"She's a piece of garbage," Sol shrieked insanely. "You'll make me a laughingstock. I spoke to Tyler about her, oh yes." I couldn't help swaying, which the old man picked up on, because he sneered, "Yes, you little hussy. He told me the whole story: how you claimed to be Jamie's true love and then threw yourself at him in the parking lot. I saw the footage. And now the little whore is crying rape. She's just like the last one. You were supposed to protect Jamie from girls like this, not bring them into your house."

"Does this mean you are backing out of your agreement with me, Solomon?" Gareth asked. I'd say he used his scary voice, but it'd be inaccurate. There really is no word in the English language adequate to convey the menace in that question.

Jamie looked ready to faint, while Daniel and Johnny both paled and began raising their guns. Only Solomon was unaffected. "You'd really

237

bring down your own house for this girl," he chuckled, looking like he'd won. "She's that important to you." Daniel had been right. Solomon had been looking for Gareth's weak point. "You seem to forget something. What's jail time to a man my age, Gareth? Right now, it would feel like a fair trade. You stole my grandson, so I steal your girl."

The room went silent. I don't know what we were waiting for. All I know was that I was practically catatonic with fear. I wish I'd fainted— perhaps elegantly slid into Gareth's arms? Tumbled daintily onto a settee? At least I might have resembled the heroine of a gothic romance. They usually have gorgeous deaths. Instead, I did something much, much cooler.

I puked my guts out all over the floor.

Chapter 25

You'd be amazed how much chaos that caused.

Johnny and Sol jumped back in horror. I think Sol called me a filthy bitch, which for some reason made me laugh maniacally. "You want me to clean this up?" I giggled at Daniel.

Daniel started laughing too (which made him look really handsome!) "What a shitstorm. Come on, Cat, let's get you cleaned up." With a nod from Gareth, Daniel grabbed my arm and dragged me into my room. As soon as the door was closed, he pulled me into a tight hug. "You've got a future in the CIA, Cat. You have a definite gift for diversionary tactics."

"It wasn't on purpose," I moaned, utterly humiliated.

He chucked my chin. "I know, kiddo. But we all owe you. I think you just saved everyone's lives out there."

Well that caused a complete meltdown right there. I let out an agonized gasp, as tears started streaming down my face. Daniel calmly took a seat on the bed and pulled me into his lap. And then, he just held me and made sure I didn't shatter into pieces while I sobbed my eyes out.

"They won't hurt Gareth?" I choked out.

"Shhh. I promise. Sol was on one of his crazy rants, but this broke it. Gareth can talk him down." After a few minutes, I started to calm down, until I looked at my dress and started sobbing again. My beautiful dress—that I'd puked on. Daniel must have decided I was beyond functioning, because he carried me into the bathroom, undressed me to my bra and underwear, and put me under the shower.

The water finally cleared my head enough to function, barely. I peeled off the wet bra and panties and tossed them on the bathroom floor, then hopped out of the shower long enough to grab my toothbrush. I frantically brushed my teeth until the gums bled, trying to eradicate all signs of the puke—all signs of this night. I stayed in there long enough to resemble an especially succulent and attractive prune— with a sunburn.

So feeling a bit less confident than my usual monstrously confident self, I wrapped a towel around my pink, puffy skin and exited the bathroom—to find Gareth.

I silently cursed Daniel for leaving me to the proverbial wolf, which was feeling rather less than proverbial at that moment. I'd never seen Gareth like this before. He looked...possessed. Whatever demon was riding him, however, did not detract from how heart-stoppingly sexy he was. But it was more than I could handle—more than anyone could handle, I think. I instinctively looked for an exit, but he was between me and the door. It briefly crossed my mind to lock myself in the bathroom, but he shook his head.

"Are you angry at me?" I managed to gulp out, proud that I'd retained some shred of self-preservation. If he'd said yes, I was going to scream for Daniel.

He made a tiny shake of his head, still keeping that predator's gaze trained on me. "Come here!"

"Gareth," I pleaded.

"No," he shut me down. "It's time." His voice was calm, which was actually even more freaky. I knew what he wanted. He wasn't trying to

240

hide it. I wanted it too, desperately, but there was something in his face that made me hesitate. At least my mind balked. My feet, like the rest of my body, apparently decided to shift allegiance and obey Gareth for once. Anyway, they walked me right over to him. When I was in front of him, he lightly gripped my chin to force me to meet his gaze.

I probably could have stopped things at that second if I'd wanted to enough, if I'd been stronger, but I wanted him so badly, not just sexually, but emotionally. But this wasn't unfolding like the great passionate consummation I'd fantasized about so often. That wasn't affection I was seeing in his expression—or even lust. They were there too, especially lust, but this was Gareth. There was something else, and that scared me.

But the second passed without my objecting.

Gareth pushed me back on the bed and began unbuttoning his shirt. I think my jaw might have gone slack at the sight of his chest. His shoulders were perfectly sculpted, the muscles on his arms not bulging, but iron-hard. And speaking of iron: he opened his pants and let them fall and stepped out of his boxers, unwrapping the whole package, as they say. I'm usually not one for admiring the visual aspect here—as opposed to the *tactile*—but his cock was beautiful, not porn star huge, but powerful and perfectly proportioned.

He only gave me about five seconds to ogle before he was on top of me, pinning my arms over my head with his left hand. His right grabbed my chin and held my face while his tongue plunged into my mouth in one of those brutal kisses of his. There was no tenderness, just aggression and dominance. I arched up, helpless under the onslaught of desires firing through me. As he continued the punishing kisses, his hand moved

241

from my chin to my breast, kneading it just to the point of pain. I tried to cry out and turn my head away from him, but he grabbed my chin again in a clear warning not to try to pull away.

At the same time, he used his knee to force my legs apart, shifting himself into position. He moved his hand down again, this time to my sex, pushing in to test my readiness. He shifted so his left thigh was pinning my right, while his other leg forced my legs even further apart until my sex could feel the coolness of the air in the room. Even with Jamie, I'd never felt quite so exposed and I tried to pull out of his hold, but he'd pinned me too securely.

"Hold still," he ordered and then he began teasing caresses to my clitoris that made staying still next to impossible, except that he'd pinned me so that I felt all the urge to move, without the ability. My mind and body were screaming that I needed to come, but I had no power to bring myself relief.

I groaned aloud, half agonized from the sensual torture. He seemed utterly in control of himself and yet in the grip of an overpowering emotion. I know it sounds like an oxymoron, but there is no other way to explain it. He dragged the teasing out until I was sobbing from frustration, never once taking his eyes from me, not missing a single detail of my reaction. He stopped without letting me climax, his expression warning me not to protest. It was so far beyond Jamie's worst teasing, I felt in danger of going mad. At least every touch of Jamie's had pleasure as its ultimate goal. Whatever Gareth was doing, the goal was not pleasure.

He gripped my chin again, forcing my eyes to stay on his, a silent warning of what was about to happen. I had a brief moment of clarity. This wasn't sex, this was a claiming.

And then he thrust in, and all clarity was gone.

He refused to let me turn my head away, and every time I tried to close my eyes, he squeezed in warning.

Again, I felt the raw pressure of primal need start to build, each thrust of his pounding into my body and brain that I would not come until he allowed it.

I realized I was screaming in sheer desperation. My body tensed over and over again until every muscle felt like it was being twisted into Gordian knots that only a sword blow could disentangle.

Without meaning to, my eyes fell closed and for a moment I wondered if I would black out. Gareth roughly yanked my hair and then whispered low, directly in my ear so that the words felt like they were coming from some traitorous lobe of my brain. "There will be no further doubt on your part: You can fuck Jamie and marry him, but you both belong to me. Is that clear?"

"Gareth...."

"Is that clear?" he whispered.

"Yes!" I wailed.

"Good. Come now." And just like that, he moved what felt like a tenth of an inch, and a year—a lifetime's—pent up need exploded out of me in a series of convulsions that went on far too long.

His lip curled up in satisfaction, and he began thrusting like a pile-driver, harder and harder. The only sign he gave me that he was coming was a slight tightening of the skin around his eyes—that and he pulled out and deliberately shot his load all over my stomach and breasts.

I yelled at him in protest. I felt like I was territory being marked, and the glow of satisfaction in his eyes told me I was exactly right. He refused to let me move at all, holding me with one hand while he trailed a finger through the spunk that he'd spattered over me, spreading it over my breasts, in my arm pits, and then up my neck, along the ridge of my chin. More was painted behind my ears, rubbed into my eyebrows, along the sides of my nose—all in this highly deliberate manner. Finally, he nudged my mouth with his finger. "Open." When I didn't obey, he pinched my nipple, which gained him access. I licked the remaining spend off his finger, feeling an irrational fear that somehow it would serve as the chemical catalyst that would cement his control over me.

He raised his eyes in question, making sure I understood, and I could only nod even as I felt something chill inside my heart. I did understand. I'd just been claimed. That had been the point: to hammer home for all time that I belonged to him.

To belong to Gareth was not to date him. It wasn't even to periodically have sex with him. It was no more or less than to be owned by him, to be one of the people whose lives he controlled.

The sex was for my sake: so I was under no confusion that I'd been claimed. He'd taken me in my room so it was clear it indicated no further change in our relationship.

I felt like those cuffs were being permanently welded to my wrists, binding me to my corner, to my place in his house. The control felt so absolute it was terrifying. I understood that look of exhausted resignation

244

that I sometimes glimpsed on Daniel or Jamie's face. To be brought into Gareth's orbit was to be captured by a gravitational force that no mere human power could escape from.

All three of us loved him in our ordinary, flawed human way, but what Gareth felt for us was something far more intractable. On the one hand, there was a profound sense of safety in that kind of loyalty—a loyalty with no limits, that would kill to protect the ones it claimed. Like me, Jamie and Daniel had both lost their parents, and what Gareth offered us was tantalizing, addictive even.

But an unfamiliar part of myself piped up with the reminder that I was only eighteen. Even if Gareth made excellent choices and I made shitty ones, was I really going to hand over complete control of my life to someone else? Because Gareth would accept nothing less. That was the price of his loyalty.

And looking back over our history I could see that I'd never even decided to pay that price. *He'd* decided. He'd chosen me and then methodically set about taking away all of my options until he was the only one left.

I loved him, but he owned me.

Chapter 26

The next hour proved how very true that was. As soon as he finished with the "marking," Gareth stood and got dressed again. He fished out a pair of sweat pants from the bureau and the Boys Don't Cry tee that Jamie had given me earlier that night, along with a cotton bra and panties and tossed them at me. "Get dressed," he ordered.

He only smirked when I used my still-damp bath towel to rub some of his semen off my face, but I was too exhausted and freaked out to challenge him otherwise.

When I was dressed, he said quietly, "No trouble, Natalie."

"What's happening?" I saw the answer in his eyes. "Gareth…" I tried to plead.

"Not another word, Natalie. You will do as I say," he warned in a tone that I'd *finally* learned to respect. Probably for the best since I was gearing up for some pretty abject begging, and every motion, every expression of Gareth's was proclaiming loud and clear that begging would be useless.

Out in the great room, Sol and Johnny were gone, but a bunch of special-ops -looking guys, all sporting Tacticool vests and goggles and big-ass guns, had taken their place. No doubt these were the dudes responsible for the red dots.

Daniel stood next to Jamie, who looked as shell-shocked as I must have. In the midst of them was a short, balding, grey-haired guy with glasses, who actually did look like a judge. And whatdya know? He was a judge.

So here it is—the part you've all been waiting for. *Reader, I married him* and all that.

Actually, it was more like a burlesque than a romance novel.

Mini-mart Cashier Snags Billionaire Bad Boy! A modern-day shotgun wedding. Cinderfuckingrella.

The truth is I barely remember any of it.

Gareth did not bother with any preliminaries. He pulled me to stand next to Jamie in front of the judge guy. I think the wedding ceremony lasted all of two minutes—no exaggeration. Gareth squeezed my arm when it came time to say "I do," which I did of course, being as I'm so obedient. Jamie was deathly pale—nothing like the beaming groom. He had to try a few times before he got the two little words out. Apparently he was suffering from some sort of bachelor cold feet—to go with my bridal jitters, perhaps?

At some point after the ceremony, I noticed there was a plain gold wedding ring on my finger as well as Jamie's, but I have no memory of how or when they got there.

There was no "kiss the bride" moment—I'm positive of that. As soon as the judge pronounced us married, Gareth pulled us over to sign some documents, giving me a warning pinch when I tried to scan them to see what I was signing. Based on my three-second glance, I figured them for New York State forms for the marriage certificate. There were definitely no thick, expensive-law-firm-bonded-paper type documents in the pile—no pre-nup or post-nup.

But then why would there be? Gareth was that fucking sure of me.

The judge guy took about ninety seconds to check the documents over, pack them up and then left without saying a single word to us.

Gareth's man all right, just like the rest of us. The special ops guys walked him out, I suppose to make sure all those papers got filed properly.

So then there were four of us.

No champagne, no cake, not so much as a canapé in sight.

Not that I could have eaten. I felt like I should scream or puke or faint—go into conniptions maybe? But I'd already emptied my stomach and sobbed my eyes out within the last hour, so I was quite literally empty of drama.

Fortunately, the groom hadn't had his chance yet. As soon as the door closed on the judge, Jamie let out a violent yell and punched the wall hard enough to injure his hand, which he followed up by knocking over the end table and smashing the lamp.

"Jamie, to me!" Gareth ordered sharply.

And just like that Jamie redirected. He threw himself into Gareth's arms, shaking and pale. Gareth pulled Jamie over to the couch so they both could sit and then put his arms around him, patting him reassuringly.

And then Jamie pounded his lips against Gareth's in a ferocious, open-mouthed kiss.

That did surprise me.

Equally surprising—to me at least—was the fact that Gareth…accepted it? allowed it? I'm honestly not sure what word I need

248

here. He participated, doubtlessly, kissing Jamie thoroughly, as in tongues twisting, full saliva exchange.

I still can't believe I didn't pass out from not breathing. I was stunned—and so turned on I thought I would go into convulsions. I've *never* seen anything so hot as the two of them.

Jamie was out of his mind. I don't think he even realized that Daniel and me, Natalie, his, *ahem*, wife, were still in the room. He began frantically kissing Gareth's neck, his ears, and when that wasn't enough, he dropped to his knees, nuzzling the front of Gareth's pants like he was going to give him a blow job right then. Gareth caught him by the arms and pulled him back up onto the sofa and then his lap, whispering reassurances into his ear, running his hands up and down his back, trying to bring him back from his freak-out. Jamie was shuddering and gasping, clinging to him, and finally Gareth unzipped Jamie's pants, pulled out his cock and started to jerk him off.

After I picked my jaw up off the floor, I tried to make for my door. I mean obviously my husband and er, employer, were sharing a private moment. But Daniel caught my arm, preventing me. "No, you need to see this," he whispered.

"I'm seeing it," I said shrilly. "They're gay?" I was too stunned to feel hurt yet, though I could already imagine a point in time when that information would seriously suck.

Daniel made one of his humorless laughs. "Forgive my nosiness, Cat, but you did just fuck Gareth in your bedroom, right?" He looked as exhausted as I felt, which was a little consolation. "I promise there's nothing for you to be jealous about. This is something else."

Something else indeed. Jamie, *my new husband*, was at that moment shooting his load into Gareth's fist. He collapsed right after, sobbing and doing his crazy apology number. It reminded me of the nightmare car ride after House of Correction.

Gareth was murmuring calming words, clutching him. "Natalie, come here," he ordered without looking at me. So he hadn't forgotten I was in the room.

Daniel gave me a firm nudge, and I walked over mechanically, wondering offhandedly if my brain would collapse in on itself like an imploding star with the number of blows it was taking tonight.

As soon as I was close enough, Gareth grabbed my wrist hard and pulled me until I was half on his lap, close enough to smush against Jamie. Gareth gently brushed his hand along the back of my head and then abruptly grabbed my hair and pulled me in so he could plunge his tongue into my mouth. I could have sworn I caught the trace of Jamie's taste.

Predictably—if any aspect of this utterly wacked out situation could be called predictable—Jamie wanted in on the action too. As Gareth took deep kisses, Jamie moved so he could wrap himself around my back and began nuzzling my neck and fondling my breasts.

"Is that spunk I taste?" Jamie joked, as he licked behind my ear. "Someone was feeling territorial. He does that to me too. Get used to it," which made me practically come on the spot. Jamie was obviously over his earlier crisis and apparently had no problem with Gareth banging and creaming all over his wife—or was it more accurate to say Jamie had no problem with me banging his boyfriend?

250

Truly, in my most demented moment, I could not have dreamed up a situation this fucked up.

Gareth shifted me until I was fully straddling him, which allowed Jamie better access to create some sort of Natalie sandwich.

Gareth had his hands on my head, controlling me, but Jamie's hands as usual were wandering—which I noticed when I felt a long finger plunge into my sex. I screamed against Gareth's lips then and tried to flinch away, but Jamie shifted to pin my arms, and Gareth gave a sharp warning yank to my hair.

"Please, Gareth," Jamie pleaded. "Can we finally fucking do this?"

Gareth paused a moment and then ordered, "Take her upstairs. I'll be there in a minute." Next thing I was in Jamie's arms, being carried up the staircase towards a part of the house I'd never been allowed to see before. As we went through the door, Jamie made a groan-worthy quip about carrying me over the threshold.

"I want a divorce," I responded, making it sound like a joke though it was the truth.

"Don't get your hopes up," Jamie murmured, correctly reading between the lines. "Well, here it is—your new room," he announced as he set me down inside the massive master bedroom.

Master bedroom, hah, hah.

It really was though. The room was enormous and decorated in that spare, minimalist style that loudly broadcast "control freak." The walls were a creamy grey, interrupted by a few stunning modern canvases, but without a single personal photograph anywhere. The California king bed was set against a partition, leaving space for a wall of closets behind it.

251

Both the curtains and the duvet were done in gorgeous indigo raw silk. Like the rest of the house, an entire wall had been given to windows, though it was too dark to see the view.

Unlike the other rooms, there was a surprising amount of clutter—except only in certain, clearly delineated areas. One half of the long Danish-modern bureau, for example, was covered by a huge pile of T-shirts that looked like they'd been emptied from one of the drawers that was in fact still open. There was also spare change, random coffee cups, and a pile of CDs not in the case. The mess extended exactly to the halfway point and not an inch over, while the other half did not have so much as a cufflink on it.

Likewise, lone shoes and dirty laundry littered the floor on one side of the bed, where the bedside table was a sea of magazines, crumpled pieces of paper, and yet more coffee cups. Again the table and floor on the other side looked as sterile as a surgical suite. It took me an embarrassingly long time to draw the obvious conclusion: Gareth shared this room with Jamie. They slept together in that bed—every night. They truly were a couple.

The reality of being in here was making me feel faint again, but I managed to say, "I don't get a side?" which sounded horribly lame as soon as it came out of my mouth.

Jamie, ever the cheese ball, came back with, "You can share my side, kitten."

I just stopped myself from saying that he was going to have to come up with a new nickname now that we were married. I was not ready to discuss the marriage with *my husband*. Instead I said, "Think I can wash this off now?" gesturing at the drying smears of Gareth's jizz.

A cool voice behind me said, "No," just as Jamie laughed, "Not a chance."

Gareth was standing in the doorway, and the way he was watching us made me shiver. "Get on the bed, both of you."

"Yes!" hissed Jamie. I could sense him going into his feral mode, despite having come less than ten minutes ago.

He tossed me onto the middle of the bed and threw himself next to me. With a quick glance over his shoulder for permission, he rolled on top of me, pulling my shirt up so he could begin tonguing my breasts, his hand already slipping down beneath my sweats. Between Gareth's "command tone" and the memory of him and Jamie going at it, I was already primed. I arched back, crying out as Jamie worked his usual magic. He brought me precipitously close to orgasm and then stopped, laughing at my protest. Smirking, he sat up on his heels over me, teasingly pulling off his shirt and then unbuttoning his pants.

Gareth had taken a position where we could see him as he watched us, which he did with his usual unreadable intensity. Despite the events that night—gunplay, weddings, claimings—he didn't seem to have so much as a wrinkle on his clothes or a hair out of place. Now that I understood better what the situation was, having him watch me and Jamie seemed a thousand times kinkier—and outrageously hot.

Once we were both undressed, Jamie widened his thighs, forcing my legs apart, and then slid down over me so that his smooth chest brushed my whole body from my ankles to almost my neck. Of course he

253

managed to land with his cock perfectly positioned. He rubbed it up and down along my sex, moistening it, and then circled the head over my clitoris.

"Oh Fuck!" I cried out.

"There you go, kitten," he murmured. "That's right."

"Don't call me kitten!" I groaned out. "I'm your fucking wife!"

"I will call you kitten," Jamie practically purred. "And since you're being such a naughty girl, now you're going to have to beg me."

"Oh fuck, Jamie!" I protested. Except for the absence of handcuffs, married sex was not turning out to be all that different from unmarried sex.

"Come on, kitten. Gareth's waiting. He can't start until we're ready."

That caused a burst of fear—start what? Because there was no way.... "If you even think about touching my ass...," I sputtered.

"Not you, babe," Jamie laughed, winking at me.

Holy fucking hell!

I only needed a second to decide I was willing to beg for *that*. "Please, Jamie. Please!"

"Say 'Please fuck me, Jamie,'" he corrected.

Cocksucker!

Literally!

"Please fuck me, Jamie," I cried out.

Jamie obliged of course. He pushed in and began pumping at a relaxed pace he could maintain seemingly forever. It was so close to what I needed, and yet not quite enough. In other words, maddening. I screamed in protest, and Jamie cooed wickedly, "You have to tell me what you want, kitten."

"Harder!" I groaned. "Please."

Jamie winked and said, "Wait for it."

That's when I felt the bed dip. Gareth knelt behind Jamie, still completely dressed, which sent shivers down my spine. He pushed Jamie's legs wider apart, massaging his ass. Jamie groaned, "That's what I'm talking about. Fuck me, Gareth. Do me, now. Please, baby. Take me rough—please, just this once."

Gareth grabbed Jamie's hair and pulled his head back sharply. "No. You know the rules, James." He gave him several sharp slaps on the ass, which were hard enough to jar Jamie deeper into me.

"Fuck that's good, Gareth. Again—harder."

Gareth took his arm way back to deliver a brutal, full-force slap, which made Jamie roar. "Legs apart, James," Gareth ordered. His pants were open, and he was rubbing something—lube I suppose—over his cock. Jamie obeyed, going up on his arms so he could angle himself better for Gareth—still managing to torture me with his too-gentle pulses.

"No one comes until I say so," Gareth said, before he gripped Jamie's hips and thrust in fiercely.

Jamie let out a wild groan. "Fuck that's good. Come on, baby. Fucking take me."

Gareth slapped Jamie's thigh—*hard*. "Focus, James."

That made Jamie grin at me like a kid—well maybe a feral kid. "And that would mean you, kitten," he said.

255

I could see Gareth's hands tighten over Jamie's hips. "Ready for it..." he said and then ordered, "Now!" With that, they began to thrust in unison, Gareth controlling the pace and Jamie matching him with perfect timing. The crazy part was I could feel it—feel Gareth's powerful thrusts pushing Jamie deep into me, feel Jamie's muscles spasm involuntarily in response to Gareth.

It was mind-bogglingly hot.

I couldn't even scream—I just made weird embarrassing noises, which seemed to delight Jamie. Surprisingly—since he was literally getting fucked up the ass at the moment—Jamie had no trouble putting all his focus on me once Gareth reminded him. He began kissing me, fingering my breasts, pushing me higher and higher, until I screamed. My vision tunneled, and I think I might have been close to hyperventilating.

"She's close, Gareth. I can't hold her," Jamie groaned.

Gareth reached down and yanked my hair painfully. He waited until my gaze was locked on his and then said, "Come now."

Everything went white. Most of the time orgasms are like a wave—a swell that starts slow and then moves faster until it crashes. This was more like lightning: the pleasure hit me everywhere at once, fast and powerful, stealing the breath from my lungs and blanking my vision, as if my nervous system had short-circuited. My body felt suspended, like I'd fallen through the mattress away from Jamie and Gareth, away from all the turmoil in my world into glorious emptiness.

Until a scream ripped through me, dumping me back into awareness and the endlessly perplexing complication of having two men staring down at me.

256

For once Jamie seemed to have lost all control. As Gareth pumped ferociously into him, Jamie gasped out an "Oh fuck," and shuddered into a too-long climax that made him collapse all his weight on me. Gareth made a few sharp jerks and then like before, pulled out and shot his load all over Jamie's back for another of his territorial "markings." I could practically feel the bone-deep satisfaction pouring off him as he dragged a finger through his spend and brought it to my lips. "Open," he said. My last thought before I passed out was that it was fucking hot the way he did that.

Chapter 27

I guess I slept for a few hours. I woke with Jamie wrapped around me, but no sign of Gareth, which didn't surprise me. It took me a moment to realize that the reason I'd woken was that my stomach was growling. I'd been too nervous to eat at the engagement party and thanks to my barf-fest, I was now starving.

As I've told you a bunch of times already, I don't tolerate that well, so I managed to disengage myself from Jamie's grip and slip out of the bed. I glanced at Jamie's watch on the bedside table. It was 3:12 a.m., hours 'til breakfast. Working from the premise that I'd graduated from sex-slave to teen bride, I decided I was no longer subject to the "no wandering" rules—in what was officially my own house, thank you.

There were still a few lights on in the living room, and I spotted Daniel sitting at the head of the dining room table, taking sips of a beer as he stared at a laptop screen. Ever alert, his head snapped up the moment I entered the room. "I'm hungry," I said before he could start an interrogation.

"Have a seat," he said. "Leftover pizza okay? Or do you want some Captain Crunch?"

"Won't Gareth pitch a fit?" I said shakily.

"I think we can cut you some slack on your wedding day," Daniel quipped.

Not quite ready to go there, I quipped back, "Wow, are you actually being nice to me?"

258

"Careful," he warned. "What'll it be, Cat?"

What the hell, it was my wedding day. "Captain Crunch."

He brought out the box, with the milk carton, spoon, and bowl, and then went back and got himself another beer. I filled the bowl and began scarfing. Daniel took sips of his beer as he focused on his computer. Finally, when I'd polished off my second bowl, I said, "Where's Gareth?"

"'Fraid that's not on the list of approved questions. Do I need to spell out why for you?" He sounded a little buzzed, which perversely made me feel better. Even Daniel had been pushed to his limit that night.

"Fine," I said. "So you and Jamie are first cousins?"

"Sure," he said sarcastically. "You could call us that, though Sol kicked my mother out of the house when she was pregnant with me. He didn't approve of my dad, seeing as he was a decorated marine and not a playboy millionaire. Jamie's mom, my aunt Rose, married where Daddy told her to. Turns out I was the lucky one."

"He doesn't know about Jamie and Gareth."

"No, and if he did, he would kill both of them himself. Gramp's a raving homophobe...and racist, sexist all-around bastard."

"How... What..." I wasn't even sure what I wanted to ask, except something along the lines of *what the fuck?* "Make me understand this, Daniel," I finally pleaded, "before I go mad."

Daniel gently brushed my cheek. "You're okay, Cat. In fact, you're holding up better than most women would. It's really not as crazy as it seems. Jamie.... After his parents died, Jamie started circling the drain—drugs, alcohol, sex, he was into everything. A lot of us, including me,

259

didn't think he was going to make it at all. Either the drugs, the booze, or that fucking Porsche of his were going to take him out.

"Anyway, Jamie had just gotten out of his third round of rehab, when we got a call from some hotel he'd trashed. There was a female involved and some rough play and she'd caught the scent of the cash. If the old man had dealt with it, she would have been fitted with a pair of concrete shoes and tossed in Lake Ontario. Gareth had been working for Sol, taking over the businesses, and he made one of his famous deals: he would get Jamie straightened out, handle everything else, pacify the woman, pay off the hotel, so long as Sol promised not to interfere."

"He didn't...." I couldn't bear to finish that sentence.

"No," Daniel said firmly. "Let's just be clear, Cat. Gareth would *never* touch a civilian or a woman. Within his world, he is one of the good guys or I wouldn't work for him. Which is not to say that Gareth didn't talk to her and *persuade* her that she was taking the wrong tack with Jamie's family if she wished to continue breathing."

"So he gave Jamie his own brand of rehab."

"I don't need to tell you," Daniel laughed darkly. "Gareth gave him whatever he needed—same as you. If it makes you feel better, Jamie practically lived in that corner for five months at least."

It did make me feel better.

"So they're, like, gay? Gareth and Jamie?"

"You think *Jamie* is gay?"

"Gareth then? Or are they bisexual? They share a bed!"

Daniel frowned impatiently. "Look, in our world, it's not an either/or. I would consider myself a hundred percent straight, but I top men pretty often, and if it's part of the scene, I have no problem fucking them."

"That's really fucked up," I said bitterly. I'm not sure why I said it, but I was just feeling fed up with all the craziness.

"By what standard would that be?" Daniel said, as angry as I've ever seen him. "The Taliban's? Or is it Brandon High School's, where they practically run a girl out on a rail because of a little PG-13 experimentation with two guys? I never thought to hear that ignorant, narrow-minded crap coming from you."

"Like you're one to talk!" I snapped back, feeling my anger finally awaken. "You haven't exactly held back on the moral judgments."

"That was over that travesty the two of you call consent. That's totally different. As far as I'm concerned it doesn't matter if you're eighteen or eighty. You have to accept your own desires and be responsible enough to actually *explicitly* consent. This is real life, not one of the Gothic romances my Nana used to hide under her bed!"

"Fine, asshole!" Before he could give me a smack for disrespecting him, I stood up. "No fucking way, Daniel. No! You're not smacking my ass. Is that clear enough to meet your consent standards? But just for the record, I don't regret anything that happened between me and Jamie. I signed the contract, and I know if I'd really refused Gareth would have protected me. And you're right, I wasn't ready to *consent*. But what I didn't say yes to, and I wouldn't have said yes to, was marrying Jamie. I never agreed to be turned into Bella Fucking Swan, and I didn't hear you speak up for me while I was getting bulldozed."

I was screaming by the end of it. Daniel watched me warily and finally said, "Who is Bella Fucking Swan?"

How the fuck does anyone answer that? My brain latched on to the sheer absurdity of explaining who Bella Swan was. I felt the anger flow out again, like the backwash of a rogue wave, and slumped back down onto the chair.

"Sorry, Cat. We're all a bit on edge, and I take your point. I shouldn't have...," he started, but then let out a whistle. "I think if I'd tried to stop it tonight Gareth would have knee-capped me. Seriously, the business with Sol got him in a state...." Daniel sighed then. "Fuck it. Doesn't even matter. I think he'd been planning for it all along, and I understand his thinking, crazy as it is."

"Right! He and Jamie need me as their alibi, a living, breathing closet."

"No," he said firmly. "Enough with the insecurity. He can't marry you himself without putting a target the size of Times Square over your head. No matter what happens, Jamie's untouchable and as his wife, so are you. And anyway, I'm sure you've figured out by now that Gareth always has at least twelve totally separate reasons for why he does anything. But those reasons always come down to one thing: control. Gareth likes to keep the people who are important to him close—or better yet, *tied* with as many different bonds and obligations as possible, financial, legal, emotional, sexual, whatever the fuck he needs. And for better or worse, you have joined that very exclusive club. Welcome to the Hotel California."

I covered my face, hoping to keep the tears in, but my eyes were burning mercilessly and my whole body started shaking. I felt warm hands around my waist and next thing Daniel was carrying me to the couch. He held me in his lap for what felt like hours. At that moment it seemed like his strong arms were the only reason I wasn't shaking to bits. I felt a weird wish then that I could just run away with Daniel. It seems a little crazy to say this, but he was the only one of the three who hadn't hurt me—really hurt me. I know he was the only one I trusted. I didn't love him the way I loved Gareth, or lust after him the way I did Jamie. It was closer to a raw neediness that made me hate myself.

I was just so desperate for the safety he represented I would have done anything. Even Gareth had never brought out anything so abject and pathetic in me. I slipped off his lap and onto my knees in front of him. I didn't fully understand what I was doing, but some part of me was convinced that if I had sex with him and submitted the way I was supposed to, maybe he wouldn't abandon me. "Please Daniel. Please. I'll do anything. Don't... I can't take it. If you leave me."

Seriously, I had joined the soap opera pantheon of hell. I think it might, *should* have been the most humiliating moment of my life.

Only it wasn't.

Daniel chuckled and dragged me back onto his lap. I tried to cover my face with my hands, but he pulled them away and pinned them easily behind my back.

"Listen to me, Cat." I tried to interrupt, but he grabbed my chin and said in his fiercest command tone, "No talking. Listen." I nodded shakily. "First. You've been through hell and you don't need to act like you

263

haven't. Second. None of this is your fault. You know that's true so act like it." He paused, so I nodded again. "Third. You've got more lovers than you know what to do with. What you *need* is a friend. Neither Jamie or Gareth can play that role for you—for a lot of reasons. I can and I will. If I'm your friend that means you don't owe me or need to be anything other than yourself. So you and I are going to be friends."

And the best part of Daniel, the best part of this whole fucking mess, was that I believed him. Tears filled my eyes, but this time it was sheer relief. There was no bullshit with Daniel, so for once I could let go the self-doubt and guilt and anger and just feel grateful.

The weirdest part was that I wanted to have sex with him more than ever at that moment, but the fact that he *didn't* want me felt comforting instead of insulting. Desire had become such a source of turmoil in my life, tearing me apart with doubts about Gareth and Jamie, forcing me to face parts of myself I feared or hated. With Daniel I could have something like a stupid high school crush without it actually meaning anything.

I must have drifted off for a few minutes in his arms, when Daniel tensed. I opened my eyes with a jolt to find Gareth staring at me. He put his hand on the back of my neck, gripping it gently but in a way that felt like a warning.

"I was hungry," I said, wishing I didn't sound like I was apologizing.

"Come to bed," he said quietly.

I don't think I'd ever felt so exhausted in my life, which I'm convinced is the only reason that I stood meekly and let him lead me back upstairs.

He lifted the duvet and nodded for me to get in the bed. Jamie must have sensed it, because he wrapped his arms around me and pulled me tight. Gareth pulled the covers over us and then lay down next to me on his side. I'd never seen him in a mood like this—contemplative, almost relaxed. He gently ran his hands through my hair and Jamie's, watching us. Daniel was right. This had been his plan all along, to bind both of us to him and to each other.

After another minute, Gareth gave me a kiss on the forehead and stood up. "The contract still stands," he warned.

"Gareth!" I protested.

"It stands—*whatever happens*." I wish I'd paid more attention to the intent behind those words, but I was reaching the outer limits of my stamina, both physical and emotional.

"I want a divorce," I said, my voice shaking badly.

"No. It's for your protection and not subject to debate." The finality of his answer left me feeling deeply defeated in a way I'd never experienced before, even after everything that had happened in my life. Hot tears started rolling down my face. Simply beginning to acknowledge my stew of emotions over this marriage was like getting a roundhouse kick to the jaw. I cared about Jamie, I loved him even, but given how I felt about Gareth, being married to Jamie felt like a betrayal of those feelings, an ugly parody.

"Go to sleep now, Natalie."

"You ask a fucking lot of me."

"I ask everything. Go to sleep." Gareth adjusted the duvet to fully cover us—basically tucking us in.

265

The movement roused Jamie enough to mutter, "Aren't you coming to bed?"

"Later," Gareth answered. "You two go to sleep." I was having trouble keeping my eyes open, but I vaguely registered that Gareth had pulled his phone out.

"It's got to be past four. Don't stay up too late," Jamie yawned, sounding just like a concerned spouse. "You've finally got both of us in your bed. It will be weird sleeping with three."

I could have sworn Gareth murmured, "No it won't."

Chapter 28

Two hours later, the FBI showed up and arrested everyone in the house.

Chapter 29

So getting arrested turned out not to be my finest moment—not that I'd been having many of those lately. They separated us right away, which produced a bit of a freak-out on my part, during which I employed enough profanities that the arresting agents started throwing around terms like, "resisting arrest" even though, *hello,* I'd already been arrested, and then something called, "aggravated harassment of law enforcement personnel." The latter apparently would have added a Class E felony charge to a resume already boasting such illustrious achievements as "slut for hire," "lottery ticket sales," and "live-in gas station attendant."

I'm sure you think I should have learned all sorts of useful lessons about kissing ass and not antagonizing authority figures from my various trials—and you can just go fuck off!

In my own defense, my behavior probably owed more to exhaustion, crashing blood sugar, and the fact that I'd suddenly become Mrs. James Fucking Vandenberger than it did to my supposed "oppositional defiant disorder." But I was apparently moments away from talking myself into actual prison time, when I was interrupted mid-rant by a knock on the door, and in walked this aging-hippie woman who was dressed like she was on her way to Woodstock—or maybe the early-bird performance for senior citizens.

"Hi, I'm your attorney, Barbara Steinman—you can call me Babs."

I responded with a polite, "What the fuck?"

Babs just chuckled. "I can already tell I'm going to like you," and then barked, "the rest of you can get the fuck out so I can confer with my client."

I did learn something that day about the strategic use of profanity, because that "fuck" of hers went a long way to convince me I should at least hear her out.

It turned out that Gareth had called Babs *the night before,* right after our honeymoon threesome, and asked her to make the drive to Albany to represent me—as in he knew we were all about to get arrested, which of course he neglected to mention. I was so mad I was working myself up to another tirade, when Babs slapped her hand down on the table.

"Enough. It's time for you to listen. First thing. I represent you and not Gareth. End of story. Second thing. Right now you need to woman up. I can get you out of here, but I'm going to need the whole story, every detail of your connection to Gareth Boyd. So no bullshit embarrassment or trying to protect him or any of that crap. I need you to think really seriously about whether you, Natalie, deserve to sit here or, Goddess help us, rot in prison for even a single minute for something he did."

I believed her, which seemed pretty crazy in retrospect. I mean, she was obviously a hippie-do-gooder, a group that in my experience can compete with Christian fundamentalists for the title of most judgmental, self-righteous assholes on the planet. Like Call-Me-Heather Saunders, she did the whole Birkenstock/patchouli thing. But there was something about her that just made you know she'd never stoop to anything low. When I asked her if she was going to blab about what I told her, she got

269

deadly serious and said, "Attorney/client privilege isn't just a line. That's my scripture, beginning to end. I won't tell. Ever."

She reminded me a little of Daniel, though it would have appalled her if I'd told her. She gave me her bio over breakfast: turns out she lived on a commune in Vermont, and was a vegetarian *and* a pacifist. She even told me that all her clothes were "Earth- and humanity-friendly" and were sewn on women's cooperatives in Paraguay and Mozambique. But politics aside, they were the two most trustworthy people I've ever dealt with, like they both lived by these personal honor codes which said that you don't use people.

Anyway, I ended up barfing up the sorry tale, telling her *everything* that had happened at pervert central, and even the stuff with Tim and Brandon that had turned my life into a PSA in the first place.

At the end of it I waited for her to start in on me for having no self-respect and selling myself and acting like an idiot, but instead she just nodded. "That, my dear, is a wild fucking story. Good job. And since you actually told the fucking truth, I can get you out."

That was *it*. No judgments, no fake pity, or even real pity. She got out a laptop and typed up this "affidavit," where I basically swore I knew bupkus about Sol Bransky, Gareth, and organized crime in New York State. She read it out to me, and then I signed it.

"So here's the deal. I'm going to make some promises on your behalf, which means as your lawyer, I'm giving them my word, not just yours, that you had no part in this. But to make sure this ends here, *today*, I need you to keep your head down. No press, no jailhouse visits. You slide off the radar."

"I don't," I swallowed. "I don't have anywhere to live."

She patted my head at that. "Got that one covered. Our enterprising friend made another call last night to a Stuart Brody. Seems the good doctor and his wife would be happy to host you until you have to go back to school."

I did start crying then, more than crying—bawling. I'm not totally sure why, but I felt this tiny glimmer of something, a bit of light in my depressingly dark tunnel. Babs gave me a pat on the head and then disappeared for an hour.

And that really was all it took. She talked to some people, signed some papers, and they released me. Babs drove me back from Albany in her Prius (which did have the "I think therefore I'm a vegetarian" bumper sticker), and we made the Brody's house by four p.m.

And just like that, I was starting my life over again.

By my own count it would be my fourth time since my dad died. But it turned out that this was the first time in ages where I actually felt a little hope.

It probably sounds as fun as watching paint dry. The Brodys were both in their sixties and lived in the middle of nowhere in this restored farmhouse. They didn't have a TV and the only computer was this desktop dinosaur in the living room with a dial-up modem. But I wasn't bored at all even though I hardly ever left the house or saw anyone but the Brodys and Babs.

I'd always liked Dr. Brody—I called him Stuart now—and Pat, his wife, was *the greatest*. She had this massive vegetable garden and could have opened up a green market with all the stuff she grew. She had also

271

literally won five statewide championships for her canned goods. I know it sounds so nerdy and Midwest—home canning—but you should try it, because it's actually really satisfying. We just did easy stuff that summer—pickles and preserves—but Pat taught me all about the pressure canner for preserving low-acid foods. There's a ton of science involved so it was really interesting, and she joked that I asked so many questions, I could have taken over her agricultural extension class on veggie processing.

It was good that I was there too, since Pat had been suffering on and off from arthritis in her hands so I could totally help her with weeding and hoeing and even with cutting up fruits and veggies to be put up.

Even though the Brodys were big on healthy eating, it was mostly stuff from their garden which made it really cool. Pat liked to say she was "the original locavore." I kept bugging her to write a cookbook, since her cooking was the best I'd ever eaten. I even promised to help her with it.

One ironic thing was that it turned out that the Brodys were big into hiking. Yeah, I know—hiking. But they invited me to come with them on this two-day hike on the Finger Lakes Trail over Memorial Day weekend, which they swore was amazing, and since they were so great to me, I did end up saying yes.

The crazy part was that the Thursday before we left, a package arrived addressed to me which contained those three hundred fifty dollar hiking boots that Daniel had gotten me with the pricy high-tech socks stuffed inside. I admit, that drove me under the covers in my room for a good hour-long sob-fest. I'd literally not heard a single syllable from any of them. Not even my husband. Not even Gareth.

Of course, I'd been scanning the newspapers for any info on them and tagging along whenever Pat had her volunteer morning at the public library so I could stalk them on the internet. There had been a gazillion stories about Sol Bransky, who had been indicted on twelve counts of money laundering, racketeering, and conspiracy, but had *allegedly* (as in anonymous sources claiming it was a hoax of some kind) suffered a stroke in the Grand Jury room.

Reporters in our neck of the woods don't get scooptastic stories like that every day, so basically the Albany journalism community was collectively creaming its jeans over our very own mafia melodrama. The upshot was that there wasn't much attention left for anyone who wasn't a dying crime lord. I could find hardly any mentions of Gareth, only that he and a long list of other people including Walter were "under investigation." That was weird enough, but there wasn't a single mention of me, Jamie or Daniel, which told me that Gareth had some powerful friends in either the FBI or the press, probably both.

I won't lie. I *missed* them. Badly. I couldn't help it. But after a lot of hard thinking I decided it was good that I hadn't talked to any of them. If someone was sending me boots, then they hadn't totally forgotten about me. Living at the Brodys was so normal, there were times it felt like the stuff at Gareth's had just been some lunatic hallucination on my part. So the boots were a little bit of tangible proof that I hadn't just dreamt it. Also, if someone was sending me hiking boots, then my gut told me they were all alive and in reasonably good shape. I just couldn't see Daniel—I assume it was Daniel—sending along some hiking boots as a little joke if

Gareth was in imminent danger of getting shanked in the federal prison yard.

But I refused to go into sad sack mode that it was just the boots and nothing else. I was finally getting back on my feet, shaking off the train wreck I'd become. For the first time since I could remember, my life felt pretty stable and was moving in the direction I wanted. I no longer felt I was destined to fuck it up irrevocably. A big part of it was that I had some truly decent adults in my corner now, the good parents I wish I'd been born with, that maybe my mom would have been if she hadn't gotten cancer. The kind of parent I'd want to be, without any other agenda than to help your kid grow up into a decent, functioning, reasonably happy adult.

I'm really not trying to be negative here or make accusations at Gareth or Jamie or Daniel. I loved them all, and Gareth would always be the person who knew me best in the world. But I was deeply grateful to the Brodys for helping me and for not asking anything else but for me to be okay.

I'm sure Daniel would have laughed his head off if he heard that the hiking trip worked out so well that I ended up going with the Brodys on their yearly vacation to the High Peaks District of the Adirondacks. They were in this club of hard-core hikers called the 46ers, where you make this public resolution to hike the forty-six highest peaks in the park. They'd each done nineteen already, and they even managed to talk *me* into registering to be a 46er. And I actually did hike Cascade and Porter during the trip.

The only other thing that happened was that two weeks before school started, Babs asked to meet with me and the Brodys. I assumed it had to do with my getting arrested, but it turned out not to at all. Seems that Gareth had set up this trust for me to pay for college—a generous one. Babs said there would have to be trustees and asked who I'd suggest. I immediately wanted the Brodys, but I was almost too afraid to speak up—they'd done so much for me already. But of course Babs told me to stop acting like a "Mary Fucking Sue" and just ask them. When they said yes I couldn't help crying. It just felt so fucking good to know that someone out there had my back and could help me make decisions. It was nothing I wouldn't have done for a kid I cared about, but like I said, my adolescence had turned out to be short on people like this.

I was grateful to Gareth too. Of course I was. But Gareth's hands were not exactly clean. Exhibit A: on a weird hunch, I asked Babs when the trust had been set up, and she told me OCTOBER! As in days after I became homeless. I'll let you just stew on the implications of that—as I did for the next two weeks, until it was time to head to school.

So the first day of September, Dr. Brody drove me to Providence with my one duffel bag, totally shocking my roommate, Bethany from New Jersey, who'd driven with her parents with their Land Rover stuffed to the gills with everything from a mini-fridge to her collection of stuffed animals.

So after all that angst and mayhem, I did actually start my really famous ivy-league college. You might not be surprised to hear that it was a bit of a let-down. Don't get me wrong: I wasn't depressed or homesick or anything, but it did feel deeply anti-climactic.

275

The stuff with Gareth had only lasted two weeks. TWO WEEKS! Could that be crazier? At the time, it felt like a lifetime. And that's because it was life-changing—legitimately. After something like that, college itself couldn't match it for sheer psychological impact. I felt older than the other freshmen and found it hard to get pumped up about the social scene in my dorm.

Luckily, my summer of introspection had prepared me for this, so I didn't beat myself up about it. And I was genuinely excited about my classes. My professors really were terrific, but it was more than that. The events from the past year had made me more determined than ever to take advantage of this opportunity. I'd learned the hard way how quickly and easily material things can be taken away from you. No matter what happened to me—whatever additional Dickensian misfortunes I was destined to suffer in my life—this education would be mine forever.

Chapter 30

I'd been at school about a month, still without hearing so much as a peep from Daniel, Gareth, or *my husband*, and I decided I'd had enough of being a lame-o shut-in. So far I'd really only made one friend, Bethany, my roommate. She wasn't too bad, though she was a motormouth and wore too much makeup, both occupational hazards for girls from New Jersey.

Under the impression that I suffered from crippling shyness and insecurity, she was constantly making validating comments about how she loved my "natural look" and promising to introduce me to hot guys if I would just come out with her. Finally, I decided to take her advice and get off the damned bench. I was at college and I was going to have a life: meet some people, party, have fun and possibly get laid like every single one of my classmates seemed obsessed with doing.

So after a bit of strategizing with Bethany, I accepted a coffee date from this guy, Tristan, from my freshman composition class who'd shown some interest. We hit it off pretty well. Like me, he's really into '80s music—his favorite band was the Pixies, which is so cool as to be almost suspect (but obviously is infinitely better than being a Maroon Five fan like Bethany). He was from Williamsburg in Brooklyn, which he seemed to think was extremely hip and authentic. I got the picture that his parents were Trustafarian types, because they ran an art gallery but he'd still gone to private school in Manhattan.

Honestly, he was a little pretentious and I wasn't that interested in him, but that actually seemed like an advantage since I wasn't looking for anything too serious. And he was extremely good-looking and dressed in this totally hip retro style. Bethany swore he was the best-looking freshman male she'd spotted, and she spent quite a lot of time on that question.

So after the coffee and then a meal with Bethany and a bunch of other first years at the Refectory, he called to invite me to a "Madchester" party being held by some juniors from his old school in this artsy fraternity, which I discovered is not an oxymoron at Brown. It was obvious that this was intended to be an actual date. I said yes and even wore a skirt to signal sexual interest. So at nine p.m. we made our appearance at the packed party which had an actual DJ playing Manchester dance classics from the Happy Mondays and the Stone Roses.

So we danced for a while, and I let it get a little sexy. Tristan was a good dancer, a veteran club-hopper as he proudly informed me. Anyway, they started playing a slow song ("Atmosphere" by Joy Division, which is a fucking awesome song) and we went full body contact, and after a couple slow turns and some tentative gropes near my ass to see if I objected, he moved in for a kiss.

At which point, we were very decisively shoved apart. "Sorry *Tristan*," Jamie sneered, because it was Jamie, "but she's taken."

Poor Tristan, who'd been sporting major wood (courtesy of my bodacious bod) was not too psyched. "What the fuck is going on?" he demanded, giving Jamie a shove.

"You're pawing my woman," Jamie replied, looming over him aggressively.

This was enough to draw the crowd's attention. Even artsy types were pumped at the idea of a fistfight.

I however was *not* enamored of the idea of being completely humiliated. "I don't fucking believe this," I shouted, punching Jamie. "What the fuck are you doing here?"

"Who is this fucker?" Tristan demanded.

"Why don't you tell him, baby?" Jamie smirked.

The threat was clear—acknowledge Jamie or I was about to be outed as a married woman. "Fucker," I muttered. "He's sort of my boyfriend," I apologetically explained to Tristan.

"Sort of?" Jamie pouted, pretending to be hurt.

I knew he was a second away from calling me kitten, which would *almost* be worse than saying we were married. That just wasn't done in the Ivy League. It was time for some shameless shoveling. "Tristan, look I'm really, really sorry. We were, like, *on a break*, cuz Jamie, here, was, like, in *Ecuador*, helping build these *latrines* for impoverished banana farmers. We totally left it so we could date other people, but I guess he decided to surprise me. It's so totally embarrassing. I wouldn't blame you if you, like, *never* wanna speak to me again." I nibbled my lip and fluttered my eyelashes apologetically.

Tristan might have been from Brooklyn, but he swallowed that whopper smooth as a hungry trout in Otisco Lake. (I got that phrase from Dr. Brody). He gave Jamie an assessing look-over and registered a flicker of disappointment that my hometown honey was at least as good-looking as he was, as well as a full three inches taller.

Jamie looked like he couldn't decide if he wanted to punch him or burst out laughing, but he drawled smugly, "Family Foundation. We do *tons* of great work with banana farmers."

Tristan seemed to grasp that this was his chance to withdraw gracefully, but he was New Yorker enough to not go down without at least one kidney shot. "Sure baby," he said, making his tone unctuously sympathetic. "I totally get it." (Read: I know what it's like when an ex won't leave you alone and sweet girl that you are, you need to let the poor loser down gently). "Don't worry *at all*—and I'll see you Tuesday in class." He was about to lean in for a kiss when Jamie grabbed me by the upper arm and manhandled me out of the room.

By this point, I was pretty evenly divided between joy at seeing him and outrage that he only showed up to cockblock me on my first date in five months. The moment we were out in the entryway, I punched his arm hard and yelled, "What the fuck, Jamie?"

Jamie ignored the punch and pushed me against the wall for a passionate kiss. "Kitten, I missed you," he groaned and then began inching my skirt up even though the entryway was *not* empty.

"Quit it, asshole," I hissed, trying futilely to shove him back. "What the fuck are you doing here?"

"You mean besides saving you from the biggest mistake of your life? Seriously, kitten, Tristan? What were you thinking? The guy's a complete wank!"

"One, it's none of your fucking business, and two, he was hot and totally doable."

"Watch your tongue, Cat." I turned to see Daniel coming through the door. That sobered me right up, because he wasn't pleased. "You should have figured by now that Gareth has limits, and *this* crossed them."

"That's very funny," I snapped back. "I haven't heard from any of you for five fucking months. I go on one date...."

Jamie cut me off with another kiss. He was downright gleeful. "Finally," he chirped. "Danny wouldn't let me come near you until you started up with that Bieber wannabe. Let's go."

I knew it was time to cut my losses. We were beginning to attract attention from random passersby, some of whom appeared "concerned." Daniel had an all-too familiar expression on his face, the one that said if I kept it up he was going to redden my ass. If I got busted getting spanked, there was no way I could show my face on this campus again. We're talking social Armageddon.

Muttering about how Tristan looked less like Justin Bieber than Jamie did, I allowed Jamie to drag me outside.

The Expedition was illegally parked in the fire lane, though Carlos was waiting with it. Daniel stopped to share some words with his operative, while Jamie and I got in the back seat. The moment the door closed, Jamie pulled me over to straddle him. "Get off of me, asshole," I protested, assuming he was going to try to screw me right there in the car.

But Jamie just hugged me close. "Shh, Natalie, don't," he murmured. "Please, just let me hold you for a moment."

281

I'd almost never seen this affectionate side of Jamie, and I wasn't fully prepared for the emotions it roused. I stopped fighting his hold. Too many sensations were bombarding me: his gorgeous scent, which I'd hardly ever registered before but which was reassuringly familiar and unbearably carnal at the same time, the sheer warmth of another body holding me, the golden silkiness of his hair, and as always those amazing clear blue eyes of his.

"Should I even ask where you've been?" I said.

"No," he chuckled. Before I could ask, he added, "Gareth's fine—he's *good*." Jamie kissed me gently on the mouth. He smiled ruefully and added, "He said to tell you not to ask for a divorce."

Screech!

"Mother fuck!" I punched him hard.

"Hey, don't blame me. I'm just the husband here." His tone was joking, but I thought I saw a lingering pain. My anger died a quick death. None of this was Jamie's fault, and I couldn't stand the idea of hurting him. It was obvious he was doing well, and if I somehow caused him to fall off the sanity wagon, I would never forgive myself.

"Jamie…" I started awkwardly.

He was always too good at reading me, though. "Shh, kitten. Stop worrying."

"I don't…I…." I didn't even know what to say to him.

"Natalie," he said firmly. "I know how you feel about him. You don't need to worry about me. It's going to be okay. I swear."

I mashed my face against his shoulder. "I really do love you," I whispered.

282

"I love you too, kitten. I love him. It's all going to be okay. Trust me." I couldn't help shuddering with relief. Jamie and I were all right. The marriage didn't make him think of me differently, expect something that I wasn't able to give him. I felt something loosen inside. I'd not realized how much worry I'd been shouldering over this marriage, but his reassurance made it feel like I'd shed a fifty pound weight.

I gave him a light kiss, which of course Jamie took as the equivalent of my lying back and spreading my legs. He grabbed the back of my head so he could kiss me deeply, while edging his other hand under my skirt—and since it was Jamie that meant a second later his fingers were deep in my sex. "Let's go quickly right here, kitten," he rumbled, reaching to undo his pants.

"No way, and I told you not to call me kitten."

"Oh babe, I cannot wait to get you to bed. You are going to scream so loud for me," Jamie quipped back and of course set to work getting me to scream right there in the car.

Luckily, or maybe unluckily, Daniel chose that moment to open the door. "Knock it off, you two!" Daniel barked. "Put your seat belts on."

"Don't blame me!" I grumbled but slid off Jamie onto the other seat and put my seat belt on. As soon as we pulled out, I asked, "So how did you guys know about that party, anyway?"

"I've had Carlos keeping an eye on you," Daniel answered, sounding pretty annoyed about it.

"You're kidding me? Carlos has been spying on me? Just to make sure I don't date?"

283

"No Carlos is here to make sure you're safe. The phone tap is to make sure you don't date."

"You tapped my phone?"

"And put cameras in your dorm room," Jamie murmured in my ear. "Danny wouldn't let me watch any of the footage. I just had to imagine you jerking off in that lonely bed of yours."

"Shut the fuck up, Jamie!" Daniel barked. "It was for security, not so you could stalk Natalie."

"And so you didn't try to bring any guys home," Jamie said, slipping his hand up my skirt.

"That too," Daniel said dryly.

I slapped Jamie's hand away, the lovey-dovey mood having evaporated at the information that they'd been spying on me without bothering to send so much as a "we're all fine" text. "Where are we going anyway?" I asked sourly.

"Surprise," Jamie answered with a smarmy wink.

Daniel just snorted from the front. I stewed in my seat, but secretly I was relieved at how unchanged they were. Whatever went on after we were separated couldn't have been too bad.

We drove into the downtown area where a recent urban renewal effort had brought in chic loft-style apartments for young professionals along with the accompanying amenities: sidewalk cafés, galleries, gourmet groceries, and a little way closer to the water, some hip (at least aspiringly hip) bars and dance clubs.

We arrived at one of the nicer properties, a converted factory right on the water which had added a top story that was all glass. There was a small driveway at the entrance with an actual valet there to park the car. Instead of entering the building lobby, we followed some old railway tracks along one side that led to a large brick warehouse next door. Once upon a time, it must have been some sort of receiving area/dock from the river. Now the flashing lights, pulsing bass line, and line of people standing outside made clear the property had been reinvented as a nightclub.

Jamie blithely walked by the line of hopefuls, nodding to the bouncer with utter confidence. The bouncer actually patted Jamie's shoulder as he ushered us in, fortunately for me without asking to see any ID. Once inside, that reverberating generic bass line resolved itself into Donna Summer's "Bad Girls," which caused Daniel to groan. "I told you no fucking disco!"

Jamie had a shit-eating grin. "A little '70s never killed anyone. Come on, kitten."

He grabbed my hand, waved at the DJ, and pulled me out on the dance floor just as the Bee Gees' "Dance Fever" came on. I couldn't help marveling at the space. So often nightclubs are dark sweat factories. This had a huge wall of windows, with sliding doors leading out to a good-sized wooden pier that in the summer could be used for more dance and table space. The décor was pretty minimalist—just a central dance floor, a front stage where the DJ was set up, and a bar opposite, second and third-tier mostly steel balconies circling the room, and another area, set off with fluorescent glowing beads, that held a separate seating area with tables and cushioned booths.

I loved it: there was something very functional and basic about it that told you the emphasis here was totally on the music and dancing, not on some sort of Vegas light show or sixteen dollar lavender martinis.

The dance area was pretty packed considering it was still before eleven. The crowd was surprisingly mixed as far as race, age, and sexual orientation went. But they did seem to have one thing in common: they were all seriously good dancers. No sign of the usual drunken skanks or Jersey Shore wannabes trolling to get laid.

Jamie pushed us through to the center of the floor like he owned the place, nodding familiarly to several dancers, all of whom looked psyched to see him. As soon as we started, I understood why Jamie liked disco so much. It really is the perfect dance for him: he's skilled enough to do the moves, but he was also fun, hamming it up, channeling his inner Travolta and just enjoying himself. I kept my own moves simple, letting Jamie strut his stuff.

The crowd adored it, with both men and women openly ogling him. I don't know how I would have reacted if he'd made moves on anyone else, but other than his usual promiscuous flirting he saved the sexual come-ons for me.

And speaking of come-ons. It happens every now and then with Jamie that you realize just how much he's holding back. Tonight he wasn't doing anything to mute his stupendous sex appeal, probably trying to remind me of the upside of being married to him.

As if I needed reminding. I had no idea what Jamie had gotten up to, but I'd just gone five months without any action not provided by my own hand—after becoming accustomed to scorching hot sex four or more times a day. I hadn't even thought I missed it that much given that I'd had plenty of other stuff on my mind, but all that pent-up desire came rushing back now.

I would have thought Jamie would be feeling me up at every opportunity, but he was too savvy for anything so obvious, nothing more than occasional brushes of our pelvises or hips, but he never took his focus off me, never let me doubt what he was thinking about.

By the end of the second dance—Chic's "Good Times"—I was about ready to spontaneously combust. I signaled that I needed a break, which made him smile triumphantly, while I put up my hands conceding surrender. No question: Jamie won that round.

He led us to a booth in the VIP area, where Daniel was sitting nursing a Guinness, sporting his usual annoyed expression. There was an array of rather recherché-looking hors d'oeuvres in front of him—untouched. It reminded me of his reaction to eating goat cheese. I'm pretty sure he would have preferred Buffalo wings and Cajun fries. He immediately handed me a fresh bottle of sparkling water. "Drink. You'll get dehydrated."

I rolled my eyes, but obediently took a long sip. Jamie had fetched a Coke from the bar and slid into the booth right next to me—managing in the same motion to get his hand up my skirt and under my panties. To my surprise, a really good-looking, almost definitely gay guy came up to the table and whispered something to Jamie. It was obvious he was asking questions, which Jamie was answering with an authority that I'd never seen in him outside of the sex act.

When they'd finished their little Q and A, Jamie said, "Miles, I want you to meet Natalie."

Miles lit up—my name obviously meant something to him. He shook my hand eagerly and gushed, "Oh I'm so…this is so great. I'm so glad you finally made it. What do you think? Isn't it amazing?"

"It's great," I said, a little overwhelmed.

"You should have told me, Jamie. Doesn't matter. You gave me the list. I'll talk to Doug."

"Wait, Miles!" Jamie whispered something else in his ear. Miles's eyes went up but he nodded eagerly and rushed off to fill whatever request had been made. As soon as he was gone, Jamie added, "Miles is my manager. He's a lifesaver."

"Your manager?"

Jamie gave me his million-dollar-smile. "It's my club. Yours too, wife." He winked at me jokingly, but I could tell he was proud too.

I was awestruck. "Oh. My. God. Jamie, this place is amazing."

He elbowed Daniel, who was still scowling. "See!"

"All I said is that you should serve fucking wings." I burst out laughing at that. "What?" Daniel said with his usual special ops menace.

"Too much goat cheese?" I giggled.

Before Daniel could answer, Creedence's "Fortunate Son" came on. "Rat bastard," he grumbled and put out his hand. "On your feet, Cat."

He didn't wait for my response but just pulled me out to the dance floor and put his hand on my waist and grabbed my left hand in his. We were immediately spinning around the floor in a rockabilly style waltz, complete with spins and dips. He was fantastic and, unsurprisingly, he could lead. When I caught his eye, he gave me a reassuring nod. I hadn't any of the hesitations about Daniel that I did about the other two. His friendship really meant something, and I wanted it.

"Are we okay?" I asked over the music.

He really did smile then. "Always, Cat."

It's a short song and was over too fast. Daniel gave me a final twirl and then to my surprise the music changed to "Oye Como Va," the old Tito Puente version.

"What the fuck?" This was seriously eclectic, but the other dancers didn't seem fazed at all, effortlessly transitioning to Salsa. I realized then that Daniel had tensed. "What?" I teased. "You don't dance Salsa?"

"*I* don't," Daniel murmured. His eyes widened, but before I could react, my hand was taken—by Gareth.

Chapter 31

It really was like a movie. We just stared silently at each other for a long minute until, finally, he gripped my hip and pulled me into the dance.

I'd never even imagined Gareth dancing, but he was extraordinary. I remembered belatedly that his mother was Cuban. No doubt he'd grown up dancing Salsa like most Latin kids. There was nothing showy in his style at all, but he owned the dance—and owned me while we were out there.

Salsa is not a dance for the faint of heart, especially if you're not Latino. But if you can attack the dance with confidence, it's the most sensual, gorgeous dance in existence. And don't believe people who tell you the Tango is sexier, because they're wrong. Tango is full-on aggression—you can believe that the dancers really are just a step from backhanding each other. Salsa requires a gentler sort of domination by the male—more coaxing, playful—and gives the female plenty of room to use her seductive wiles. It's also best as a social dance, unlike Tango which is too demanding and always feels like a performance.

I'd always adored it myself and had had a great teacher. Rodrigo used to say that *any* woman—young, elderly, slim, full-figured—is beautiful when she dances Salsa, because it's impossible for her to really do the moves without realizing how beautiful and desirable she is. He also used to say that the best Salsa dancers were couples who'd been married for at least twenty years, because they knew the dance was about more than just sex. I think he would have been impressed by us. Gareth and I had never danced together before but every motion felt so intuitive and graceful. For the first time ever I felt like we were actually a couple—a man and woman in a real relationship.

You know, the kind where you have conversations or watch TV or do dishes, and no one is tied up.

Sorry for the digression. But 'til the day I die, I will never, ever forget that dance with him.

As the dance wound down, I realized that the other dancers had pulled back and were watching us. There was wild applause as we stopped. Gareth actually smiled and made a little bow, nudging me to do the same. I was ridiculously happy that I could still make heads turn with my dancing, especially a hard-core dance like Salsa.

The moment couldn't last—not like that. The music switched back to disco. The uncertainties swirling around this reunion were oozing back into my consciousness. The awkwardness of addressing them—or leaving them unmentioned—made me feel suddenly tired.

As I'm sure you're aware (assuming you're not a complete shut-in), nightclubs are not the best places to have long overdue heart-to-hearts with the man you love. Per our usual, Gareth seemed able to read my thoughts, since he took my arm and steered me through one of the sliding doors onto the pier. We walked out to the rail and stood watching the river, romantically moonlit if you can believe it. There was a bit of a breeze so he took off his jacket and put it over me, immediately flooding me with his scent, which might as well have been genetically engineered as a Natalie aphrodisiac.

He turned us to face each other, brushing my cheek with his knuckles in a move that seemed…affectionate, like a prelude to saying something along the lines of, "*Sorry about bullying you into marrying my boyfriend, but you're still the love of my life, and I've missed you so much I thought I might die.*"

You know, typical Gareth stuff.

Instead, he frowned and said, "I'll allow you to stay in the dorm if that's what you want, but I cannot permit you to date."

Nothing had changed! I didn't know whether to guffaw or burst into tears. I'm sure you'll be astounded to hear I chose breaking out into profanities. "What the fuck! You'll fucking allow it?"

He covered my mouth to stop my tirade. "Please Natalie. Hear me out before you explode."

That was enough to cool me marginally. "Wow, did you just say 'please' to me?"

"Please," he repeated firmly. "I'll give you as much freedom as I can, but I can't…. Don't push me on the dating."

"Are you, like, jealous?" The idea seemed ludicrous. By his arrangement and orders, I'd had sex with Jamie more times than I could count.

He looked annoyed at this but answered, "Extremely, and I really can't tolerate the idea of another man touching you."

"Except for Jamie, my husband."

He smirked but said blandly, "Except for Jamie."

"This is so fucked up, Gareth. I don't hear from any of you for five months, I go on one date, and suddenly you're all back. I want a divorce." I sounded petulant, but this was seriously not coming close to my fantasy version of this conversation.

"That's out of the question. Don't ask me again."

I was on the brink of screaming my head off. He was making me so *angry*, but for once I didn't want to fight with him. I wanted my fucking moonlit scene—why wouldn't he give it me? Hadn't I earned it?

And then some mocking voice in my head said, *are you going to stand there and take it?* I swear I could practically hear Babs saying, "Time to woman up." I had let Gareth call all the shots. The sex, the marriage, every last kiss had been on his terms. I'd *fought* him plenty, but I'd yet to *ask* for what I most wanted from him. He'd made it clear I was his. Was he mine as well?

What exactly was I waiting for?

So I didn't wait any longer. I went up on my toes and mashed my mouth against his.

My face must have turned the shade of Jamie's Porsche—and not with lust. It had to be the most awkward, least seductive kiss in the history of hopeless love affairs. Worse, even after everything that had happened, it felt almost transgressive—like I'd taken this incredible liberty.

But I shoved down my humiliation. I mean what the fuck? I couldn't kiss him? Really?

Was I really contemplating having a relationship with someone I was afraid to kiss?

Fuck our contract: my limits finally were clear to me. I could tolerate Gareth's obsessive need for control, his ownership, the spankings and

293

endless sex with Jamie, but I had to be able to ask for comfort and affection when I needed it.

That was the only freedom I needed. If I couldn't have it, if he refused to give it to me, I would walk.

It felt like one of those massive realizations and yet it really was that simple: I would walk.

Not a threat, not a manipulation, simple self-preservation. I knew myself and I knew if I truly meant it, Gareth would let me go. He'd have to. I was no longer that desperate girl sponging sandwiches and showers. I had friends now, a home when I needed it, somewhere to go for Christmas dinner. I was nineteen years old and I had my whole life ahead of me. I didn't need to sacrifice my heart to someone who didn't want my love.

I gave him a challenging stare, and then I grabbed his chin and kissed him again, deeply. For once he responded without taking control, accepting my desire, sharing it without turning it into some sort of conquest.

"Come home," he murmured between kisses. "Please."

There was that rare, beautiful word 'please' again—signifying choice and respect, more romantic in its humble way than the most fervid I love you.

So he did understand. I stopped and rested my forehead against his chin.

"Come home, Natalie," he said again.

I laughed then. Was Gareth actually pleading with me? "I have class Monday at nine. It's a three-hour drive."

"It's a two-minute walk."

I gaped at him. "Excuse me?"

"Two minutes, less probably, to go next door, and then a thirty-second ride to the top floor—penthouse loft." His smiled edged into predatory. "I finalized the sale the week you were accepted."

"You are such a bastard."

"I know." He kissed me then in his usual style, demanding, dominating. Sucker that I am, I melted into him. There was nothing on earth as sexy as his kiss. His eyes narrowed in satisfaction. He was obviously sure he'd won his point. I wasn't close to capitulating yet, but I also would not have bet money on my holding out against his persuasion.

"Is it really my home this time?" I held him at a distance as I asked.

"Yes."

Well that was something.

And then he said, "I love you," and I was officially lost.

Chapter 32

I actually was lost: the sheer romance of the moment—moonlight on the water, "I love you," and such. So much that I didn't notice until his body physically slammed into mine that Jamie had decided to join us. "Did she say yes?" he demanded.

"Not yet," Gareth said, his eyes lighting up dangerously.

"Yes to what exactly?" I demanded.

"Not yet, huh?" Jamie said, ignoring me. "Are you suggesting that my lovely wife requires some persuasion to take up residence with her lawful spouse?"

"I am not your fucking wife!"

I felt a sharp smack on my ass. Gareth's eyes were amused and challenging. "The contract stands."

"It does not," I protested as the two of them pulled me inside. We bypassed the dance floor and made our way along the edge to what was clearly an "employees only" area. Which I suppose would include owners (me!) as well. Jamie unlocked a door and pushed me into what was probably an office, not that I was paying too much attention. The music had just switched to the pulsing '80s synthesizers of my absolute favorite New Order track, "Blue Monday"—one of the sexiest songs ever written.

So I'm standing there, and both of them were facing me, smirking and, I realized, very, very *hungry*.

Holy fucking shit!

It was enough to drive most rational thought from my head, replacing it with some explosive mixture of panic and ravenous desire. I backed up until my calves hit the edge of a sofa.

Jamie looked to Gareth who gave him a go-ahead nod. He danced towards me slowly, hips swaying to that incomparable '80s beat. He gripped my chin and held my gaze, as he brought our hips together. He gave me a light kiss, then deeper, while sliding his hands under my shirt to fondle my breasts. A body pressed against my back told me that Gareth wasn't going to settle for being a spectator this time. Gareth gave me nibbling kisses along my ears to my neck, slipping his arms through mine and then interlacing them until he had my arms pinned behind my back. Jamie pushed his thigh against my sex, rubbing it, forcing my legs apart. Then, with a wicked smile, he leaned over my shoulder and kissed Gareth.

I still can't figure out why I found that so effing hot, but my whole body shuddered in response. Jamie sensed it instantly and took it as an invitation to jack up the heat levels. Again waiting for a nod from Gareth, he reached under my skirt, yanked down my panties, and then dropped to his knees. Before I could stop him, he'd pushed up my skirt, thrown my leg over his shoulder, and was lavishing my sex with his tongue.

It was almost unbearable, and I couldn't help struggling. Gareth just held me tighter and murmured in my ear, "Stop fighting us. I've got you."

The words felt like some sort of final straw—or more accurately the spark on the pile of gunpowder.

Gareth had me. He wouldn't ever willingly let go. With him supporting me, I could let go, lose myself to Jamie's crazily talented tongue, accept the pleasure and not feel like I was paying some unbearably high price for it.

I arched back into him then, finally able to revel in the sensation of that firm if possessive grip. Jamie knew all too well that I had accumulated months' worth of pent-up desire. He worked his tongue delicately, repeatedly pushing me agonizingly close to climax, only to back down again until I was screaming and swearing at him to finish. Jamie looked up from his torture for a moment, to say, "Not me, kitten. Ask Gareth. Nicely."

Fuck!

Gareth's cheek was against mine as he held me tight. "Please," I groaned. "Please, Gareth."

"Easy," he murmured. "Say you'll come home."

"Gareth!" I screamed.

"Say it and then you'll come," he soothed. If anything his words ratcheted up the tension and lust tenfold. I was furious about the blackmail, but that only made the desire more maddening—it certainly didn't make it less. "Say it," he murmured in his most seductive voice.

"Fuck you both! Yes!"

"Bring her," Gareth ordered Jamie, and just like that I was pitching over the cliff. I'd never climaxed while standing up before and somehow my body felt that much more out of my own control. Tears darted to my eyes and my legs buckled until Gareth's hold was the only reason I was still standing.

Jamie jumped up, extremely pleased with himself. He kissed Gareth again. I'm pretty sure one of their silent communications passed, because Jamie turned me to face Gareth and then guided me to my knees. He knelt behind me, resting my head against his shoulder. He then unzipped Gareth's pants and pulled out his cock. "Watch and learn," he whispered in my ear. Keeping his gaze on Gareth, Jamie leaned forward and licked the head lavishly. Then he leaned back and nudged me. "Your turn, kitten. Keep your eyes on his."

FUCK but this was hot! I'd just come—for all the good it did me. The desire was already building up again.

I leaned forward but I wasn't as deft as Jamie at the whole blow job business and missed catching Gareth's cock in my mouth, so I raised my hands to grab it. Quick as a blink, Jamie pulled them down. "Bad girl," he murmured in my ear. "No hands. Just your mouth. Come on, he's waiting."

It was a little awkward, but I managed to take a long lick around the head, but before I could do more, Jamie pulled me back again. This time, he took Gareth's whole length in his mouth at once and began to suck.

No question if Gareth had a kink, it was this: Jamie and me kneeling at his feet taking turns sucking his cock. As usual, Gareth's expression didn't reveal much, but his eyes glittered. I could practically feel the waves of satisfaction pouring off of him, which just made me more turned on. Somehow with Jamie there the whole kneeling thing didn't feel so...compromising.

It gave me a different perspective in more ways than one. I was getting a glimpse of whole new dimensions of Jamie and Gareth's relationship. Jamie was beyond turned on, and he obviously adored giving Gareth this pleasure. Just as I could feel the satisfaction emanating from Gareth, I could feel Jamie's happiness. That was something new. In the past sex had given him pleasure, but it had never given him the kind of pure…I almost want to say *joy* I was sensing. Almost more than Gareth, Jamie wanted this—wanted the three of us together.

And he adored egging me on as well. He pulled off Gareth and nudged me to copy him. I didn't have Jamie's porn-star-like ability to instantly swallow Gareth's whole dick, but I did my best, again catching the warm shaft in my mouth and sucking hard. Gareth lightly brushed my cheek with one hand, running his fingers through Jamie's hair with the other. Jamie kept whispering lewd instructions and encouragements.

"You know what will make him really happy, kitten?" he whispered. "Let him fuck your mouth. What do you say? Can he?" I don't think I would have said no to anything at that point. I did my best to nod. "Good girl."

Again some signal passed between Gareth and Jamie, because Gareth pulled out. Next thing Jamie guided me to lean forward to rest on my hands and knees. He slipped his legs under mine, so I was crouched over his lap. He must have unzipped because he began rubbing his cock against my sex. Then he lay flat on his back and pulled me sharply down on his shaft and just held me there.

Gareth moved back in front of me, brushing the silky head of his cock against my lips until I opened for him. He put both hands on the side of my head and, never taking his eyes from mine, he began to pump into my mouth.

300

It was impossible to feel more thoroughly possessed. It was overwhelming, physically and emotionally. Gareth wasn't brutal but he didn't hold back. It was seriously arousing, but also physically difficult. With Jamie's coaching, I was able to relax my mouth and not panic when Gareth hit the back of my throat. It did hurt, not unbearably, but enough to make me tense. But between Jamie's encouragement and Gareth's intense desire, it was incredibly empowering. I'd never felt sexier.

It was also incredibly arousing. I'd almost forgotten that I was actually riding Jamie, but once I was in a rhythm with Gareth, Jamie started to move my hips while he made shallow upward thrusts. Again, they seemed instinctively in sync with each other. Once Jamie started, I realized how close I was to coming again.

Jamie knew immediately of course and cried out, "We're going to do this—together." He gripped my hips hard and shifted something that made him hit my clitoris with each movement. I couldn't help moaning around Gareth's shaft, which actually made Gareth's eyes roll back in his head a little.

"She's close," Jamie yelled. "Thirty seconds." Gareth nodded and his movements and expression turned fierce. I screamed as shudders of pleasure rolled through me, just as Gareth pulled out, shooting all over my breasts—clearly another of his kinks. Jamie was yelling out his own climax, "God yes, kitten."

I think I might have blacked out for a second—that or time leapt forward because the next thing I knew I was on Gareth's lap on the sofa, with Jamie's arms wrapped around both of us.

301

Suddenly, Gareth pulled me into a voracious kiss that left me dizzy. "Let's go home," he said.

I nodded. Gareth raised his eyebrows. He wanted a real answer, so I said, "Okay."

So sue me. I was in love.

"Yes!" Jamie cried triumphantly. Gareth and Jamie zipped up, and I pulled my panties back on. I was so spent, just the thought of the two minutes needed to get to the apartment seemed impossibly long. The three of us left the office and again made our way alongside the dance floor. As we headed for the exit, Daniel joined us. He gave me a wry smile and whispered in my ear, "Like I said, the Hotel California."

I elbowed him and said loudly, "I still want a divorce."

Gareth looked amused by this. "No," was all he said.

"At least tear up my contract!"

"No."

"Gareth!"

"I love you but no."

Story of my fucking life.

The End

302

Acknowledgements

I began this book almost exactly five years ago, the first piece of erotic fiction I ever wrote. Weird as it is to say this, I can't help feeling a profound debt of gratitude to Natalie, Gareth, Jamie and Daniel for not shutting up and staying hidden in the back of my brain. The nagging did pay off, and they got their *happily ever after*. Having published three other titles in the interim, I can honestly say these beings, imaginary though they are, had a pretty drastic effect on my life.

That's not to say that real people didn't do their part—they did and it was incredible. My husband, sister, and sister-in-law were my first readers, reading multiple drafts over multiple years. Old college and grad school friend, Jenny Davidson, made crucial suggestions that helped me hone the final version. Bookie from I ♥ Bookie Nookie Reviews and moderator of the Goodreads Ménage Readers Group answered my call for beta-readers, and I am so lucky she did. I can't say enough in praise of her instincts and attention to detail. As always, Jane at Crazy Diamond Editing did an absolutely fantastic job on a tricky proofreading job. Kim Killion of The Killion Group has my warmest thanks for her lovely cover design. Last but very far from least, a million-bajillion thanks to my husband and my sons for their endless support and love.

About the Author

Lilia Ford is also the author of *The Heartwood Box: A Fairy Tale* and *The Slave Catcher*. She lives in New York City with her husband and two sons.

She loves to hear from readers:

> Her website is: liliafordromance.com
>
> Her blog is: liliafordromance.blogspot.com

She has Pinterest Boards for all of her books:

> www.pinterest.com/liliaford

As far as social network sites go, she is most active on Goodreads.

She also remembers to update her Facebook page every now and then:

> www.facebook.com/liliafordromance

Other Titles from Lilia Ford

The Heartwood Box: A Fairy Tale

BEWARE THE GIFTS OF THE FAE. Battered by the attacks of the demon king, the Fae Queen, Titania, promised her greatest warrior, Declan, that his line would never fail. To keep her promise, she made a bargain with a human village. She would gift each girl with a magical heartwood box. When it came time to marry, the girl's box would change color to reveal her true love. But there was a catch: in each generation, one girl's box would turn black. She must give herself as a bride to a member of the Black family.

When Genevieve Miran arrives for the first event of the Bridal Week, the other girls are in a panic. Damian Black has joined this year, and one of them will have to marry him. Genevieve is too inexperienced to see what is obvious to the others: that Damian Black is a man who will demand complete submission from his wife. When the gorgeous warrior sets out to charm her, Genevieve can't resist: her heartwood box turns black the same afternoon.

After his brothers failed to find brides, Damian Black knows he must be ruthless. If he fails to marry, Faerie may fall. The moment he sees Genevieve, his path is clear. Marry her and get her safely locked up in his castle before she can escape him. But Damian never dreamt that he might have rivals for the shy Genevieve—or that the rivals might be his own brothers.

Warning: this novel contains graphic sex, spanking, bondage, three smoking hot alpha brothers, and a shy heroine who must learn when to say "no!" and when to say "yes, yes, yes!"

The Slave Catcher

Genre: Science Fiction, LGBT

16,000 words

Star City, best known for its brothels and casinos, is one of the few planets in the quadrant that outlaws slavery—for everyone, that is, except the galaxy bullies, the Borathians. Telepaths and recent conquerors of a backwards planet named Earth, the Borathians are simply too powerful to refuse. A special treaty allows them to bring their pleasure slaves or "bonds" onto the planet, and if one escapes, they have five days to recover him.

Sam Beron, private locator, may have been born on a Maradi space cruiser, but Star City is his home now and he'd say he despises slavery as much as any native. Unfortunately, a run of bad luck at the casino tables leaves him flat broke and scavenging expired military rations out of a neighboring dumpster. Next thing he knows, the Borathians are offering him a fortune to track down one of their escaped bonds, a beautiful

Earth boy named Liam. What's a hungry locator to do?

Pet to the Tentacle Monsters!
Genre: Science Fiction, LGBT
17,000 Words

It's been more than twelve years since the alien invasion wiped out much of the human population and forced those who were left into Refugee Communes. As far as Benji Tucker is concerned, a life devoted to bare survival is boring as hell. But when a stupid prank threatens to bring disaster down on the entire commune, the Galactic Enforcers show up and announce Benji is now eligible for adoption—by the invaders!

He wakes in a plain white cell to find three very different monsters determined to make him their pet.

www.ingramcontent.com/pod-product-compliance
Lightning Source LLC
Chambersburg PA
CBHW071248170626
46809CB00001B/130